GIFTI

CW00499194

BOOK ONE OF THE HIGHLAND MAGIC SERIES

FOR JIMMY AND LINDA

Prologue

The girl with no name scurried down the corridor, hiking up her skirt to avoid the hem from trailing along the dusty floor. She'd already been in trouble once today for her appearance when the cook had cuffed her ear for wearing a stained apron. The fact that it was stained simply because she'd been in the garden and picking mudberries on the cook's orders didn't seem to matter. It was one thing, however, to be told off in the kitchen; it was quite another for it to happen in the grand hall in front of goodness knows who.

She hadn't been in the Bull's presence for months. The last time she was summoned it was to make up numbers at a cocktail party. Not, of course, as a guest; it was her role to hold up canapés to the mingling party goers - no mean feat for someone who was short for her age and surrounded by towering Sidhe adults.

She barely lasted ten minutes. Once the Bull spotted her, staring at her with dark glittering eyes, his skin suffusing with a mottled angry red, she was ushered away and scolded for drawing attention to herself. Since then she'd kept well out of his way, even risking the wrath of the cook by taking the long way round the dusty palace and arriving even later for her daily duties than she normally did. Frankly, she'd do just about anything to avoid the

Bull's terrifying gaze.

Rounding the corner at high speed, and worried about what was expected of her, she was less alert than she should have been. Colliding with the delicate, elfin form of Tipsania, she sent them both crashing to the ground; her bare feet became tangled with the other girl's ornate skirts, the heavy fabric inextricably wrapping itself around her ankles.

'You stupid bitch!'

The girl yanked hard, attempting to free herself. There was an ominous rip of fabric as she finally pulled away, then she received a hard kick from Tipsania for her efforts.

Ignoring the sharp burst of pain, she scrambled to her feet then bent down to help the other girl stand up. Tipsania glared at the proffered hand as if it belonged to a cockroach instead of a child. She still took it, though.

'You should bloody well watch where you're going,' she hissed. 'Now I look as if I've been dragged through a muddy puddle. Don't they teach you how to keep clean?'

The girl ducked her head down, mumbling an apology.

Tipsania clicked her teeth in disgust. 'Byron will think I've been raised in a hovel. I'll simply have to go and change.' She spat, an astoundingly unladylike gesture for someone of her rank.

The girl's eyes flew upwards. 'Byron?' She'd heard of him, of course. The privileged son of the

Sidhe Steward Aifric Moncrieffe was well known around the court for his youthful misdemeanours. Only seventeen years old, he was already living up to his namesake as mad, bad and dangerous to know. It didn't make sense, however, that he'd be coming here. Little as the girl knew, even she was aware that the Moncrieffes held little love for the Scrymgeour Clan, even though they worked together from time to time.

She swallowed the knot of pain that appeared in her throat. Was that why she'd been summoned? Was it an opportunity for the upper echelons of Sidhe royalty to sneer at her, as well as the lower ranks she normally dealt with?

Tipsania's lip curled. 'You don't think he's going to be interested in you, do you? A dirty urchin?' She leaned in more closely, her smooth honey-coloured hair tickling the girl's cheek. 'A bastard?'

The girl drew back. Her parentage wasn't her fault. If she could change it, she would. It was incredibly unfortunate for her that her pure white hair and violet eyes reminded everyone of just who her father was.

She opened her mouth to answer back then snapped it shut again, thinking better of it. Tipsania had made an art form out of underhand cruelty that could extend for weeks when she thought she had been slighted. There was no point in antagonising her unnecessarily, tempting as it might be.

The girl dipped her head again, casting her eyes

downward and hoping that her act of submission would encourage Tipsania to forget the flare of rebellion that had flickered across her face.

A door opened several metres away and the low hum of voices reached the girl's ears. Her eyes snapped up, wary of who was about to join them. She received another sharp kick from Tipsania in response.

'Well, well, well,' drawled a deep voice. 'What do we have here?'

This time, the girl kept her head firmly down.

'Byron!' Tipsania tittered, her previously harsh tone now muted to a breathy giggle. 'Are you lost? We're supposed to be in the grand hall.'

'Just exploring, Tipsy,' he replied easily. 'Who's this?'

The girl with no name felt his gaze burning into her. She told herself not to look up.

Tipsania's lip curled. 'She's the one.'

'Really?' Byron sounded curious. He reached out, his fingers brushing under the girl's chin, tilting it up so that she was forced to meet his eyes.

She shrank back, terrified of the new horrors that were about to visited on her. Byron's appearance certainly lived up to the hype. His hair, so golden in colour that it mimicked burnished bronze, fell artfully across his forehead. His skin was tanned, without a blemish, and his eyes glittered emerald green. He towered over her, a tiny furrow on his forehead as he took in her appearance.

'She's a filthy thing,' Tipsania dismissed. 'I don't know why you'd want to bother with her. Look at what she did to my dress! She's going to pay for that.'

Byron's expression turned stony, flecks of frozen ice reflected in his brilliant irises. He flicked a glance at the older girl then back again. 'You're right,' he said finally, 'she *is* pathetic. If I were you I wouldn't even speak to her.' Without another word, he withdrew his hand and bowed in Tipsania's direction. 'My lady,' he murmured. Then he strode off.

Both girls watched him go. When he was out of earshot, Tipsania turned to the girl again. 'You're lucky he didn't want more from you,' she hissed.

The girl with no name dropped her head again. Her stomach felt tight and uncomfortable. She clenched her fists and dropped her shoulders. Please, she thought, just leave me alone. I'm nobody.

Her submissive posture seemed to do the trick; Tipsania sniffed loudly and stomped off, no doubt to find another example of gold-edged finery with which to impress the Sidhe princeling.

The girl with no name waited, counting to twenty in her head to ensure Tipsania was not about to return and cause more grief. It would make her eventual appearance in the grand hall even more delayed and she risked the Bull's anger increasing. She was already late by now, however. One minute or ten - either way she'd get her ears boxed for her troubles. Not from the Bull, of course. He never touched her himself.

Trembling from her encounter, she took several short, rapid breaths. Byron Moncrieffe's supercilious attitude, combined with Tipsania's venom, swirled around her head. When she was older, she decided furiously, she'd make both of them pay. She sniffed to herself.

She dusted down her apron and set off once more, her mind working feverishly as to why she'd been summoned and just what the Bull could possibly want with her. A door at the far end opened and bright sunlight spilled in. There was a shout and the guard, who'd been standing there silhouetted against the sun, turned to answer the call, leaving the gateway open.

The girl gazed out at the bright light, then back at the dark corridor behind her. She gnawed her bottom lip and looked again. After a brief moment of indecision, she began to run.

She wasn't a prisoner. She'd never been told she couldn't leave. But until that moment, with the glow of the outside world and its golden uncertainty contrasting with the darkness that no doubt awaited her in the grand hall, she'd never considered leaving. There was nowhere else for her to go.

In years to come, she'd describe her action as foolhardy and reckless. The right move, without a doubt, but one in which the possibility of success was hampered by lack of planning and foresight. Still, sometimes the stars simply align and the time is right.

She skidded down the corridor, emerged outside and blinked at the light. Without pausing, she veered left –towards freedom.

The guard, startled by the sudden movement, turned to watch her. His companion arrived, shading his face from the sun and squinting in her direction. Even without her long white hair whipping behind her and the determined set to her chin, her intent was obvious.

'Isn't that…?'

'Yes.'

'Should we stop her?'

One side of the guard's mouth crooked upwards. 'Leave her be. I'm only surprised she's not done it sooner.'

'What about the prophecy?'

He shrugged. 'What about it? It's mumbo-jumbo. Even the Sidhe don't believe it.'

'She's still alive though, isn't she? After what they say her father did…'

The guard tutted. 'Who's going to kill a kid?'

The girl was oblivious to their attention. She zipped ahead, down the well-worn path and away. No-one stopped her speedy descent down the drive and out past the ornate gates that were standing open to admit the Moncrieffe heir and his entourage. The Sidhe were far more concerned with keeping people out than forcing them to stay in. It was a hangover from the days of the Fissure and probably pointless now.

She ran out, pushing past the magical barrier that separated the Sidhe world and all its Clan members from the Clan-less, with little more than a shiver. Then she emerged onto a narrow country road and simply kept running until she reached the dual carriageway leading to Dundee in one direction and Aberdeen in the other. Confronted by the speeding cars and the lack of pedestrian walkways, she came to a stumbling halt in a layby. Less than a minute after she collapsed, breathless and shaking, a car pulled in.

Like a frightened rabbit caught in headlights, she froze. The vehicle was far removed from the gleaming sports cars and limousines that she was used to. This one was battered and rusty and gave every appearance of being unroadworthy. Indeed, after it came to a juddering halt, the exhaust coughed up a belch of black smoke.

The door swung open and a man peered out. Human - not Sidhe. Thank heaven for small mercies.

'Need a lift?' he asked, his voice rasping in the cold air.

The girl blinked. This was far from what she'd been expecting. She looked him over. He had carroty orange hair, a quick smile and a friendly light in his eyes. He didn't look particularly strong and he was definitely human. It didn't mean he was good, though.

As if sensing her indecision, he held up his palms, indicating that he was weaponless. 'I'm not very trustworthy,' he said. 'But I'm not going to hurt you.'

She considered his words. 'I'm Sidhe,' she answered finally.

'I can see that.'

'It means I'm very powerful,' she lied.

He nodded his head gravely. 'I have no doubt.'

She weighed up her options. Climbing into a car with a perfect stranger wasn't ideal but there was something about the man that made her trust him - and she had little alternative. If he tried anything, she could always make a grab for his groin and twist. She'd seen Tipsania do just that to one of the guards. It had seemed to hurt. A lot.

The girl pursed her lips then slowly nodded. His face broke into a smile and he jerked his thumb towards the back seat. After some difficulty, she opened the door far enough to squeeze herself inside. The radio was blaring, some political pundit jabbering away. 'What Sidhe royalty lack is integrity,' he argued. 'They're not like the rest of us.'

She stiffened. She'd thought that once she was out of the Clanlands, she'd be free of the Sidhe. Less than five minutes into her escape and already they were being discussed on the radio. That didn't bode well.

'What Clan are you?' she asked.

The man flicked her an amused look. 'I'm not with any Clan. I don't hold to those Sidhe ideas.'

She frowned. 'But everyone's in a Clan.'

He laughed. 'No, they're not. I'm Clan-less. I

don't follow their rules. If that bothers you, you can still change your mind.' He gestured towards the door.

She glanced outside. 'No. I'm here now.'

He pointed downwards. 'Seatbelt then.'

The girl stared at her new benefactor. He frowned and repeated the word. Finally understanding, she hastily pulled the seatbelt across her body, clicking it into place. With a satisfied grunt, he re-started the engine. 'Anyone asks,' he said, 'you're my niece, alright? We're on our way to see your grandparents.'

Confused as to why anyone would care, she bit her lip and nodded. He opened the glove box and rummaged around, then tossed her a faded baseball cap. No less baffled, the girl put it on, tucking her hair inside. Her stomach had a strange squirmy sensation that she didn't like very much.

Less than half a mile down the road, when the talking on the radio had given way to a jazzy song, blue-and-red flashing lights appeared and the man threw her a meaningful glance. The car rolled to a stop and the unsmiling face of a uniformed policeman appeared.

Certain that this was for her, she squeaked and shrank back in her seat. While the police might technically be considered Clan-less and they certainly had no jurisdiction within the Clanlands, their wages were paid out of the twenty-four Clans' pockets. There was no doubting where their allegiance lay.

'License and registration.'

The man calmly handed them over. The policeman inspected them briefly then turned to her. In a fit of desperation, she burst out, 'We're going to see my gran. She's sick. She needs us.'

The policeman's expression softened. He waved them on, already focusing his attention on the car behind them.

Once they were safely away, the man spoke, glancing at her in the mirror as he drove. 'That was good work,' he said. 'A bit shaky but the improvisation was clever.' He nodded. 'It's been a real stroke of luck meeting you. Perhaps we can help each other out. I'm Taylor. What's your name?'

The girl, eyes wide and hands clenched tightly in her lap, took a deep breath. 'Integrity,' she said suddenly, her voice clear. 'My name's Integrity.'

Taylor laughed aloud. In fact three hours later, when they finally pulled into a dark Aberdonian street, he was still laughing. It was a long time before she realised why.

Chapter One

You have to do bad shit to get ahead. Taylor had told me that a million times and for a long time I'd bought into it. After tonight, however, things were going to be different. A new leaf and a new me. That was what I was planning.

I'd been thinking about it for a long time but since I'd received the letter in elegant, handwritten script demanding my appearance at the Sidhe court, I felt I had no choice but to step up my plans to vamoose out of the city. I didn't want anything to do with those bastards. Not unless it meant ripping them off. Frankly, I'd rather head down to the Lowlands - and the Veil - than venture near the Clanlands.

At least Taylor had promised that my final hurrah was going to be a straightforward job. 'In and out,' he'd said. 'The place will be empty.'

'You know I'm leaving after this one,' I reminded him. Not that it was likely it would have slipped his mind but with Taylor sometimes certain points bore repeating.

'Of course, of course! As if I could forget.' His eyes took on a knowing look that I chose to ignore. 'You'll miss it though. You won't get many thrills from tramping around the countryside.'

'It's not tramping around the countryside. It's mountain rescue. I think saving lives will be thrilling enough.'

He grimaced at that. 'You'll be bored.'

I simply smiled back. We'd had this conversation often enough in recent weeks. My mind was made up and even he couldn't change it.

'I'll always be here,' he said. 'If you do want to come back, that is.'

I hugged him impulsively. 'I might not come back to work but I'll always come back. You're my family.' I meant every word. We'd had a few rough times over the years but who hadn't? Taylor had been there for me when no-one else was, even if his motives weren't always pure. I worried about him more than he'd ever know.

He looked abashed at my heartfelt words and ran an awkward hand through his hair. It was no longer the carroty mop he had when I first met him all those years ago. Now it was more silver, far closer in colour to my own locks, which still drew curious looks and the odd question about my ancestry, even amongst the Clan-less underbelly. For the most part I shrugged them off.

It was a very long time since I moved in Sidhe circles. I crossed the road to avoid passing close by any of my kin, no matter how distantly related they were. And one of the reasons I was leaving Aberdeen was because they'd contacted me.

It wasn't that I was afraid of what they might do if they got hold of me, although that was a part of it. I just wanted a quiet life. My childhood with the Sidhe was little more than a distant memory; in fact sometimes I felt as if it had happened to someone else.

I ignored the gossip mags and whispered rumours about what each Clan was up to. I lived in the underclass, far away from them. I didn't care whether Aifric remained Steward and was therefore still in charge, or which man Tipsania Scrymgeour was currently stepping out with. I didn't even care that her father, the Bull, appeared to be making more money than Bill Gates. The Sidhe could spend their days worrying about politics, jockeying for position and doing whatever they could to rise above other Clans. I only cared about me and mine. And none of mine were Sidhe. Or Clan.

I tested my kit, adjusting the harness at my back to ensure it was secure, and skirted round the back of the building. It might be the middle of the night during a bank holiday weekend but I still needed to be circumspect. It would be sod's law if I got nabbed on the very last day I spent as a career criminal. Tapping my forehead three times with my index finger to signal to my waiting crew, I gave one last look around then sprang up.

My fingertips curled easily around the first ledge. Despite the typical Scottish chill, I was barefoot. It made it far easier to gain purchase on the smooth glass surface of the towering bank. I also admit that I rather enjoyed it when I glanced down and caught a flash of the sparkly nail varnish adorning my toenails. It felt appropriate for this job; we were, after all, going after some more sparkles –

albeit of the more expensive kind.

Clambering up with fluid, nimble ease, I made fast work of my ascent. Beads of sweat were only just appearing on my brow when I reached the assigned floor. Piece of cake. I tightened my grip with my left hand, using my right to reach behind and unclip the glass breaker that was hooked to my belt.

It was a nifty piece of kit, designed to help trapped motorists break out of their cars. While I'd never heard of anyone actually using one to save their own life, I found mine particularly useful. It was a gift from Taylor when I graduated from simple manipulation tactics and dull look-out posts to full-blown thief. The others might scoff at its hot pink colour but I'd had it for seven lucky years and it had never let me down. I might wear black to stay camouflaged against the night sky but that didn't mean that everything I carried had to be boring monochrome too.

Leaning back as far as I could, I swung it into the centre of the pane of tinted glass, shattering it instantly. Thanks both to the glass breaker's and the window's design, all the shards of glass fell inwards just as I wanted.

Flashing a satisfied smile to my inner thief, I heaved myself inside with a leap, landing far enough in to avoid catching my skin on any of the dangerous broken pieces. I pivoted round and grinned, curtseying at the now-gaping hole. Then I checked my watch. Less than ninety seconds from pavement to entry. That was impressive, even for me.

Without wasting another minute, I unclipped my harness and tested the nearby wall. The plaster seemed sound enough so I pulled out my tiny drill, made a hole in the wall and carefully inserted the climbing wire. I gave it an experimental tug; it would hold. Less than thirty seconds later, I was lowering the rope out of the window and whistling down softly.

Three dark shadows broke away from different corners of the street. As the rope grew taut with the weight of the first climber, I surveyed my surroundings. Taylor had insisted that this floor would be the easiest one for entry. Looking around at the low-spec furniture, I was inclined to agree. The employees on this level were clearly not the wealthy bankers who occupied other areas of this building and were universally despised by the rest of the world. The guys who worked here looked like they filled their days with dull data entry whilst suffering zero-hour contracts.

I wrinkled my nose and made my way along the narrow aisle between the cubicles until I reached the office, which was separated by walls rather than flimsy partitions. Frankly, it was a wonder that more people didn't turn to a life of crime. Working here would drive me insane.

Inside the manager's office was a heavy walnut desk and swivel chair. It looked considerably more comfortable than the chairs out front. I sat down experimentally and swung myself around. Yup - it was pretty damn fine. I examined the collection of family photos of beaming children and heavily lipsticked trophy wife; I resisted the temptation to find a Sharpie and draw a moustache on them.

The frame was marked with the Macfie Clan colours. Typical. I bet Mr Manager here had aligned himself with them, whereas his minions in the larger room outside remained Clan-less. The Macfies were always into bloody banking. If they'd chosen a different path, we wouldn't be targeting them so bloody often. I shrugged. Their fault.

I helped myself to several boiled sweets from a crystal jar, raised my legs up, crossing my feet on the desktop, and waited.

The crunch of glass signalled Speck's arrival. He hated heights so he had to be forced to go up the ropes first. If the warlock was left until last, he'd never pluck up the courage to clip on his carabineer. We'd learned that the hard way a couple of years ago and lost out on a fat purse as a result. I had tried coaching him through his fear but nothing seemed to work – other than a swift kick up his arse. With Lexie following on his tail, of course, that wasn't a problem.

Speck appeared in the doorway, cursing. 'We didn't have to climb. I could have bypassed the front door in less time than it took to get up here.'

'Relax.' I gestured towards the sweets. 'Have some sugar and calm down. You know this was the sensible option.'

He grumbled at me, reaching out for the jar with a trembling hand. I knew better than to comment. His terror would subside by the time Brochan, the last of our motley crew, joined us. To point out that Speck was shaking like a leaf served no purpose. He could be rather sensitive, even at the best of times.

While he crumpled up the sweet wrapper into a ball and tossed it carelessly onto the floor, I opened up a drawer and peered inside. Lying on top of several heavily perfumed envelopes was an ornate letter opener. I lifted it out. It was an expensive tool, especially in today's digital age. Made entirely from silver and with a perfectly balanced blade, it seemed a travesty to leave it where it was. I regarded it seriously for a moment then slid into one of my many zippered pockets. It would make a nice souvenir.

When Lexie appeared, grinning broadly at Speck's pale face, I got to my feet and scooped up the jar of sweets. It wouldn't be long now. I went back out to the main room, depositing one sweet next to each keyboard.

'One for you,' I sang out, 'and one for you, and one for you.' I paused at one cubicle laden with Star Wars memorabilia and pursed my lips. 'You deserve two.'

'You're such a geek,' Brochan told me, appearing silently from behind with the coil of climbing rope.

I winked at him and rattled the now almost

empty jar. 'Want one?'

He patted his flat stomach. 'Watching my weight.'

I rolled my eyes. 'Are we clear?'

'As a mountain stream.'

I shot him a look, wondering whether that was a gibe at my upcoming change of career. His expression was innocent but I caught the faintest hint of merriment in the back of his eyes and stuck out my tongue.

'If the wind changes…'

I waved a hand in the air. 'Yeah, yeah. We're not in Sidhe territory, remember.'

'Well you're the one who'd know.'

I tossed back my hair and ignored the rejoinder. 'Come on. Let's get going.'

Leaving behind the depressing office space, the four of us moved quietly out towards the bank of lifts. We required little in the way of communication by this point; we'd worked together long enough to have an almost telepathic understanding of what was required. Still, out of respect for this being our last mission together, Speck glanced at me and I gave him a nod of acknowledgment. He unscrewed the button panel in the wall, short-circuiting the system and disabling all the elevators in one fell swoop. He jerked his thumb at Brochan who immediately stepped forward and wrenched open the doors to reveal the cavernous drop.

'First one to the bottom is a rotten egg,' he smirked.

Speck sighed. 'Can't we just take the stairs?'

Lexie tutted, giving him a sharp shove. Speck stumbled through the gap, his curse echoing as it bounced off the walls.

'We are trying to stay quiet,' I reminded her with a frown.

She shrugged. 'No-one's here, Integrity. We'd be waiting forever for Speck to make a move if I'd not done that.'

I didn't entirely disagree; I didn't entirely approve either. 'There's no point in taking unnecessary risks.'

'Your impending retirement is making you boring.'

I folded my arms and gave Lexie a stony glare. Unfortunately I wasn't able to maintain it for long before a smile tugged at the corners of my mouth. 'Yeah, you're right. I can still get to the bottom quicker than you though.'

The other woman grinned. 'Go on then.'

I took a deep breath and jumped. Although the drop to the bottom should have been lethal, Taylor had cleverly modified all of our jumpsuits so it was a piece of cake. He was a regular Q. Each suit was fitted around the shoulders with a small canopy-style parachute. It was no good for heights of more than eighty metres, as sheer velocity would negate its gliding power. For something like this elevator shaft, though, it was perfect. Less than one floor down and I'd already released it, enjoying the air rushing past my cheeks as I descended with Lexie a heartbeat after me on the other side of the narrow drop. She might have beaten me if Speck hadn't somehow gotten in her way and forced her into the wall instead of directly on top of the roof of the frozen lift.

'Oops,' he said, entirely unrepentant.

'Idiot!' Lexie hissed. 'I've been trying to beat Integrity at this for months and you know this was my last chance to do it.'

'Tell you what, Lexie,' I said. 'I promise I'll meet up with you in a few weeks once I'm settled in Oban and we can have a jumping session then. As many times as you want.'

Brochan joined us, his large feet clanging loudly against the metallic lift. His merman body was better designed for water rather than land, even though he had a profound fear of the sea. Any footwear he ended up with looked like outsized clown shoes. It was a miracle he managed to stay as quiet as he did. 'Waste of time,' he dismissed.

'Why?' Lexie demanded. 'You don't think I'm good enough?'

'She's Sidhe. You're not. You're a cute pixie but you're not like her.'

I stiffened. What did that mean? Fortunately I was prevented from asking by Speck's obvious snigger. 'She's Sidhe. That's funny.' Brochan looked at him blankly. 'Sidhe? She? You know. Sidhe is pronounced she and you said she is…' His voice faltered at Brochan's expression. 'Never mind,' he muttered.

Lexie sniffed. 'Integrity is not Sidhe. Not like the rest of them are, anyway. She's better than that.'

I gave her a grateful look even though we all knew the truth. 'We need to get a move on,' I said, changing the subject. 'We've been here far too long as it is.'

Working together, we easily unscrewed the air vent panel opposite. I went first, wriggling my way through, followed by Speck, Lexie and Brochan respectively. It was unfortunate that Brochan was somewhat larger than the others and ended up getting stuck halfway. With considerably hilarity – muted though it was – we managed to pull him through. He landed with a rather painful sounding thump, rubbed the base of his spine and grimaced.

'You really do need to watch your weight after all,' I commented, dodging out of the way of his playful swipe. Then I winced melodramatically. 'Ouch. If looks could kilo…'

'Watch it,' he growled back, jabbing his thumb ahead to focus me on our goal.

With only one barrier left, we all took a moment to admire the not-inconsiderable steel door in our path.

'It must have cost a pretty penny,' Lexie said, her eyes wide.

'Hundred and twenty thousand,' Speck answered. 'Retail, anyway.'

'Waste of time when you think about it.'

We shared a grin.

'Are you sure the drill isn't going to be too

loud?' Lexie asked, gnawing at her bottom lip.

'Worry wart. We've tested it. No one's going to hear a thing.'

'And,' I added, 'even if they do, they'll associate it with the building works next door. They'll assume some poor sod has been pulled in over the holiday to speed up the construction.'

'I could still cast a spell,' Speck began. All of us shook our heads in vigorous denial. Speck pouted. 'Just because the last one went slightly wrong…'

'Slightly? I almost lost my eardrums!'

I patted him on the shoulder. 'Really, Speck, there's no need. This drill is the business.' I pulled out several parts from my small backpack while the others did the same. We assembled the heavy-duty piece of machinery in next to no time then I hefted it and gave an experimental tug on the button. It was definitely audible but no louder than our normal speaking voices. I raised it in Speck's direction. 'Would you like to do the honours?'

He held up his palms. 'This is your last gig, Integrity. You should do it.'

I glanced at Lexie and Brochan, both of whom nodded solemnly in agreement. For a brief moment, a hard knot rose up in my throat. Bugger. 'I'm really going to miss you guys.'

Brochan turned his head away while Lexie blinked rapidly several times. Even Speck grabbed my hand and squeezed it. 'It won't be the same without you.'

I cleared my throat awkwardly and tried to pull

myself together. This was neither the time nor the place to get all maudlin. At least they weren't trying to change my mind. I'd miss my life as part of Taylor's crew more than I could possibly admit, even to myself, but I knew I was making the right decision. 'Let's get a move on then,' I whispered.

Brochan tapped the wall thoughtfully then measured out four points, marking each with a small piece of chalk. He stepped back, allowing me to take his place. We exchanged a quick smile before I pulled a mask over my mouth and nose and got started.

The diamond-tipped drill made fast work, piercing through to the other side at each point in less time than it would take to brew a cup of coffee. A cloud of fine dust filled the air, coating the gleaming vault door right next to us.

Lexie traced out a giant smiley face on it. When Brochan gave her a funny look, she shrugged. 'It might make them happy when they walk in here first thing on Tuesday morning.'

'Somehow I don't think they're going to be happy.'

'They've got insurance. They'll get over it.'

I straightened my shoulders, massaging my neck and eyeing my handiwork. 'A bit wonky,' I decided, 'but it'll do. Off you go, Lex.'

The blue-haired pixie grinned, using the edges of the gap to hoist herself up while Speck and Brochan helped steady her. 'Are you staring at my arse, Speck?' she called out.

He coughed, going slightly red. 'Course not,' he mumbled. 'I respect you too much, Lexie.'

'Oh,' she said, sounding disappointed, 'that's a shame. I've been doing extra squats just for you.'

Speck went even redder. I pressed my lips firmly shut, trying not to laugh.

Even with Lexie's petite form, it was a tight squeeze. It took almost as long for her to shimmy through as it did to complete the drilling. It was just as well that this particular model of vault had a failsafe button on the other side in case anyone got trapped inside. There was no way the rest of us would have made it through that gap.

When her feet finally vanished and she stood up, Lexie peered back at us from the other side. 'Peekaboo!'

'Open the damn door,' Brochan growled.

'What's the rush?'

'Well, let me see,' he said sarcastically. 'We're breaking and entering into what is supposed to be one of the most secure vaults in the country to steal a gemstone that's worth more than most people will make in their lifetime. If we get caught, we'll end up in prison until we're all grey and wrinkled. So, sure, take all the time you need.'

She jabbed a finger through the gap. 'Pixies don't go grey. And Integrity's hair is already pure white. So it's only you and Speck who have to worry about that side of things.'

'Lexie...'

'Okay, okay. Give me a moment. It's pitch black

in here, after all.'

Brochan started to mutter something under his breath.

'Counting to ten?' I asked, amused.

'I could count to a thousand and she'd still annoy me.'

'You love her really.'

There was a loud creak as the vault door began to open. Speck pushed forward, tripping over his own feet in his haste to get inside.

'I can't believe you're leaving me on my own with these two,' Brochan grumbled.

I smiled and gestured at the door. 'Moany mermen before shady Sidhe.'

'I'm not moany. Not any more than you're shady, anyway.'

'I'm a thief,' I said simply. 'I'm about as shady as you're likely to get.' I gave him a gentle nudge. 'Come on. Weren't you getting worried about the time?'

He blew air through his cheeks and followed the warlock in. I held back for a moment, savouring the last time I would ever do this. It had been a hell of a ride. Then I entered the dark vault too.

Speck had recovered enough from his stumble to click his fingers and create enough light for the four of us to see what we were doing. The vault was lined with box after narrow box. It reminded me of Doctor Who's TARDIS. Even with its huge door, the size of the vault and the number of safety deposits boxes were surprising.

'What number is it?' Brochan asked.

'A724,' I answered. 'Further down the back.'

'Did I ever tell you that I'm slightly claustrophobic?' Speck asked.

'Only every time we do this,' Lexie replied. 'Is there anything you're not scared of?'

He seemed to think about it for a moment. 'Spiders,' he said finally. 'I quite like spiders.'

The pixie shuddered delicately. 'Ugh.'

'There it is,' Brochan said, breaking into the conversation. He strode over, examining the box in question with a practised eye.

'You know,' Speck said, 'there must be a lot of wealth hidden behind all of these. We don't just have to take the jewel.'

'Do you want to be the person who steals some poor grandmother's family heirloom?' I asked, watching Brochan carefully. 'Or Joe Bloggs' life savings?'

'You have an interesting sense of morality. We are here to nick the Lia Saifir after all.'

'The lordling who owns it is as rich as Croesus. He won't miss it.'

Speck snorted but I ignored it. 'Can you open it, Brochan?'

'I reckon so.'

'Do you need some tools?'

He drew back his fist and smashed it into the box. The door sprang open. He looked at me from over his shoulder. 'Nah,' he grinned. 'I'm good.'

My eyes danced. There was nothing like sheer

brute strength. I stood next to him and gazed down. This was always my favourite part, the heart-stopping moment before the big reveal when all our hard work and preparation would pay off. With a deep breath, I reached out and slid open the drawer.

I stared, my mouth dropping open. Crap-a-doodle-doo. Brochan cursed and spat.

'What?' Speck asked. 'What is it?'

Lexie squeezed her way in and gazed down. 'Shit. It's gone?' She shoved her hand into the box and felt around. 'Maybe it's rolled to the back?'

I shook my head. Frustration, disappointment and just the tiniest edge of relief mingled together in my stomach. 'No. It's empty.' I sighed. 'Taylor was so sure it would be here.'

'A month!' Speck shrieked. 'It's taken us a month of planning to get here and the stupid gem's not there? Now what?'

There was only one answer to that. I slammed the box back into place. It clanged, the sound reverberating around the vault. 'Now we go home. We're done.'

Chapter Two

I stood at the back, leaning against the wall with my arms folded while the others yelled.

'You know how long we took in planning that operation? Goddamnit, Taylor!'

'How could you have gotten the intelligence so wrong?'

'I could have died climbing up that building and all for nothing!'

Taylor glanced at me. 'Wouldn't you like to join in as well?'

I shrugged. 'We went for the Lia Saifir and it wasn't there. End of.'

His mouth twisted. 'Everything I had led me to believe it was there. My contact said…'

'Well, your contact was bloody wrong, wasn't he?' Speck exploded.

'This isn't over,' Taylor said calmly. 'We'll still get it. You'll still get your payday.'

Lexie squared up to him. There was something very amusing about the tiny pixie with her fists at the ready while Taylor's large, hulking shape gazed implacably down at her. 'You're damn right we will. I still want my money. It's not our fault the jewel wasn't there.'

Taylor scratched his temple. 'It wasn't mine either.'

'But it was your plan! Your orders!'

He sighed. 'Okay, I admit, I may have been slightly hasty and didn't double check everything. But I'm in rather a tight spot and time was of the essence.'

I had a sudden sinking sensation. There was something about the tone of his voice. This was familiar territory as far as Taylor was concerned.

'How much are you in for?' I asked quietly, fixing my gaze on him.

The other three swung their heads in my direction then back towards Taylor. Brochan frowned. 'What does she mean?'

Taylor waved his fingers in the air in an attempt to be dismissive. It didn't work. 'A small matter. I might have borrowed some money and had a punt on the horses.'

Lexie's nose wrinkled. 'Gambling?'

'Just the horses?' I asked. I would have crossed my fingers if I'd thought it would help.

Taylor wouldn't meet my eyes. It was even worse than I thought, then. 'Well, I went to the casino once or twice.'

I took a deep breath. 'How much?'

'A hundred grand. Give or take.'

I mulled it over, slightly taken aback. It was peanuts as far as Taylor's usual indiscretions were concerned. 'Less than the cost of a state-of-the-art bank vault door,' I commented. 'It's bad but it's not horrific. You've been in worse states.'

'Are you saying,' Brochan growled, 'that we're not going to get paid because you've been betting on Princess Pony to win the bloody Grand National?'

'Actually, I lost most of it on Appaloosa at Ascot.' Taylor pursed his lips. 'But it was very good odds and I had an amazing tip.'

Speck threw up his hands. 'Unbelievable. Absolutely frigging unbelievable. Did you travel down to England too? Because the cost of avoiding the Veil and the Lowlands…'

'There's a fabulous new invention, Speck. It's called the internet. I can place bets without leaving the comfort of my own home.'

Speck flipped up his middle finger and turned away in disgust.

I was still focused on Taylor, not taking my eyes away from him. Something about this didn't fit. 'So pay those three then pay the loan back. Arrange for instalments or whatever with your usual broker. I can wait until you're back on your feet.'

He took in a deep breath. 'Under normal circumstances, of course that's what I would do.'

Lexie stared at him. 'Normal circumstances? How often does this happen? We've worked for you for more than five years.' She turned to me. 'Why didn't you tell us this was a problem?'

Because until now it hadn't been any of her damned business. I didn't take my eyes off my old mentor as I framed my answer. 'Because it never really has been before,' I said, keeping my tone level and calm. 'There have been a few times when things got a bit hairy but we always sorted it before we reached total disaster. What's different this time? What's happened, Taylor?'

He shifted his weight, a shadow crossing his face. 'Someone else has bought the loan.'

I cocked my head. 'People can do that?'

'Yeah,' he muttered.

'Why would someone bother?'

His mouth flattened into a grim line. 'To make a quick buck.'

I drew in a breath. 'So talk to whoever bought it. Do a deal with them.'

'I tried,' he said helplessly. 'They won't talk to me. They're demanding immediate repayment.'

Begging the question of why. I tightened my jaw. 'Stall them.'

'I did. I don't think they're prepared to wait any longer. I had a buyer lined up for the Lia Saifire and I thought that would solve all our problems but…'

'All our problems?' Lexie asked, incredulous. '*Our* problems?'

Taylor gazed helplessly at me. I shook my head. Lexie did have a point. I sighed and raised my eyes heavenward. 'Tell me who they are and I'll talk to them.' I'd done it before. I could do it again.

Taylor's response was heavy. 'I don't know who they are. We only communicate through a courier.'

My eyebrows flew up. I'd not heard of that one before. 'That's rather old-fashioned, isn't it?'

'I figured they didn't want to leave a digital footprint. You should see the delivery guy though.

He's a brute. At least seven foot tall and almost the same distance wide again. He has a massive scar from his eyebrow to his mouth. No visible Clan markings.' Taylor shivered. 'He's dangerous. And he's just the errand boy.' He flicked me a look. 'Wild Man, of course.'

Of course. I passed a hand over my eyes. I'd bailed out Taylor many times in the past so my own savings weren't as substantial as they should have been, given my career. They'd be enough to tide him over, though. 'I have about a hundred and twenty thousand. That'll cover your loan and leave some left over to give to Speck, Brochan and Lexie.' I glanced at them all. 'If you can wait for the rest, I'd appreciate it.'

Brochan shook his head. 'Nuhuh. No way are you paying for us. I've got money. I can wait.'

Speck's hand shot up in the air as if he were still a pupil at school. 'I can wait too. It's not like I ever really spend much money anyway.'

They both looked at Lexie. She pouted, her expression stubborn, but it took her less than five seconds to crack. 'Fine! I'll wait. Jeez.'

The relief on Taylor's face was palpable. 'I'll make it up to you, I promise.'

I nodded. 'I know you will.' I meant it too. He always put things right – sooner or later.

He beamed at us. 'I think I have a new lead on the Lia Saifire. What we need is…'

'Whoa.' I put up my palms. 'This was my last job. I'm out, remember?'

Taylor winced. 'But you didn't get the gem.'

I was sympathetic but adamant. 'Not my fault. I'll help you out with the money but I'm done. I'm due in Oban in five days' time. I can't start planning a new heist.'

'Tegs, I need you.'

I met his eyes. 'I'm sorry but Lexie, Speck and Brochan are capable enough and you have others you can contact if you need a fourth. I made my decision and I'm not backing down.'

He gave a pleading look that stabbed at my heart but, when it was clear he could look at me like that all day long and I still wasn't going to break, he nodded imperceptibly and sighed. 'I understand.'

The others remained silent, unwilling to get involved in what was essentially a family matter. I pushed myself off the wall and walked over to them giving Taylor a hug first. 'I'll send the money over this evening,' I told him. 'But I need to get home, get some sleep and start packing.'

'Okay.' He hung his head but didn't quite let go of me.

I forced a smile at the others. 'We're still on for drinks before I leave though, right? At the usual place? You might need to buy those drinks now, of course but…'

'We'll be there!' Lexie cried. 'Of course we will!'

The pixie rushed towards me, ignoring the fact that Taylor's arm was still round my shoulders. Speck rushed in too and then Brochan. All of a sudden all five of us were embracing in a warm, tight, group hug.

'Guys,' I squeaked. 'I can't breathe.'

They broke apart. 'I'm going to miss you kiddo,' Brochan said gruffly.

I smiled tremulously. 'Drinks first, remember? I'm not leaving just yet.'

'It's still the end of an era though,' Lexie sighed, her chin wobbling.

I took a step backwards. Despite – or perhaps because of – our failure at the bank and the drama of Taylor's admission, this was all getting a bit too much. I had to leave before I collapsed in floods of tears. I wasn't usually ashamed to cry but I was afraid that if I started I'd never stop. 'Saturday night?' I managed to get out.

They all nodded. Then, very quickly and before my first tear escaped, I made my escape.

*

Dawn was just breaking. I wound my way through the familiar Clan-less streets while the sky broke apart into streaks of pink and purple, promising a perfect day. It was a long walk along the banks of the River Don but it helped me to get my head together. It was also a chance to take in the familiar landmarks and make my own silent goodbyes.

Crossing the invisible boundary into Old Aberdeen, I passed the High Kirk of St. Machar, pausing for a moment in front of its grubby, sandstone façade. In all the time I'd lived here, I'd never been inside. The place still gave me a shiver though. Along with numerous bones belonging to ancient bishops from the Clans, the left quarter of William Wallace's body was buried deep inside. His brutal execution signalled the very last time that a person of Clan-less birth was ever allowed a position of leadership.

Things might have improved over time, if it hadn't been for the Fissure. The Sidhe took full advantage of that terrible war with the Fomori demons – and the ensuing Veil, which smothered the borders of Lowlands from the Firth of Clyde right down to England itself. Now they ruled without challenge. Either you played along and gave allegiance to one of the remaining twenty-four Sidhe Clans or you were out in the cold with the Clan-less and grubbing about to make a living. But then, Scotland was never known for its warmth.

I shoved my hands into my pockets and continued walking. A group of boisterous Bauchan fell out of a nearby pub, laughing uproariously to themselves. I gave them wide berth, resisting the temptation to follow them home. They looked like roughnecks, enjoying the fruits of several weeks' labour out on the North Sea. They'd be loaded – and far too drunk to notice a tail. They were Clan-less though. I had some morals.

I wandered across the Brig O'Balgownie, raising a hand in greeting to Rab the Troll, who pulled himself up onto the stone parapet. 'How's business?' I asked.

His grey face twisted. 'Bollocks. Haven't seen a

Sidhe in weeks. Other than your fine self, of course.'

I lifted an apologetic shoulder. 'I don't count.'

'When times are desperate…'

I narrowed my eyes at him. 'Don't get cute.'

'Yeah, yeah. You see any of your kinsfolk, send them my way.'

As if. I just smiled.

By the time I got back to my flat, the pretty dawn sky had given way to a crisp blue morning. It was a shame I'd spend most of it in bed, catching up on the sleep I missed thanks to last night's activities. Usually I loved early mornings. I had no idea whether it was a Sidhe thing or just a me thing, but the break of day was the best time to be up and about as far as I was concerned.

I unlocked my door, dropping my equipment as soon as I was inside and peeling off my black jumpsuit as I walked to the bathroom. At least at this time of the morning the water would be hot. My one indulgence when I moved in was to get a power shower installed with all manner of angled jets and sprays. It was well worth it. It didn't matter how much money I paid, though – this was still Clan-less territory and I lived in an old building. It was undeniably beautiful, with a sold granite structure outside and cornices and stained glass inside. Perfect plumbing, however, was a luxury reserved for others.

I turned on the shower and got in, yelping as I half scalded my skin. Still, it was so good to get clean. I scrubbed away all the traces of grime and oil from my climb up the building and my ascent down the lift shaft – not to mention the clinging dust from the drill.

It was a crying shame that I couldn't wipe away my guilt at the same time. I felt guilty for leaving Taylor in the lurch when things looked so dire for him, and guilty for enabling his gambling habit by paying off his debts. I dreaded to think what I would have done if he hadn't helped me out all those years before. I wasn't naïve enough to think that he'd not used me but he'd never once judged me for who or what I was, and he'd always been there when I'd needed him. Maybe Saturday would be a good time to mention Gamblers' Anonymous again.

It was a good twenty minutes before I stepped out of the shower, my skin pink from the heat. I stared at my reflection in the mirror. My white hair hung down past my shoulders, an unfashionable length for a Sidhe. My violet eyes blinked back out, with just the faintest trace of shadows underneath them. I looked even paler than normal. It didn't matter how many hours I spent in the sun, there was never a tan or a blush of sunburnt glow to my cheeks. I never even got any freckles. Other people often commented on my skin, saying that they wished for the same kind of flawless complexion. I just thought it was boring. It might seem strange to desire a bout of acne but I actually did. If nothing else, it would make me appear less Sidhe – although with my eyes and hair, I was probably not going to pass myself off as anything else any time soon.

Giving up on my appearance, I towelled myself off and wandered through to my bedroom, pulling on a comfy pair of worn pyjamas before lying down on my bed and closing my eyes. I was dog tired and should, by rights, have fallen asleep within seconds.

My brain, unfortunately, had other plans. No matter how hard I tried to turn off my thoughts, my worry about Taylor wouldn't let me rest. I ran through scenario after scenario. There had to be a way to help him out so that this kind of situation never arose again. I gnawed over the problem for three-quarters of an hour when, still wide awake, I got up again. Maybe some hot cocoa would work. Unfortunately I'd forgotten about my discarded jumpsuit and, while rubbing my eyes, I didn't see it. My foot caught up in one of the sleeves and I went flying, sprawling on the floor in an ungainly heap.

'Bollocks,' I swore, picking myself back up again. I could scale buildings, abseil down mountains, perform feats of extraordinary acrobatic skill - but when it came to walking along a small corridor, I failed. My only saving grace was that I lived alone so no-one else had witnessed my clumsy collapse.

I turned round and eyed the offending clothing then scooped it up, heading towards the kitchen and the noisy old washing machine. It had a nasty habit of juddering its way across the floor in a thunderous motion which sounded more like a volcanic eruption than a mere spin cycle. I'd been meaning to replace it for years but it was low on my list of priorities. Now I was leaving it didn't seem to matter although it was hardly likely to induce sleep. But right now it didn't appear that the land of nod was anywhere on the horizon. The least I could do was get the last of my chores out of the way. It would make packing easier.

I patted down the pockets and pulled out a few errant sweet wrappers, a plastic Hello Kitty pinky ring that I'd completely forgotten I owned and which made me smile, and the letter opener I'd taken from the office. I threw the jumpsuit, along with my last remaining dirty items of clothing, and turned the machine on, then stared at the small knife. The handle was rather remarkable. My finger traced along its ornate carvings. Here in the light of day, it seemed much less elegant and graceful than it had in the dim office. There was something about it that drew me to it. Goodness knows why. It wasn't even pink.

'Like a moth to a ruddy flame,' I muttered, pulling the knife out from its sheath.

The blade was stained. Clearly its previous owner hadn't cared for it very much. The heady and unpleasant perfume from the letters it had been used to open still clung to the metal. Grabbing a nearby dishtowel, I gently rubbed along its length, wiping away the grime and, hopefully, the smell.

The washing machine began to kick into high gear, starting its shuffle across the marbled floor. That's probably why I didn't notice the strange buzzing sound to begin with. It was the odd scent of cinnamon which caught my attention first.

Wondering if it was a base note from the perfume, or perhaps remnants of a long-forgotten cleaning agent, I sniffed the blade again. As I did so, a blinding flash of light seared my eyeballs. What the hell was that? Crying out, I dropped the knife and covered my face with my arm.

'I can still see you, you know. It doesn't work for ostriches and it doesn't work for you.'

I froze. The booming voice sounded as if it had come from right in front of me. Baffled, and still squinting, I lowered my arm and stared. The knife lay on its side where it had clattered to the floor and the washing machine continued to rumble - but there was definitely no one else in the room. I was going mad. Or dreaming.

I turned slowly, wary that someone might be behind me. There was nothing more than the battered ironing board propped up against the far wall and the kitchen table covered with old bills and bits of paper that I'd left out so I could file them away in carefully labelled folders, ready for transportation.

'Honestly, for a faerie, you're pretty stupid.'

Okay: I definitely hadn't imagined that. 'Hello?' I asked cautiously, wondering whether it could be a ghost.

'Great Scott!' The voice said, utterly exasperated. 'I'm down here!'

Rubbing my eyes again, I stared at the floor,

feeling like an idiot. 'Where?'

'Here!'

A flicker of movement caught my eye and I saw him, crouching down next to the discarded letter opener. A tiny man wearing what appeared to be a tuxedo. He wasn't any larger than my thumb. I did what any girl would do in such a situation. I gaped.

'I knew a goldfish who did that once,' the little man commented.

'Who are you?'

A grin spread across his face. I realised that he was the most perfectly apple-cheeked being outside of the toddler three doors down that I'd ever seen in my life.

'I'm Bob!' he answered cheerfully. 'Who are you?'

'Uh,' I licked my lips, still not sure if any of this was real, 'Integrity.'

'Uh Integrity? That's a strange name. I'm guessing it's not your true one.'

Something inside me closed off. 'You mean because I'm a Sidhe,' I said flatly. 'Well, we're not all the same. I don't have a true name.'

'Every Sidhe has a true name. And a magical gift to go along with it.'

'No.' I put my hands on my hips. 'They don't.'

Bob put a hand on his hip too, obviously mimicking me. Then he flounced. I definitely did not look like I was doing *that*. Whoever this strange intruder was, he was making fun of me. That was okay. I liked daft jokes – but I still dropped my hands.

'Ooooooh,' Bob said. 'Touchy.'

Folding my arms, I glared down at him. 'What the hell are you and how did you get into my flat?'

'Well, duh! Isn't it obvious?'

A prickle of annoyance ran down my spine. 'If it was obvious, I would hardly be asking you, would I?'

He shrugged. 'It's true that you don't seem to be the smartest owner I've ever had but, hey, it's not like I had much of a choice.'

My eyes narrowed. That was an interesting – and incredibly distasteful – choice of words. 'Owner?'

'Of course!' He pointed to the letter opener. 'I am Bob. The Genie of the Sword.'

I looked from the fallen blade to him and back again. 'You mean letter opener.'

'No, no, no, no,' he declared. 'This is a sword.'

'It's really not.'

He flicked a disdainful glance at it. 'Alright,' he conceded, 'it's not a sword. But it is a very fine example of a dagger.'

'It's a letter opener.'

'No, it's a…'

I held up my palm to forestall him. 'Let's agree to disagree, shall we? Besides, I thought genies lived in lamps. How do you live in a letter opener?'

'Dagger. And there was one genie who lived in one lamp a very long time ago who gets all the sodding credit and is in all the sodding stories. Most of us aren't that lucky.'

'You live in the metal?' I asked doubtfully.

'Of course!' He sprang back to the blade, grinning. 'Watch.'

There was another painful flash of light. I swore again, wincing because my eyeballs felt like they were on fire. When I recovered enough to see properly again, I picked the knife up gingerly between my finger and thumb. Sure enough, reflected there in the flat surface, was Bob's smiling face. He gave me a two-dimensional wave. Then the air filled with a hum once more. At least this time I was smart enough to cover my eyes.

'So,' Bob said cheerfully, 'what would you like?'

I frowned. 'Excuse me?'

'What wishes would you like? You get three, you know.'

No way was I going to fall for that trick. Anyone with a scrap of intelligence knew to steer clear of anyone offering wishes. 'I'm good,' I told him with a definite edge to my voice.

'I don't care whether you're good or bad. What do you wish for first?'

'Nothing. I don't need anything.'

'Hah!' he scoffed. 'Everyone needs something. Go on. You can tell Bob everything. I can make it happen.'

'No thank you,' I said primly.

He gazed at me, disappointed. 'Why ever not?'

'I know how these things work,' I told him. 'I ask for money and the next thing I know I'm receiving compensation for having my leg chopped off in a freak accident. I've read the stories. Everyone's read the stories.'

He pouted. 'You're no fun.'

That stung. 'You know what the psychiatrist said to the genie, right?'

Bob looked at me suspiciously. 'What?'

'That his feelings were all bottled up.'

He deadpanned me. 'I don't get it.'

I thought about explaining and then decided against it. Life was too short. 'Look,' I said, 'jump back into the let— I mean the dagger, and I'll take you back to where I found you. You can give the banker his wishes instead.'

'Whoa! Hold your horses, Uh Integrity! I don't want to go back there!'

I waggled my eyebrows. 'Well, you're certainly not staying here.'

'He's never once cleaned the blade. I've been trapped inside that thing for years! I can't go back to that.' Bob got down on his knees and clasped his fingers together, holding them up beseechingly in my direction. 'Don't make me!'

'So what do you suggest?' I said. 'I'm certainly not going to pass you along to someone else so they can get burned by wishing for stupid stuff they don't need.'

Bob gazed at me with an air of unmistakable desperation. 'I take back what I said before. You're obviously very smart for a Sidhe. Let me stick around. Even if you don't use any of the wishes, I'm sure I can still help you.'

'First of all,' I said, ticking off my fingers, 'I don't need any help. And second of all, I'm not really a Sidhe.'

His brow furrowed. 'Of course you are.'

'I've renounced my heritage.'

Bob threw back his head and laughed. 'It doesn't work like that, you stupid…' His voice faltered mid-sentence. 'Oops. I didn't mean that.'

The washing machine suddenly groaned as it switched gears. Shaking dramatically, it began its inexorable path across the kitchen floor. Bob, alarmed, jumped about a foot in the air. 'A monster!' he yelled. 'Don't worry, Uh Integrity! I'll save you!'

Good grief. How long had he been stuck in that letter opener? 'It's not going to hurt you. It's just a machine.'

His eyes went wide and saucer-like. 'You mean it's a robot?' he whispered.

I hissed through my teeth. 'No. I'm going to bed. If you're going to stay here then don't touch anything. I have to get some sleep.'

'But it's morning. Why do you have to go to bed in the morning?'

'Sometimes I work nights,' I said shortly. I waved a finger at him. 'And I meant what I said. Don't touch a damn thing. I'll decide what to do with you later.'

'Sure, sure.' He nodded his head vigorously. 'There's just one thing though.'

'What?'

There was a sudden loud thump on the door.

'Someone's here to talk to you,' Bob answered cheerfully. And with that he hopped straight back into the blade.

Chapter Three

Whoever was at the door was feeling anxious. What began as a single loud thump turned into a battering ram of knocks that gave the washing machine a run for its money in the noise stakes. I pitied my poor neighbours. I also didn't open the door immediately. Hours earlier I had, after all, been engaged in serious criminal activity. The last thing someone in my position wanted was the door to shake in its frame. Despite our failure at the bank, I was convinced we'd covered our tracks well but it was possible we missed something. Surely though, if this really were the police, they'd have announced themselves by now. Or broken down the door.

Remaining cautious, I grabbed Bob's knife and slid it back into its sheath, hiding it underneath one of my piles of paper. Then I grabbed my kit from where I'd dropped it, shoved it into the wardrobe and jammed the door shut. Satisfied that there was nothing else incriminating on show, I nervously opened the front door.

The second I saw Taylor, I let out a sigh of relief. When I took in his dishevelled appearance, however, my wariness returned.

'You took your time,' Taylor huffed, pushing past me and pivoting to stare worriedly down the corridor as if angry hordes were on his tail.

'What is it?' I asked, alarmed. Taylor lived his life in a cloud of blithe calm. Even taking his money worries into consideration, his present demeanour was uncharacteristic. 'What's happened?'

'The others left not long after you. I went out to get a pint of milk and saw the muscle on the way back.'

I was momentarily confused. 'The muscle?'

'The Wild Man I was telling you about. The Incredible Hulk with the scar. He kicked in my door.' Taylor grimaced. 'He means serious business. If I'd not popped out then…' He swallowed, his voice trailing off. This was a different Taylor to the one I was used to. He was definitely scared.

'He wants the money and he's not prepared to wait,' I surmised.

'That has to be it.' He scratched his neck and look at me helplessly. 'What do I do?'

I took his arm and guided him gently in the kitchen, sat him down and put on the kettle. 'It's fine, Taylor. Give me the name of the courier service and I'll get the money wired over immediately. Once your creditor has that I'm sure he'll call off his attack dog.'

'Yes.' Taylor's Adam's apple bobbed up and down. 'You're right. That'll work. The money is all they want.' He fumbled in his pocket and pulled out a crumpled piece of paper. His hands shook.

I raised my eyebrows. I'd expect this kind of reaction from Speck but Taylor was normally laid back to the point of being horizontal. He was the very definition of blasé. Whoever this scarred Wild Man was, he had Taylor seriously rattled.

'Integrity, he was carrying a gun. And I'm certain he meant to use it.'

That troubled me. From the very beginning Taylor taught me that, no matter what we did, violence was not our gig. We didn't carry anything on any job that could be construed as a weapon: we were thieves, not thugs. It was a concept I stringently adhered to. There was always an alternative to fighting, even if it meant doing nothing more than running away. We usually avoided getting mixed up with people who were liable to be violent. Taylor really had got involved with some dodgy people this time.

I smoothed out the paper and looked at the phone number scrawled on it. I cleared my throat and tried to stay calm. 'I'll call them now and tell them they'll have their money within hours. Relax, Taylor.'

He pressed his lips together and nodded while I searched for my phone. Eventually finding it behind a wilting spider plant, I jabbed out the number. It rang three times before a disembodied voice answered, 'Yes?'

I took a deep breath. 'I'm calling on behalf of Andy Taylor,' I said. 'I have your money and I will send it to you now. You'll get what you want so there's no need to get all worked up.'

There was an almost imperceptible pause. Then the voice spoke again. 'The payment is late. There is a penalty.'

My fingers tightened around the phone. Loan sharks had no damn shame. 'How much?'

'Double the original amount.'

I choked. 'That's ridiculous! He's not that late.'

'I take punctuality very seriously. Double the amount or a he's a dead man walking.'

'You're being unreasonable,' I began.

'He owes me.'

I tried to think quickly. 'We'll need more time.'

'You have seventy-two hours.'

I closed my eyes briefly. 'Thank...'

'Oh, and Integrity?' the voice interrupted. 'Tell Taylor that if he tries to run I'll personally make sure that he never walks again.'

The phone clicked off. I pulled it slowly away from my ear and stared at it. 'He knows my name,' I whispered. I looked at Taylor. 'Just who in hell have you got yourself mixed up with?'

He glanced up at me, misery etched into every line of his face. 'I'm so sorry, Tegs. I've really screwed up.'

*

We went round and round in circles, trying to come up with a quick-fix solution.

'Perhaps I can ask around,' Taylor said heavily. His shoulders were slumped. 'Get a bit of money from someone else. Borrow from Peter to pay Paul, so to speak.'

Normally I'd counsel against creating debt to pay off debt but this situation felt very dangerous. I was pretty certain that neither Brochan, Lexie nor Speck would be keen to help. As much as they professed loyalty and had agreed to delay their own payment for last night's failed heist, Taylor would burn every bridge he had if he borrowed money from them. He couldn't afford to alienate them, not if he wanted a chance of turning a profit in the future; the fastest way to lose friends or colleagues is to mess things up financially.

Discarding them as potential lenders, I considered. 'Who could you ask?'

'There's Boon.'

I sucked in a breath. Boon was a distinctly sinister moneylender. Much like everyone else in my little underworld, he was Clan-less. That didn't mean he wasn't scary. I'd heard stories about what happened to borrowers who defaulted on his loans and, unless Taylor was keen to have a section of his soul cut away, it wasn't much of an option. 'I don't think…' I began.

'Who else is there?' Taylor asked. 'As long as I keep up the repayments, Boon won't create problems.' His face shadowed. 'I've taken money from him before.'

I stiffened. 'When?'

'Before you.'

I studied his expression. How had he gone from being so bright and confident the day before the bank job to so desperate now? 'There must be another way.'

'Can you think of anything?'

My gaze fell on the sheet of paper on top of the letter opener. There was always Bob. I narrowed my eyes suspiciously. Was it merely a coincidence that I'd come across the genie now – when desperation might lead to me using him? I nibbled my lip and decided his appearance was too far-fetched to be anything more than serendipity. Serendipity that I'd be a fool to make use of. Going down the wishing road could cause more problems than it solved.

I held off making a decision for now. It wasn't like the genie was going anywhere. 'It won't do any harm to ask Boon for terms,' I said finally. 'Don't commit yourself to anything. Just see what he says.'

Relieved to have something to do, Taylor nodded. I passed him my phone, then gave him some privacy to speak. In the bathroom I splashed cold water on my face, then leaned against the sink and pressed my forehead against the cool mirror. If only the damn Lia Saifir had been where it was supposed to be, we wouldn't be in this mess. So much for my big move to Oban. I couldn't leave until things were straight with Taylor. I owed him too much.

When I went back to check on him, he was even paler than before – if that were possible. 'Let me guess,' I said drily, 'the terms are too steep?' I wasn't particularly surprised. Boon was a bloody charlatan.

Taylor shook his head slowly. 'He won't do it,' he croaked.

I blinked. I hadn't been expecting that. 'What

do you mean?'

'He won't give me the loan. He said he knows who's bought it and he doesn't want to piss them off. I got the impression they'd already been in touch with him. He refused point blank to tell me who it was.'

'That doesn't make any sense.' I sank down into my chair. Except it did. This wasn't about money at all; this was about someone wanting to destroy Taylor. No wonder they knew my name. 'Who is it? Who really took the loan?'

He looked me in the eye. 'I don't know. I was telling the truth, Tegs. I really don't know.'

'You must have pissed off someone.'

'Not that I can think of. The last time I really did that was before you came along. I've been keeping my nose clean.'

Other than arranging for a series of high-profile thefts, I thought. Apparently reading my mind, Taylor sighed. 'You know what I mean. I've not upset anyone in the underworld.'

'Could it be someone we've stolen from in the past? Someone wanting serious revenge?'

A spark flared in his eyes. 'I might not be much of a gambler, Tegs, but I am good at my job. No one knows who we are.'

I had no idea what we were going to do. 'Okay,' I said. I'd have to make this up as I went along. 'This is what we're going to do. Um...'

There was a sudden thump at the front door that made us both jump. I looked at Taylor. 'Stay there,' I told him, every muscle in my body tensing up.

It was nothing more than the morning paper. I cursed myself for being as jumpy as a kitten and picked it up. 'It's alright,' I called out to Taylor, picking it up from the doormat. 'It's just the newspaper.' I tossed it down onto the kitchen table with the rest of the detritus.

'I'm sorry,' Taylor said miserably. 'I've screwed everything up. Here you are trying to pack, trying to make a new life yourself and...'

'Stop.' I mustered my sternest look. 'Yes, you've messed up. But we'll deal with it.'

His head drooped. 'How?'

I straightened my shoulders. Sneaky was my middle name. But when sneaky didn't work... 'I'll find this courier and talk some sense into him. If we can get the name of the guy who bought the loan, we can find out what he really wants. Because I'm betting it ain't money.'

Taylor jerked his head up in alarm. 'The Wild Man will squash you, Integrity! This isn't someone you want to mess with.'

I shrugged, trying to appear nonchalant. 'Maybe he'll find out that I'm someone *he* doesn't want to mess with.'

Besides, at this moment we were out of damn options.

'I should come with you then.'

'No. Right now you're the target. It makes more sense for you to stay here. It'll be easier for me to talk my way out of things if I'm alone.'

He sighed. 'Once upon a time, it was *me* giving the orders.'

'Once upon a time, you weren't a decrepit old man.' I winked. 'Don't worry. We'll sort all this out.'

Chapter Four

From where I was standing, Taylor's little house looked empty. The door was closed, the curtains were drawn and there were no signs of life. A few people scurried along the street, one or two of them with faces I recognised. Wanting to avoid getting drawn into a chat about the weather, I stayed in the shadows. I couldn't afford to get distracted. You're tough, I told myself. I nodded at the tiny voice inside my head that chirped: 'And when the going gets tough, the tough get going.'

I could do this. I *had* to do this.

As soon as the street was clear of pedestrians, I darted forward. It was possible that the hulking brute had vanished when he realised Taylor wasn't around. That wouldn't help my cause; I needed to confront him. He knew who I was and that meant he probably also knew I was Sidhe. I would bet, however, that he didn't know that I had no Sidhe Gifts to work with. I could play with that. Assuming he showed up again.

When I reached Taylor's door and examined it, the splintered frame was easy to see. The lock itself was completely bust. I pushed open the door stealthily but it took only one touch for it to creak ominously, fall forward, drop off its top hinge and slam against the wall with a loud crash. So much for a discreet entry.

With little choice, I folded my arms and stalked inside, yelling as I went, 'Hey Scarface! Where the hell are you?' I injected a gravelly growl into my tone. Ha! Take that, scary enforcer man.

Without slowing down, I stormed through the hallway and into Taylor's living room – to be greeted by a scene of utter devastation. He was normally fastidious about tidiness. When I lived with him after fleeing the Bull, he snapped at me for so much as leaving an empty glass on a table. If he could see how things looked now, he'd have palpitations. Oh wait. He already was having palpitations.

Taylor's computer monitor, which normally sat neatly on the desk in the corner, was lying smashed in the centre of the room. There was a huge rent through his watercolour of the Aberdeen skyline, and there was paper everywhere. There was also a strong smell of cloves.

'Where are you?' I snarled. I marched over to the rug in the middle of the room and picked up one of the cushions from the sofa. It appeared to be stained with some sort of icky brown liquid. 'You better have wide pockets,' I shouted. 'Because you're going to have a hell of a dry cleaning bill!'

As threats went, that was hardly going to have a thug quivering in his boots. I had to do better. 'You lily-livered guttersnipe! Come out and show yourself!' Nope. That wasn't much of an improvement.

Just then there was a thump. I froze and slowly

lifted my eyes to the ceiling. There was another thump and, as I watched, a crack appeared in one corner of the plasterwork then snaked its way across. Okaaaay. Upstairs then.

Trying not to be terrified at what sort of creature could cause structural damage so easily, I balled up my fists. Bring it on.

I thumped over to the stairs. I wasn't going to cause any cracks to appear but at least I could make myself sound unafraid. 'Show yourself!' I yelled.

A strange rumble reverberated through the house. I swallowed hard. That didn't sound good. Before I could place one foot on the bottom stair, a vast shadow appeared. There, directly above me, was a monstrous dark shape. I couldn't make out any features but, whoever he was, he was possibly the largest being I'd ever seen in my life. It was a wonder he'd ever made it up the narrow staircase. No doubt this was Taylor's Wild Man then. The only saving grace was that I couldn't see any sign of the aforementioned gun.

I ignored the rapid flutter of my heartbeat and frowned upwards. 'I'm guessing you like to disco,' I called up. 'Because you're doing a bloody good impression of the boogieman.'

For a moment there was silence, then I heard a tiny wheeze. Was that a good or a bad thing? 'You like jokes?' I asked. No response. I took a deep breath. 'What does one penny say to the other penny?'

There was still no answer. I provided it for him.

'Let's get together and make some cents.' Nothing. 'Okay, okay. So it's an American joke,' I said. 'It's still good though, right? You can still understand it. And, you know what? This, right now?' I waved my arm. 'You being here? It's making no sense. Your boss, whoever he is, will get his money. But seventy-two hours is ridiculous. We need more time. You tell him that you don't scare me. You want a fight then I'm here and I'm ready.'

I puffed up my chest, emboldened by the continued silence from the enforcer. It was all for show, of course. I didn't fight. Ever. 'What's your boss's name again?'

Unsurprisingly, the monster-shaped man didn't answer. I was going to have to be a damn sight cleverer than that. 'Strong and silent, eh?' I asked. 'I'm betting you're actually a real softie at heart. You probably hate violence.' I took one step up. 'You play the part of the bully but really you like puppies and pansies and crying at romantic comedies.' I took another step up.

There was another loud rumble. I forced myself not to clutch at the banister as the entire house shook. It took me a moment or two to work out what the sound was. Shit. It was laughter. I shrugged.

'Okay then. I pegged you wrong. You *do* like violence. You *are* a bully. But you know what? Most bullies can be beaten. You probably live off your size. People run away in fear before you even raise your little finger. Well,' I said, hoping to hell that I sounded bold and confident, 'I'm not scared of bullies. Not any more. Until you've faced a vicious Sidhe teen girl, you don't know the meaning of the word bully. So you? You're nothing.'

He still didn't bloody move. This was like talking to a brick wall. I stepped up once more. I was getting closer. And he was still a freaking statue.

'I'm Sidhe, you know,' I said casually, hating myself for bringing up my heritage. What the hell. I was leaving town anyway. 'You want to know who my father was? Gale. From Clan Adair. He was a mean wanker with more power in his pinkie than you could ever even dream of.' So I'd been told. I flicked a cold smile up at the statue. 'Clan Adair might not be around any more but I've got his power. I *am* his daughter.'

He didn't so much as flinch. My words might be tough but I didn't have a single thing with which to back them up. I tossed back my hair. 'So get your boss on the blower and tell him to back the hell off. If he does, he'll get his money. But if it's not money he's really after, then tell me what he wants and I might just let you go.'

In a world of ridiculous notions, that was about the silliest thing I could have come up with. I was a third of this guy's size. But I was banking on the fact that it was so ridiculous, it might actually work. Unfortunately I was wrong.

The huge man wheezed again. He started to move down towards me, one step then another. I ignored the tremble in my knees and held my ground. It was all I had. If I ever got out of this, though, I was going to wring Taylor's neck.

The reek of cloves got stronger. I peered at his face but it was still shadowed. I lifted up the corner of my mouth in a rueful smile. 'You're going to be sorry if you come any closer,' I told him.

I'd barely finished my sentence when he reached out with one huge hand and grabbed the front of my T-shirt, hauling me off my feet. Quashing my terror, I began to mumble incoherent nonsense. I screwed my eyes shut. 'Qaleghqa'mo' jIQuch! LwlIj jachjaj' I ignored my legs dangling helplessly in the air and waved my arms around as if I were about to cast a spell. Then I opened one eye and peeked.

His face was still shrouded in darkness but I could make out the scar that Taylor had mentioned. It was clearly an old wound but it was an angry red colour, cutting a jagged line from one side of his face to the other. His nose was large and bulbous but his eyes were nothing more than shaded chasms of black. Uh oh.

He cleared his throat. 'Since when do the Sidhe know Klingon?' he grunted in a deep voice.

I winced. So much for that. Without further warning, he thrust his free hand in a tight fist at the side of my head. For a brief second I felt a burst of pain and tiny lights danced in front of my eyes. Then the world slid into darkness.

*

When I came to, I was completely disorientated. I thought I was back in my own bed and had dreamed up the entire thing, until I tried to sit up and felt the pain in my head where he'd struck me. I raised my hand and gingerly touched my temple. It throbbed and was tender but I didn't appear to have suffered any lasting damage. Then it occurred to me that the brute of an enforcer might still be around and I leapt to my feet.

I was back in Taylor's living room, lying on his sofa with my head propped up on a cushion – which made no sense whatsoever. Of the monster man there was no sign.

'Hello?' I called out cautiously. There was no response. I cast a wary glance upwards to the ceiling. Had he gone back upstairs? The crack seemed to have grown, threading its way out across the white surface. I stared at it and made a decision. Whether my attacker was there or not, I was done. It was time to get the hell out of Dodge.

I half ran and half stumbled out of the door, almost colliding with the warm, familiar figure of Brochan.

'Hey!' he said, catching my arm. 'What gives? I came round to see if Taylor was alright and I saw his door.' He pointed at the semi-destroyed frame. 'I'm going to guess that wasn't you.'

'We need to get out of here,' I told him. 'Now.'

I filled him in on the details as we half walked, half ran back to my flat. Brochan listened, his face expressionless. When I was done, he stared at me with an intensity that I rarely saw. 'You should leave, Integrity. This is Taylor's problem. Not yours.'

'Taylor's problems are my problems. And vice-versa.'

He shook his head. 'You can't spend the rest of your life beholden to him.'

'If it wasn't for him, I don't know what I would have done.'

'You've paid him back tenfold.'

I straightened my spine. 'And I'll continue to pay him back.'

Brochan sucked air in through his teeth. 'It sounds to me like you're in over your head.'

'And that's the fun part,' I said lightly, punching his arm. 'Besides,' I joked, 'I live for danger.'

Brochan didn't crack a smile. 'I know what it's like. We all know what it's like. We're just as Clan-less as you. It might be a bit different for you because you're Sidhe…'

'It's not different,' I interrupted. 'I'm not different just because I have Sidhe blood running through my veins.'

'Every Sidhe has a place. Every Sidhe has a Clan. That can't be said for the rest of us.'

'There are mermen in the Clans.'

He nodded. 'Sure. Just like there are pixies and warlocks. And all the rest. But they only *work* for the Clans. They're not tied to them like the Sidhe are. And there are plenty of us who aren't in the Clans either. You're the only Sidhe in the country in that situation. You're bound to feel the need to belong somewhere. It doesn't mean you need to kill yourself because of it.'

'Believe me,' I snorted, 'I have a very strong survival instinct.'

He spoke quietly. 'Not strong enough. Pack up your stuff, Integrity. Get out of here and go to the mountains like you planned. Taylor will manage without you. He got himself into this situation. You said he's owed money before and got himself back into the black again. He'll cope.'

I thought of the hulking Wild Man in Taylor's house who'd laid me out with one single swat. 'No,' I said, shaking my head. 'There's something about all this that's different.' I tilted my head up to the sky and felt the faint drizzle on my skin. 'I can delay Oban for a few more days if I have to. Besides, this guy – the one who's bought the loan – he's given us seventy-two hours.' I checked my watch. 'My train leaves in seventy-five so I'll probably still make it.'

'You might not be in one piece, that's all,' Brochan muttered under his breath.

I laughed, trying to sound more confident than I felt. 'If this moneylender guy wants a piece of me, then he's got good taste.'

'Let me speak to the others. I'm sure between the three of us we can scrape together enough money to sort things out.'

A part of me really wanted to say yes but it wasn't fair. 'If you don't think *I* should be involved,'

I said firmly, 'then you lot definitely shouldn't be. Taylor and I will work something out. There's still time.'

'Integrity…'

I met his eyes. 'I promise that if I can't find an alternative solution then I'll come and talk to you, alright? I'm sure it won't come to that though.' It definitely wouldn't. I'd use Bob's wishes before I involved the crew. The scarred man was dangerous, even if he'd laid me down on the sofa after knocking me out. I remained convinced that his boss wanted something more than money - and until we knew what that something was, it made sense to keep things between Taylor and me. 'This isn't your problem,' I reiterated.

'Why is it,' he complained, 'that you can say that to me and believe it, but I can't say it to you?'

I smirked. 'Sheer stubborn contrariness, of course.'

He gripped my fingers tightly, bare seconds before there was a squeal of tires and the sudden sharp howl of a siren. My stomach dropped. Oh shite. We were cornered and there was nowhere to run.

'Iain Brochan! You're under arrest for assault. You do not have to say anything but it may harm your defence if you do not mention when questioned something which you later rely on in court. Anything you do say may be given in evidence.'

I gaped. Assault? What the hell? A burly police

officer jumped out of the car, snapped a pair of handcuffs round Brochan's wrists and flung him into the back seat.

'Wait!' I shouted. 'He's not done anything! You can't do this!'

The car door slammed shut. From the other side of the window, Brochan stared at me with wide eyes. 'Get the others,' he mouthed.

'Stop!' I shrieked again. It was pointless. The police officer didn't give me so much as a glance; he simply clambered into the driver's seat and the car took off, leaving me standing there frozen with shock. Dry leaves skittered across the road in the wake of the car's departure.

With shaking fingers, I pulled out my phone. Before I could dial, however, it rang and Lexie's name flashed up on the screen. Thank the stars.

'Lexie,' I said, urgently, 'listen. Something's happened. Brochan…'

'It's Speck,' she broke in. 'He's been arrested. He sent me a text message just now. They broke in his door, Integrity.'

The tendrils of dread curling round my heart squeezed further. 'Why?'

'I don't know,' she babbled. 'There wasn't time for him to explain. It has to be the bank job. How did they get onto us? How…'

Cold rationality replaced my fear. 'Leave now, Lexie,' I told her. 'Don't pack anything. Get out of your house and find somewhere to lay low. Someone's after us and I don't know why.'

'But…'

'Do it! Dump your phone too. I'll come and find you when I know what's going on.'

'I'm scared.'

I swallowed. 'Me too. But go, Lex. Now.'

I sprinted the last few hundred metres home, flung open my door and bolted inside. Taylor's strained expression greeted me.

'Who else knows about the bank job?' I demanded.

He blinked. 'What?'

'The Lia Saifire, Taylor. Who else did you tell about it?'

Confusion was written across his face. 'No-one. I'm not stupid. What's happened?'

I cursed, flipping on my laptop to scan the news. There was nothing. It was still the holiday; in theory no one would have noticed the break-in yet. But then why had both Brochan and Speck been arrested?

'Tegs,' Taylor said again, 'what's happened?'

'Brochan was just arrested for assault, right in front of me.'

He rose up from his chair, staggering slightly. 'Assault? But he would never…'

'I know,' I answered grimly. I pulled out my phone again, smoothing back my hair and trying to adopt a calm, professional tone. It took seconds to find the number I needed. 'This is Joanna Smith,' I said into the receiver. 'I believe you've just arrested a client of mine, Mark Specton. What are the charges?'

I waited while the person on the other end tapped at a keyboard. When I got my answer, I muttered a brief word of thanks and hung up.

'Speck's been arrested for hacking,' I told Taylor grimly.

He sank back down into his chair. 'Now that I could believe,' he said, 'except for the fact that Speck's too damn good.'

I agreed. Never mind being one step ahead of the cyber-crimes unit, Speck was about a thousand. He was too skilled to leave a trail and get caught. I shook my head. 'This isn't a coincidence. Your loan. Brochan. Now Speck … it's all connected.'

'What about Lexie?'

'Hopefully she's safe. I told her to get away.'

'I don't understand,' Taylor whispered.

I was right there with him. We were criminals - all of us - and we knew there was always a possibility we'd screw up and the police would come knocking at our doors – but for stealing. Not for these other things. And why the hell didn't they scoop me up at the same time as Brochan?

Taylor's phone chirped with an incoming message. We exchanged a look of dread then he reached down to check it. He squeezed his eyes shut, confirming my worst expectations. I peered down.

Get my money and your friends will be released.

I felt sick. 'Who has that kind of power?' I asked. 'Who has the police in their pocket like that?

It couldn't be a Sidhe. Not unless it's a previous target who's found out who we are and wants revenge.'

Taylor opened his eyes again and stared at me miserably. 'If that's the case,' he said flatly, 'then we're fucked. But truthfully, I have no bloody idea who is behind all this.'

'Whoever he is, we need to pay him. We need to get that money and get him off our backs. What else do you have? There must be other jobs on the back burner that I can…'

'There's nothing.'

'But…'

'There's nothing, Tegs.' A shadow crossed his face.

I glanced at the paper-strewn table. Bob was going to get his day of glory, after all. I started to reach for the letter opener but Taylor jumped back up. He adjusted his cuffs, drawing my attention to his hands. My eyes narrowed. He might be getting old but he didn't make any movement that wasn't deliberate.

'What's going on?'

'You mean apart from being threatened by a Wild Man? Nothing.' He fiddled with one of his buttons.

I hissed through my teeth. 'Seriously, Taylor?'

He blinked at me innocently. Too innocently. 'What?'

'You trained me. Everything you know, I know.'

He shrugged. 'So?'

I pointed down. 'Do you really think I'm not going to notice that kind of sleight of hand?'

He cursed. 'I knew I should have kept back a few tricks.' He sighed and slid a rolled-up piece of paper out of his sleeve.

I recognised the photo immediately. It was taken not long after I'd joined him. Both of us were beaming into the camera; both of us looked so young. 'You didn't need to steal this,' I said softly. 'I'd have given it to you if you'd asked.'

He looked away. 'I didn't want to come across all soppy.'

I tutted. 'Taylor, come on. I think after all we've been through…' I paused and my eyes narrowed. Hold on a second. 'Smart. Real smart. Use an old diversionary tactic. What are you really hiding?'

His eyebrow twitched. Tell-tale giveaway. Sometimes he forgot that I knew him almost as well as I knew myself.

'What have you really got hiding there?'

'I don't know what you're talking about. There's all your junk, today's newspaper and some daft knife.'

Was this more trouble to deal with? 'It's a letter opener.' I met his eyes. 'And? What else are you covering up?' I demanded.

'And nothing. How did it go at my house? You were quite a while.'

'I bumped into your friend.' Or rather his fist bumped into my head. Whatever. The Wild Man was the least of our problems. 'It didn't go very well.'

Taylor's eyes widened. 'Are you alright?'

'I'm fine.' This wasn't the time to skirt around the truth. My gaze hardened. The only thing that I hadn't seen was the newspaper. That must be what he was trying to conceal. 'Hand over the paper.'

He shook his head vehemently. 'There's nothing there. I was just reading the horoscopes. You don't want to know what mine said.'

The day that Taylor was superstitious and believed the bumph the newspapers printed was the day I stopped liking hot pink. I lunged towards him, feinting right then grabbing the newspaper with my left hand.

'Integrity!' he howled.

I backed away and smoothed it out – and saw the headline.

'I could leave the country,' Taylor started. 'I've heard Belize is nice at this time of year.'

I ignored him, scanning the story. And I'd thought things couldn't get any worse. I should have known better.

'You'd have somewhere nice to come and visit on holiday,' he continued.

'And what about Brochan and Speck?' I sighed. There was no choice. 'No,' I said, pointing to the huge picture on the front of the paper. 'I've got a far, far better idea.'

Taylor squinted. 'You can't.'

I nodded to myself. 'I can. It's the Lia Saifir.

And look who's got it.'

He stared at the smooth good looks of the man in the photo. 'Oh.' He sank down, deflated, into the nearest chair. 'I didn't see that,' he mumbled in a blatant lie.

'He's staying at the Astor Hotel. He's in town, Taylor. We can still get the jewel.'

'No, Tegs. You can't do it. It's not fair.'

I touched his arm. 'We steal from the Sidhe all the time, Taylor.'

'Not like this. Not when there's a chance you'll be recognised.'

'Every time I step outside I might be recognised! It's been sixteen years. If they cared where I was, they'd have found me by now.' I refrained from mentioning the letter I'd received summoning me back to the Sidhe court. Taylor had tried to hide the newspaper because he didn't want me to get that up close and personal with a Sidhe who knew my real background. He'd go nuts if he discovered I'd been summoned back 'home'.

'I think I can handle one Sidhe,' I said decisively, although I had no idea whether that was true or not. But how hard could it really be? 'What choice do we have? I get the jewel and you get the money to get us out of this messed-up hole.'

'But *him*? He knows you, Tegs.'

I smiled grimly at Byron Moncrieffe's photo. 'He's a playboy with nothing more on his mind than wine and women. It'll be a piece of cake.'

Taylor regarded me soberly. 'You're supposed

to be leaving.'

'Next week.' I shrugged. 'I can't leave now, can I? Besides, I steal the Lia Saifire from Byron in the next seventy-two…' I checked my watch, 'make that sixty-eight hours, and I'll still have plenty of time to pack and say my goodbyes. Whoever the bastard is who's pulling the strings of this loan and screwing with our crew, they can't argue if we actually pay up. You just need to make sure the buyer is still in place. And see if you can find out who the money lender is. We need to know so we can stop this happening again.'

Taylor still looked troubled. 'Stealing from this Sidhe could go very badly. You shouldn't do it. If he recognises you…' His voice trailed off.

My eyes flickered again to the spot where Bob's letter-opener was hiding. The genie was a last resort but he was still there if we needed him. But nicking a gem from a spoilt Sidhe Clan heir should be easier than taking candy from a baby. I could solve all our sudden problems in one fell swoop. And if Byron recognised me … well, I'd spin him a line or two. I was pretty damn good at manipulation when I put my mind to it. Not when it came to burly Wild Men or the arm of the law when I hadn't had time to prepare but with this idiot … no problemo.

Chapter Five

Taylor wasn't happy when I'd told him to get lost. It was, however, for the best. He wasn't going to be able to help me with Byron. At this short notice, the only plan I had time to put into place was that of femme fatale. As much as I hated doing it, it wouldn't be the first time. And I had to admit that it was almost always successful, even if I normally passed the dubious honour of acting as bait over to Lexie who enjoyed that kind of role-playing far more than I did. For now, it was more important that both Taylor and Lexie were safely tucked away from the moneylender's reach until we had the necessary coin to get him off our backs. Whether he was after something else or not, he wouldn't be able to argue if we paid him back.

Once I was sure that Taylor was out of the way, I sprang into action. Desperate times called for desperate measures. I depilated, plucked and pruned myself to within an inch of my life, before liberally dousing my skin with the expensive scented moisturiser which I saved for special occasions. Then I grabbed The Dress.

Every girl has one of these – an item of clothing that says 'shag me but don't you dare screw with me' written all over it. Mine was hot pink, naturally – and very, very tight. It cost me an arm and a leg but it was well worth it, even if I'd only ever worn it twice before and felt distinctly awkward on both occasions. The cunning stitching around the bodice created the illusion that my breasts were far larger than they really were and the fabric panels around my hips accentuated my waist until I looked like some kind of sculpted Barbie doll. It was bloody uncomfortable to wear and sitting down was not a feat for the faint-hearted. I had to go for it, though – I had no choice. It helped that the vast majority of men were generally pretty stupid when it came to such matters. I had no doubts that Sidhe men – even Sidhe men who had females throwing themselves at them every minute of the day – would be no different.

I was less successful with my make-up, carefully applying eyeshadow before stabbing myself with the mascara wand so my eyes watered and I looked like a Pierrot clown in the rain. I was clearly out of practice. I wiped it all off and started again, more slowly this time. When I was done, however, and looked at the results in the mirror, I felt satisfied. The effect was that of a wide-eyed sultry temptress. Byron would have no chance. Or so I hoped.

I ignored the tremor of fearful butterflies rippling in my belly. I wasn't a terrified child any more, I reminded myself. I grabbed a bag, flinging extra lipstick and powder inside. Then, as an afterthought and because you simply never knew, I shoved Bob's letter opener in too.

Tottering out on high heels, I almost collided with Charlie, my dodgy black-market-dealing neighbour. I usually avoided him. This time his reaction to my appearance served me well. For once, I got what I wanted.

'Whoa! Integrity, wherever you're going, I want to come too!' He leered at me, his eyes dropping to my chest and lingering there.

I pushed away the creeped-out feeling that was threatening to overcome me and smiled. 'Sorry, Charlie. Invitation only.'

'I can be your plus one.'

I placed my hand on his arm. I needed both the practice and the affirmation. 'That's so kind of you,' I purred. 'But no.'

He almost dropped his bag. Given the fact that it contained his takings for the day and he usually clung onto it like a drowning man to a raft, it was the response I'd been after. He licked his lips. 'Check this out,' he said in a low whisper. He dug into his pocket and took a small silver sphere. Threads of red ran through it. I peered down.

'What is it?'

'Poison. It's from a plant which grows along the Veil. It almost killed me to retrieve it. Give this to your worst enemy and they'll drop dead in seconds.'

Ugh. 'Why are showing it to me?'

'It's brand-new stuff, Integrity. And expensive. I'll let you have it for free.' From the lascivious look on his face, he had a different kind of 'payment' in mind.

'I don't want it. Anyway, you shouldn't be venturing near the Veil. It's dangerous.'

'You're worried about me,' he said, his eyes suddenly gleaming.

'No,' I replied flatly. 'I'm simply giving you sensible advice.'

'The Veil is secure, Integrity. Nothing gets out of there and nothing's getting in. You should check it out some time. I could take you.'

'No thanks. Whatever the Lowlands hold is of no interest to me.'

'Are you scared of a little Fomori demon?'

I gave him an irritated glance. 'Have you ever seen a Fomori demon?'

He pouted. 'No.'

'Exactly. No one has seen a Fomori demon and no one wants to. The Fissure isn't some cautionary tale to keep children in line, Charlie. The Fomori annexed half of Scotland.'

'That was almost three hundred years ago. Who cares?'

I rolled my eyes. I was done with this conversation. 'You can keep your poison. I'm on my way out.'

'Why go out when you can party with me here?'

I smiled and pointed at his chin. 'I think you're drooling,' I told him. Then I sauntered off, appreciating the fact that I could feel him staring after me. For good measure, I threw in a little extra hip swing. There was an audible sigh from behind. Charlie was a sleazebag for sure but I felt better knowing that my outfit was such a success.

Thankfully, the taxi was already waiting; I didn't like the idea of hanging around on the street looking like this. I arranged myself on the seat, running through the moves I'd need to make to attract Byron's attention. When I'd covered various different scenarios and was confident of the possible outcomes, I finally started to relax. Maybe this could even be fun. Maybe.

The moment the taxi pulled up outside the Astor Hotel I slipped into character, nodding imperiously at the doorman who helped me out of the car. There was a nervous moment when I realised just how high my dress was riding up on my thighs but I pulled it down in one fluid movement and strolled inside. From the looks I received from both the staff and guests milling around at the front, my plan was already working.

Taking tiny mincing steps, I made it to the bar without falling over. Then I crooked a finger to grab the bartender's attention and ordered a glass of champagne. Normally, of course, I drank beer but right now I was selling an image.

It took less than three minutes for the first guy to approach me. 'Hello there.' His voice had a definite Cockney twang. That was surprising in itself. Most English people avoided coming to Scotland if they could possibly help it. That was due mostly to superstition about breaks in the Veil but it was also a difficult journey to make. He would have had to cross the Channel to France and then gone overland across Europe and up to Scandinavia. Flying anywhere near the Lowlands was a big no-no. Whatever was going on there caused jiggery-pokery to electrical systems. It just wasn't worth it.

His lip curled up in a good impersonation of Elvis. 'I couldn't help but notice you from my table. That's some dress. You have good taste.'

I flicked him a look. A human coming onto a Sidhe? That was pretty daring, even for a guy as overtly good looking as this one. 'I do have good taste,' I told him. 'And that's why I'm not interested.'

He affected an expression of mock hurt. 'Why so hasty?' His gaze drifted down my body. Irritatingly, my dress had begun to wiggle back up my thighs again. It was like the damn thing had a mind of its own. 'Nice legs. When do they open?'

Oh, he so did not want to go there. I fixed him with my coldest look and brushed my index finger against his lips. 'Nice mouth. When does it shut?'

A spark flared in his eyes. 'Wonderful! I like my women feisty.'

When was the last time a man was called feisty? I resisted the urge to put him down further; I was here for a reason and, while I needed him to back off, I didn't want to appear too haughty. I couldn't see any Sidhe in the bar but that didn't mean there weren't already others here who were in some way related to Byron. 'Thank you,' I murmured, softening my smile. 'But I'm really not looking for anything other than some peace to enjoy my drink.' I tapped the side of my glass for emphasis and turned away.

He stood there for another moment or two as I prayed he'd piss off. Eventually he got the message.

Breathing a sigh of relief, I sipped my drink and covertly checked the time. It was still early evening but I was feeling the effects of my sleepless night. It would be really nice if Byron could show up right about now. If he waited until later - or, worse, if he didn't make an appearance at all - I was liable to end up snoozing on the bar before I could put any of my plans into action.

'You alright there?' the bartender asked.

I nodded, looking him over. He was human but wearing the Fairlie Clan badge. That was unsurprising considering the Fairlies owned this hotel. No Sidhe - even a lower-class member - would be caught dead serving drinks. It was typical for the Clans to press others into service to do the jobs they had no desire to do themselves. The bartender might have pledged allegiance to the Fairlies but that didn't mean he was blindly loyal to them.

I dropped a tenner and raised my eyebrows. He glanced from the money to me and back again. 'What can I do for you?' he asked finally.

I kept my tone casual. 'You got many Sidhe staying here this weekend?'

He shrugged, sliding his hand over the note

and palming it with professional ease. 'Quite a few. They usually end up down here. Which Clan are you?'

I tapped the side of my nose as if it were a secret and winked. I might have been honest about my origins with the Wild Man but that was in pursuit of a greater cause. Advertising that I was the last remaining member of the Adair Clan wouldn't serve me now. Fortunately, the bartender got the memo and nodded knowingly. If he was curious about my reasons for keeping my Clan secret, he was too polite to show it.

I passed over another ten-pound note and lowered my voice. 'I might sit here for a while,' I said. 'I like people-watching.' I tilted my head. 'I don't particularly enjoy getting drunk though.'

The bartender stroked his chin. 'We have a wonderful sparkling cider that's entirely alcohol free. And it's very similar in colour to champagne.'

I grinned, briefly forgetting my role as temptress in favour of acknowledging the bartender's understanding. 'That sounds wonderful.'

He smiled in return. 'Last night, Byron Moncrieffe arrived around seven,' he told me.

I decided to brazen it out. 'Am I that obvious?'

'You're not the first woman who's heard that he's in town. You're not even the first Sidhe.' He jerked his head to a table over to the right. I discreetly followed his movement, registering the three young Sidhe girls dressed up to the nines and giggling.

I lifted a shoulder in rueful acknowledgment that he'd caught me out. As if. 'Any tips?'

The bartender's looked quickly left and right, as if someone might be listening in. Then he leaned over. 'He prefers doing the chasing himself.'

'Noted.' By the sound of things, the playboy princeling was as predictable as I had imagined. I had no idea what the bartender thought of me trailing after royalty and I didn't much care. It would suit my purpose if he lumped me in with all the other hangers on.

Less than twenty minutes later, when my champagne glass had been helpfully filled with cider rather than anything that might cause inebriation, three snooty-looking Sidhe swept into the bar. I was in luck. A helpful nod from the bartender confirmed my suspicions.

The Sidhe ejected a family from the best table in the centre of the room and set about checking the surface for minute traces of dirt and ordering drinks. Ah ha. The advance entourage.

I straightened my posture and angled myself away from the table. Just as another group entered, Byron Moncrieffe included, I flipped out my hair in a move calculated to garner attention. Then I pointedly ignored them all.

The hum of voices from the other patrons quieted to a hush, although the group of giggly Sidhe girls found it impossible to stifle their excited laughter. I was almost surprised that there wasn't a trumpet to herald his arrival. Honestly, for someone who was in his position for no other reason than the circumstances of his birth, the reaction he received was ridiculous.

I twisted my head slightly so that I could see the table reflected in the mirror hanging across the bar. I counted seven people in total: the three who'd entered first, two women, a cheeky-looking dimpled friend and Byron himself. They were all Sidhe and, by the insignia they were sporting, all from Clan Moncrieffe. That was good. A tight-knit group who kept to themselves would be less likely to know about me - even if I had once had the displeasure of meeting Byron himself.

Surreptitiously - and still using the reflection in the mirror - I eyed him. He had an easy smile which contradicted my memory of him. His bronze hair and golden skin remained the same but he'd definitely grown into his body. Trying to remain dispassionate, I took in the roped muscles on his arms. His clothing, while casual, was as well-designed to display his buff physique as my dress was designed to show off other, uh, attributes. Nah. He wasn't that good-looking. Maybe he was alright if you liked your men golden and muscled and charismatic. Shite. Okay, he was as sexy as hell.

I noted a small scar underneath his eye that I didn't remember. It must be fairly recent. Unfortunately, it worked for him, taking away his disturbing perfection and giving him more of a rakish air. Probably the same air that the stubble around his jawline was meant to provide. I leaned slightly to one side to get a better glimpse of it. And that was when I realised he was watching me right back.

I choked slightly as Byron raised up his glass in greeting. Don't blush, Integrity. I raised my fake champagne to him and offered a distant smile. Then I caught the bartender's attention and engaged him in a conversation about the weather. I didn't look into the mirror again.

It didn't take the three Sidhe girls long to make their first advance. The prettiest one waltzed up and, although I didn't see what she did, her voice was loud enough to make it clear that her approach was welcome. In less time than it took the bartender to pour me another drink, her two friends joined in, pulling over chairs and simpering. I remained aloof. If he liked the chase, then that's what he'd get.

I let a tiny Mona Lisa smile play around my lips. I was mysterious and interesting. And bloody uncomfortable sitting in this dress. There was a spot on my back where my bra strap was rubbing against the zip. It was very itchy and very annoying but interesting, mysterious women don't do contortions in public to give themselves a damn good scratch. I twitched my shoulders but it wasn't going away. That was okay though. I could saunter my way to the bathroom - drawing attention to myself along the way - and take care of it there.

Nodding my intention to the bartender, I slung my bag over my shoulder, then carefully descended from the stool. The door to the restroom was in the far corner. Perfect: I'd have no choice but to walk past Byron's table. I flipped my hair over my shoulder again and strutted off.

The Cockney guy who'd approached me before glowered in my direction. This time I gave him a sweet smile, filled with sultry promise. His Adam's apple bobbed in his throat as he swallowed. Then I tilted up my chin and walked past Byron, the Sidhe girls and his entourage, telling myself that this would be a really bad time to trip and fall flat on my arse.

When I eventually made it to the safety of the bathroom, I immediately found the itchy spot and moaned in satisfaction as I scratched it.

There was a muted flash of light and Bob's booming voice floating up from my bag. 'Don't tell me you're doing what I think you're doing,' he said.

I cursed and unzipped the bag. 'How did you get out?' I complained. 'I thought you had to wait until I rubbed the blade.'

Bob thrust his hips forward. 'Uh Integrity, you can rub my blade any time.'

Oh for Pete's sake. I started to zip the bag closed again but he made a good show of protesting. 'Oh come on! That's not fair! Until you take all three wishes, I can appear whenever I want to, okay?'

That certainly didn't sound right. 'I thought I was your owner.'

'You are! But if you're going to keep ignoring

what a wonderful opportunity you have with these wishes, then I'm going to keep appearing to remind you of what you've got.'

'Until I give you back to the guy who owned you originally,' I said shortly.

A crafty expression crossed Bob's face. He held up his miniscule index finger and gave me a shit-eating grin. 'He never cleaned the dagger. I never appeared to him.'

'So?' I asked sourly.

'You don't know much about genies, do you, Uh Integrity? I'm yours until you take the wishes. You can give me away, hide me in a drawer, drop me in the ocean if you like. I'll still come back to you.' He gave me jazz hands. Actual jazz hands. 'It's magic!'

I stared down at him. 'That can't be right.'

'It is! Try it. Go on. Try it.' He craned his neck upwards, glee in his eyes. 'We're in the ladies room? Please try it, Uh Integrity! Leave me here! I love being in the ladies room!'

'You're disgusting.'

He beamed at me. 'Thanks.'

'What happened to your begging me on hands and knees to keep you around?'

He gave an indolent shrug. 'Twenty-four hour cooling-off period.'

'What?'

'You get twenty-four hours after picking me up to change your mind. That passed, oooh, about thirty minutes ago.'

I gritted my teeth. I should have dumped him the second I realised what he was.

'In my experience,' Bob continued, 'this generally goes better when the owner thinks they're in control and making all the decisions. I like you though. I can tell you're a bit different.' He winked as if he were paying me a wonderful compliment. Or softening the blow. 'Now tell me, who are you trying to impress? I can help. I'm good at true love wishes. Sometimes. Okay, almost never. But I can still help. Who's the lucky guy?'

'Never you mind,' I told him as the door opened and one of the Sidhe girls strolled in. She gave me a funny look; she probably thought I was holding a conversation with myself. There certainly wasn't a trace of fear in her expression so she didn't recognise me. It was a relief to know that my face wasn't plastered on Wanted posters all over the Clanlands.

I snapped the bag shut and firmly zipped it. There was a muffled squawk of irritation from Bob, which I covered with a cough. I gave her an airy smile.

'I was drinking a glass of champagne,' I told her, 'when I heard someone say hello. Then I realised it had to be the drink talking.'

Her mouth fell open slightly as my feeble joke sailed right over her head. She looked me up and down and edged away. 'Are you from Macquarrie Clan?'

'No. Why do you ask?'

She shook her head. 'No reason.' She backed quickly into one of the stalls and firmly closed the door. I shrugged and walked back out. There will always be haters.

This time, when I walked back past their table, I fixed on the handsome dimpled Sidhe who was sitting next to Byron. He caught my eye and smiled. I smiled back slowly. His eyes danced. Yahtzee. I continued to saunter past and, just for a moment, there was a brief lull in the conversation. Well, well, well. It appeared I was already getting somewhere.

I jumped awkwardly back onto my bar stool and smiled at the bartender. 'Hey,' I said. 'What do you know about the Macquarrie Clan?'

He opened his mouth but was forestalled by a smooth voice from behind. 'Other than the fact that insanity runs in their family?'

I glanced round, my gaze falling on none other than Byron himself. 'Insanity, huh?' I murmured. 'That makes sense.'

The corners of his chiselled lips lifted . 'I'm Byron,' he said.

I gave a tiny smile back. 'I know.'

His emerald green eyes laughed at me. 'Then you're at an unfair advantage. Aren't you going to tell me who you are?'

My tongue darted out and wet my lips. His eyes followed the movement and I felt a frisson of unexpected lust in my belly. That was quite enough of that, I told myself firmly. I sniffed. 'I'm here incognito,' I told him quietly. 'I could tell you…'

'But then you'd have to kill me?'

I shrugged. 'I'm a pacifist. But, yeah, at the very least I'd have to tie you up in a room somewhere while I made my escape.'

'Sounds like fun,' he murmured. 'Can I get you a drink?'

'Don't bother, mate,' grunted the Cockney, appearing at my other side in a bid to get the bartender's attention. 'She's not interested.'

Perfect timing. I waved a hand in the air. 'He's right,' I said cheerfully. 'You should go back to your friends. I'm just enjoying a quiet drink.'

Byron folded his arms so that his biceps bulged. I wondered how many times he'd practised *that* move in the mirror. 'Right now,' he drawled, 'it's far more interesting here.' He gestured to the stool next to me. 'May I sit down?'

I did my best to look nonchalant. 'It's a free country.'

He sat down. My dress was already riding high again but, to Byron's credit, his eyes didn't once drift downwards. I caught a whiff of spicy aftershave that almost did me in. Then I remembered what he was really like and what I was here for.

'I'm surprised that you're not aware of the Macquarrie Clan's reputation,' he commented. 'It's well advertised across the Sidhe world.'

That throwaway observation meant that he didn't recognise me from our encounter in the Bull's palace all those years before. It had lasted only a few seconds so that wasn't completely surprising but it meant that, despite my white hair and eye colour, he hadn't connected me to my father. He'd pegged me as one of the lower-class Sidhe, probably from a minor Clan. My chances of success had just quadrupled.

'I don't get out much,' I told him. Then I crossed my legs. It was deliberately calculated body language to give off the vibe that I wasn't interested. 'Hard to get' would win the day.

Byron beckoned the bartender, who'd finished serving the annoying Cockney. He gave a deferential bob of his head and poured him a neat whisky without asking what he'd like. I guessed that this wasn't Byron's first evening here. And he probably took a different girl home with him every night. As long as I was that girl tonight, nothing else mattered.

'One for the lady too,' he purred. 'But make it the really good stuff.'

Shite. 'I'm good with what I have.'

'I'm sure it's nice. I happen to know, however, that there are wonderful vintage bottles in the cellar. They only bring them out on special occasions.'

The last thing I wanted was for the bartender to pop a cork right in front of us. 'Well,' I said lightly, 'this occasion isn't that special.'

Byron's eyebrows shot up. 'In that dress? I'd say it was very special.'

Watch it, I thought. You're verging on sleazy now. 'I'm not wearing this because I'm looking for attention,' I said, coolly. 'I'm wearing it because I like it.'

His eyes glittered. 'You like hot pink?' he asked, emphasizing the word 'hot' so it was laden with innuendo.

'I do,' I replied, irritation flashing down my spine.

Byron appeared amused. 'Then make that bottle pink champagne, Timothy,' he instructed the bartender, who nodded again and walked off, no doubt to the famed cellar. So much for my bribe then. I had to admit, though, that it was interesting Byron had taken the time to learn the man's name. I hadn't.

If I protested any more, I'd end up going too far. Beaten for now – at least in the alcoholic stakes – I caved. 'It's very kind of you.'

His eyes held mine. 'You can thank me later.'

I shivered. 'No,' I said firmly, 'I'll thank you now.'

Byron threw back his head and laughed. 'Very well. Thank me by telling me your name.'

I turned back towards him, deliberately relaxing my posture as if I were warming to him. Which I most definitely wasn't. He was a wanker who'd once treated me as if I were a piece of dirt. He'd called me pathetic. Well, I wasn't so pathetic now. I was going to wrap him round my little finger, take from him exactly what I wanted, and then never, ever see him again. 'What would you like it to be?'

He reached out and placed his hand on my bare arm. His touch seared my skin and, involuntarily, I jerked away. That wasn't in the script. 'Tell me,' he repeated.

I hadn't had a name when he knew of me before and the best lies are those that are wrapped around the truth. Deciding it wouldn't do any harm, I told the truth. 'Integrity.'

'Interesting name.' He leaned forward. 'So, Integrity, do you live up to it? Are you honest and morally upright?'

'If I wasn't, would I admit it?' I asked. Both of us were amping up the flirtation. It was faster than I'd have liked but I had to follow his lead. I had to make sure I didn't screw this up.

He laughed again. 'I guess not.' He reached out again, this time taking my hands. I managed not to flinch. His thumb stroked the centre of my palm in a manner that was too familiar for someone I'd just met. Damn, but he was good. 'You have very soft skin,' he told me.

'Actually, I have eczema all over my chest,' I said with a straight face.

For the first time he appeared taken aback. 'Really? That's awful.'

'Yes.' I cast my eyes down and tried to look sad. 'I have a cracking pair of tits.'

For a horrifying heartbeat I thought I'd completely misjudged the moment. Then Byron's eyes crinkled and he laughed again. Without taking his eyes off my face, he purred, 'I can't disagree with that.'

I winked saucily just as Timothy returned with the bottle. Without so much as a flicker of apology for breaking our earlier deal, he presented the label to me. I swallowed. That was seriously expensive stuff. I gave a tiny nod - what else could I do - and he pulled out the cork in an expert motion. Without spilling a drop, he filled my glass.

I murmured my thanks and sipped. Although champagne wasn't my usual tipple, this was damned good. 'Aren't you having any?' I asked.

'I'm more of a Scotch man myself.' His eyes danced. 'Even if whisky does make me frisky.'

I sucked in a breath. I opened my mouth to match his comment with one of my own when one of the other giggly Sidhe girls elbowed her way between us. 'Your highness!' she cooed. 'Why don't you come back and join us?'

I caught a flash of annoyance in Byron's emerald green eyes. Then he turned to her and smiled. 'There's no need to be so formal,' he said to her. 'Call me Byron.'

Her mouth parted and she licked her lips. She moved away from me so I was presented with her back and started to regale him with an anecdote about her girlfriends and another local bar. It wasn't particularly interesting; besides I was prepared for competition. She was too young and too eager. I knew he'd get rid of her before long. And I could play this game too.

I shuffled away on my bar stool to give myself

more room, took another sip of the delectable champagne and glanced casually around the bar, my gaze falling on the Cockney bloke. Feeling my eyes, he looked up and glowered. I shrugged in apology and offered a half smile. His mouth tightened and I thought he wasn't going to take the bait but he wasn't that unpredictable. Less than twenty seconds later he was back by my side.

'You've changed your tune,' he snarked.

I toyed with my glass. 'I didn't mean to be rude before. I've had a bad day. Now I've got a drink or two inside me, I'm starting to relax. Perhaps I can buy you one to make up for how I acted.'

'I don't let women buy me drinks,' he threw out in typical Neanderthal fashion. Then he looked at Byron and the girl behind me. 'I guess you've been given the brush off too.'

I smiled. 'I guess so.'

He leered down my dress. 'Why don't we leave this place and head upstairs? Then maybe you'll open those legs for me after all.'

Ick. Ick. Ick. I held up my palms. 'Er, actually I…'

There was a sudden crack in the air and he was thrown backwards, falling several feet through the air and landing dazed against the wall. My mouth dropped open.

'I think you owe the lady an apology,' Byron growled. He was on his feet, his brows snapped together and his mouth tight. I'd expected a reaction but not that fast and not that violent. The Sidhe girl backed away, her hand clasped to her mouth as she looked from the sprawled Cockney to Byron and back again.

'What happened?' she squeaked.

I frowned at him. 'I don't need a hero,' I told him. 'I was handling that.'

His expression grew even darker. 'It didn't sound like you were handling it.'

I wondered if I was now seeing the real Byron, heir presumptive to the Sidhe stewardship and all that entailed. If that was the case, he certainly had a temper.

I made a quick decision. The flirtatious banter had gone and was unlikely to return. I still needed to be in full control of this situation and with Byron's friends on their feet and the tense atmosphere in the bar, I wasn't going to achieve that if I stuck around. I threw some money down and stood up, putting my bag on my shoulder. 'I told you I was a pacifist,' I said softly. 'This is a little too rough and tumble for my liking. Thank you for the champagne. It was lovely meeting you. I'll have something to tell my grandchildren.' Then, without another word or glance at either him or the Cockney, I walked out.

Something poked me in my ribs. There was a muffled protest coming from my bag: Bob. I jabbed him back and began to count, crossing my fingers as I did so. One. Two. Into the lobby. Three. Four. Five. Shite. This was taking too long. Past the table with the elaborate flowers. Six. Seven. Up to the doorman. Arse. I'd misjudged the situation.

'Integrity!'

I allowed myself a tiny smile. No, I'd got it right after all. I turned slowly, reluctantly.

'Byron,' I said with a sigh. 'I think my quiet evening has been ruined. It's time to head home.'

He regarded me seriously. 'I can't let you do that.'

He would have to do better than that. Come on, Golden Boy. Give me something to work with. 'I don't think it's up to you.'

'But it is. How can I possibly let you go with what happened there as the only story for your grandchildren? It'll hurt my reputation immeasurably. You need to give me another chance so that they'll think better of me.'

Better. I gave a silent round of applause. 'I promise I'll paint you in a very favourable light, my liege.'

He winced. 'Don't call me that. My father might be Steward but that doesn't mean I will be.'

'Byron.' I softened my voice and looked at him up through my eyelashes, noting his reaction. Yep. He might be a pretty face but he was also pretty dumb. 'I can't go back in there,' I told him, gesturing towards the bar. 'It really is better if I go home.'

He tilted his head, a bronzed curl falling across his eyes. 'We were getting along very well, Integrity,' he murmured. 'Let's not ruin things. I have the penthouse suite. I can get Timothy to send up the champagne. No one else is going to drink it and it would be a shame to let it go to waste.'

I did an imaginary dance. I am a sexual goddess. At least for tonight anyway. 'I don't know… I've got work tomorrow and…'

'Please. Just one drink.'

I met his eyes and something inexplicable flared between us. What the hell was that? 'Okay,' I said finally. 'Just one. But only because you've paid for that champagne and it's so expensive.'

A smile tugged at the corner of his mouth and he held out his arm. 'One drink,' he breathed. 'I promise.'

Chapter Six

We stepped into the lift. As the doors glided to a smooth close, I turned to Byron. 'So that's your Gift, is it? Telekinesis? Throwing things around with the power of your mind?'

'It's one of them.'

Surprised, I asked, 'You have more than one?' That *was* unusual.

He gave a dismissive shrug. 'Comes with the family. I only have two though. Not as many as my father unfortunately.' He paused. 'What's yours?'

'Not worth mentioning,' I demurred. I didn't have any. I'd left the Sidhe lands before I could receive either my true name or my Gift. Like I cared. I got along quite well without either of them. It wasn't too much of a big deal – plenty of lower-level Sidhe didn't have much zap behind their Gifts.

To avoid further interrogation, I kept the focus on him. People love talking about themselves. 'Your Gifts must be very strong,' I purred. 'What's it like?'

Byron grimaced. 'It's easy to push out lots of strength like I did in the bar. It was actually a dick move. What's far harder is being delicate and targeted.'

'Oh yes?' I asked innocently. 'Like what?'

Mischief danced in his emerald-green eyes. 'I'll show you.' He blinked languorously like a cat. That's when I felt it. The zip at the back of my dress tugged. What the hell? I jumped and he chuckled –

but he didn't stop. Without touching me, he continued to lower my zip. My fingers scrabbled at my back.

'Stop that!'

He smiled. 'Okay.' The strap on my shoulder began to slip down instead, exposing my bra. 'Mm. Hot pink underwear to match your hot pink dress. You *do* like that colour.'

I squeaked, 'That's enough!'

'If you insist.'

'I do!' I wagged my finger. 'One drink, remember? Nothing else.'

'As if I could forget,' he murmured. 'Come on, turn around. I'll fix you back up.'

I didn't ask why he wasn't using his Gift to return my clothing to its appropriate state. I already knew. His fingers brushed against my skin, lingering as he gently pulled my shoulder strap back up. Then he slowly pulled up the zip. 'I can't believe our paths haven't crossed before,' he said in a low voice.

Oh, he knew all the right things to say and all the right moves to make. I reminded myself that he was a playboy. I knew that, even though I avoided reading the tabloids and gossip sheets whenever the Sidhe were involved.

Control, Integrity. You're in control.

'Just our bad luck,' I whispered.

A bell sounded as the lift arrived at its designated floor. Both Byron and I flinched then I turned round to catch his eye and laughed nervously. He stared at me for a moment before smiling. 'Here we are,' he said. 'Home sweet home. At least for the next three nights anyway.'

He took my hand and led me into the penthouse and through a heavy self-locking door which I took careful note of. Once inside I made a point of looking around casually. Damn. This was pretty swish. I walked over to the large window and gazed out. 'You're a lucky guy,' I commented, 'getting to experience all this.'

'Believe me, I know.'

'And you're only here for three nights?'

He nodded. 'I have some business to attend to.'

I got the impression from his tone that he didn't want to talk about it. That suited me. I only wanted to know where the Lia Saifire was being kept. I offered a brilliant smile. 'I've never been in a penthouse before. Can you give me the grand tour?'

His mouth quirked up. 'It would be my pleasure.'

I followed him around. The place was impressive. And ostentatious. I exclaimed over the elaborate chandeliers and cooed over the soft furnishings. I wasn't expecting to see the gem on display, of course, but there was bound to be a safe somewhere. I strolled over to a large painting of two hunting dogs gazing up at a bird of prey.

'Beautiful artwork,' I said as I tried to work out whether it was a front for a wall safe.

'It's not really to my taste,' he said. 'Come on. I'll show you the bedrooms.'

I trailed after him, hoping it was clear that this was a tour and nothing else. Fortunately, after the little show of power in the lift, he was now on his best behaviour. He pointed out the vast bed and the modern painting hanging above it, as well as the ensuite. His tone remained neutral. Thank goodness.

We were returning to the main living room area when I saw it. One of the vast wardrobe doors was open less than an inch and, nestled there inside like a gift from the gods, was a safe. My stomach flipped. Bingo. I could feel my skin prickling in anticipation. Now I was getting somewhere.

'Do you mind if I use your bathroom?' I asked.

Byron grinned at me. 'Be my guest. You can use the ensuite or there's another one to your left, next to the second bedroom.'

As tempting as it was to scoot back to Byron's own bedroom and see what I could make of the safe, I wasn't stupid enough to burn all my bridges just yet. I gave him a rueful smile, suggesting that I wasn't brave enough to venture back into his bedroom, and pointed to the other bathroom. I received a lazy smirk in return.

'Don't be long.'

My stomach flipped again. Goddamnit. The sensation was because I was so close to my goal, I told myself. It had nothing to do with the smoky look in his eyes or the rasp in his voice. I did not want Byron Moncrieffe. I wanted the freaking Lia Saifire. Everything depended on it.

I shut the bathroom door and carefully locked it, then leaned against and put my hand to my forehead. This was a job, like any other. It was time to stop acting like an idiot and start being more professional. Byron was ripe for the picking; everything he'd done up till now had proven that. I knew where the Lia Saifire was. I was on easy street. I just had to remember that.

I opened my bag. Bob grinned at me and gave a little wave. 'Hey! How's it going?'

'Get back into your blade,' I growled. 'I don't have time for this.'

He pouted. 'Aw, come on, Uh Integrity! Where are we?' He pulled himself up, peered over the edge of the bag and gave a low whistle. 'Damn, girl! This is seriously posh! High living!'

'Bob,' I said through gritted teeth, 'so help me God, if you don't get back into your blade and give me some peace I'm going to throw you out the window.'

He stuck out his tongue. 'I already told you, you can't get rid of me that easily. Not any more.'

'Maybe not. But it'll still hurt when you hit the ground. And keep your voice down.'

'Why? Are you playing hide and seek? I love hide and seek! I'm so good at it! Let me join in.' He began jumping up and down, making the bag bounce. 'Come on. Let me join in!'

I gave him the nastiest look I could muster. He sighed dramatically. 'You're really mean.'

'That's right,' I told him. 'I really am. Now shut

the hell up and get into that blade.'

He pulled another face. 'You didn't say I wish.'

'Bob...'

He retreated. 'Fine, fine. Honestly. Women!'

I covered my eyes as he flashed back in. Relieved that he was doing as he was told, I rummaged around for my lipstick and quickly unscrewed the bottom of the tube. Two small white tablets fell out. I palmed them quickly. Byron might be Sidhe but these babies were enough to knock out an ox. They were harmless enough, though. He'd wake up in the morning with a sore head - by which time I'd be well away.

After flushing the toilet and checking my make-up, I left the bathroom. Byron was gazing out over the night sky, his back turned. Timothy had sent up the champagne and two chilled glasses were sitting on the table top. Perfect. With one fluid movement, I dropped the tablets into the one that was furthest away. The tablets fizzed slightly but dissolved to nothing within moments. I gave myself a mental high five.

I cleared my throat. 'You're switching to champagne?'

He turned. 'Like I said, whisky makes me frisky. And I promised you one drink and one drink alone.' He reached behind me and grabbed the nearest glass by its stem, handing it to me before taking the other – the spiked one – for himself.

'You're a true gentleman,' I murmured, raising my glass up to his then taking a sip. 'Slainte.'

'Slainte,' he replied. Then he drained his glass in one gulp. Hurray!

I smiled and took a sip from mine. 'This really is good.'

'I'm glad you approve.' He leaned towards me and I felt a lurch in the pit of my stomach, sure that he was making a move. Instead, he reached around me again and returned his glass to the table top. Then he pulled back. 'So, Integrity. I know you like hot pink and you hate violence but I don't know much else. What do you do for a living?'

'I'm in security. It's pretty boring.'

'Security?' He glanced up and down my body until I was forced to repress a shiver. 'Forgive me, but you don't seem built for that kind of position.'

I needed to get him sitting down. The last thing I wanted was the current Steward's son keeling over in mid-conversation and banging his head. I didn't need to be accused of attempted regicide, whether Byron claimed he held no actual title or not.

I put down my own glass and met his eyes. 'What kind of position do you think I'm built for?' I asked. There was no mistaking my meaning.

He ran his tongue across his top lip. 'Well, I can tell from your attitude that you enjoy being on top. Being in control.'

He had that right. I smiled, turned and walked over to the large sofa in the centre of the room. 'You're right. I do like being on top.' I sat down, making zero effort to stop my dress from riding up, and leaned back against the cushions.

Byron stayed where he was. 'The trouble is,' he muttered, 'I like being in charge too.'

I tucked one leg underneath me. It wasn't easy but it was worth it to see the flare in his eyes. Come on, Byron. Get your arse over here and sit down before you fall down. 'I suppose that makes us incompatible then,' I said with a tinge of sadness. 'Nothing more than ships that pass in the night.'

He still didn't bloody move. 'Don't say that, Integrity,' he said. 'I have a feeling that we're going to know each other for much longer than that.'

'Really?' I patted the seat next to me. 'What makes you say that?'

He seemed to make a decision. He strode over and sat next to me, his thigh dangerously close to mine. I could smell his aftershave again. Delicious.

Byron smirked. 'What is?'

I started. Had I said that aloud? 'Er,' I stuttered, embarrassed. 'Your scent. It's delicious.'

His smile grew. 'Really? Because I think you're delicious.'

It was the type of comment that would normally have me rolling my eyes. Instead, my chest felt tight and it was like I'd forgotten how to breathe. Byron stared into my eyes, his emerald depths darkening to a deep jade. There was a question lurking there.

My senses swam. Oh, why the hell not? He'd be unconscious before this really got anywhere. I gave the tiniest nod of my head. I'd almost achieved what I'd come here to do; I could allow myself a bit of fun in the process. It would hurt him more tomorrow when he discovered the theft of his sparkly jewel. And he deserved the hurt after the way he'd spoken to me when I was a kid.

Byron didn't take any further convincing. He gave a faint groan and leaned in, his lips brushing softly against mine. Screw that. If I was going to make this kind of error of judgment, I was going to go all in. I grabbed the back of his head and deepened the kiss, pressing into him. He tasted of whisky and champagne mixed together. His stubble scraped my cheek. I felt dizzy and exhilarated all at once. A kiss shouldn't feel this good. Especially a kiss with such a wanker. I pulled back, breathing hard. He stared at me, a stunned expression on his face.

'I told you I liked to be on top,' I said, hooking one leg over him so I could sit astride him. His body was rock hard. I ran my hand up his chest and he shuddered. He must have put in an extraordinary number of hours at the gym to achieve that sort of physique. He adjusted my weight, shifting my body so he could get more comfortable.

'Oh really? Because I think you'll find I'm the one in charge here.'

'No chance,' I whispered, leaning in once more. Then I pulled back abruptly.

He frowned. 'What's wrong?'

I put one hand up to my head. It didn't feel good. 'Something's not right,' I muttered.

'Integrity,' he rasped, 'this is so right.'

'No.' I shook head. My vision was beginning to blur. 'I feel strange.' And then, for the second time that day, I keeled over.

Chapter Seven

This time when I woke up, I was more aware of my surroundings than I was when the Wild Man knocked me out. That was mainly because there was an arm wrapped tightly round my waist and a leg thrown over my hip, pinning me into place. And that damn aftershave was everywhere. It was as if I'd been sprinkled liberally with it.

I groaned and tried to move my arm, eventually managing to squeeze it out from underneath me. I rubbed my eyes. I glanced down at myself and froze. My pink dress was gone. All I was wearing were my bra and panties. At least I wasn't naked. I wasn't sure if I could take that sort of shame. I'd never live it down if Lexie discovered I'd let myself be this vulnerable.

What the hell had happened to me? Everything was going so swimmingly … I ran through the events in my mind. It had to have been the champagne. Somehow - and I had no idea how - I must have drunk from the spiked glass instead of Byron. That would explain why I'd felt the sudden urge to throw caution to the wind and fling myself at him. And the current wham-wham pounding in my head. Frankly, it was a bloody good thing that I'd passed out before things went any further.

I scowled. He didn't have to strip me though. And he could have put my unconscious body in the second bedroom. Or on the sofa.

His breath, hot on the back of my neck, was soft and even. I'd just have to hope he was a sound sleeper because I was getting into that safe and getting the Lia Saifire right now. Enough was enough.

As gingerly as I could, I wriggled my hips forward to extricate myself from his leg. Then I reached down for his arm and tried to loosen his grip. He murmured something in his sleep and tightened his hold. Crapadoodle. I tried again.

Inch by slow inch, I slid down and forward, trying to create enough room so I could roll free. I could climb up glass-faced buildings, jump down elevator shafts and perform acrobatic feats that the general public would find impossible, yet freeing myself from one stupid, sleeping Sidhe was almost impossible. In the end, I pulled myself away with a sharp tug. I hadn't had much choice.

I sprang backwards and looked at Byron. He was still fast asleep, long lashes curling against his cheek. His hair was rumpled and he remained as sexy as hell. Mentally I slapped myself. Get a grip, girl.

Spying my dress on a nearby chair, I tiptoed over and grabbed it. I shimmied into it, just managing to pull up the zip, then edged to the safe. Byron hadn't moved a muscle. This was good. I'd just reached the wardrobe, however, and was sliding it open to access the safe when there was a sudden cough. Shite.

'What are you doing?' he asked, sleep blurring his voice.

'Uh, just looking for my shoes!' I sang out. Damn it.

He sat up. 'You're leaving?'

Not without the Lia Saifire, I wasn't. 'Yes,' I said, doing what I could to look guilt-ridden. 'Walk of shame.'

Byron ran a hand through his hair while I tried very hard not to notice the ripples in his chest. Not hard enough. 'You can stay,' he said. 'I can order in breakfast.'

There was a traitorous part of me that loved that idea. We could sit across the table from each other, nibbling at croissants, then… 'I really should go. I've got, um, work.'

'Oh. Okay then.'

Was that disappointment or relief in his face? 'Well,' I said airily, 'it was nice meeting you. Thanks for the champagne and sorry about the, you know, falling unconscious part. I should remember to eat next time.' Not that there would be a next time. I pivoted on my heel.

'Integrity, wait.'

I turned slowly back. 'Yes?'

His eyes fixed on me, freezing my body into place. 'Nothing happened last night. I'm not that kind of guy. You conked out so quickly that I was worried. It made more sense to keep you with me so I could check on you.' He inhaled. 'I'd really like to see you again.'

I almost snorted. He'd not achieved end-game status yet; that was why he didn't want this to be over. So predictable. 'Sure,' I said. 'I'll call you.'

'You don't have my number.'

I shrugged. 'The hotel is pretty well known. I'll find you.'

Before I could leave, Byron got to his feet. Without meaning to, my eyes drifted down. He was wearing a pair of silky black boxers and nothing else. I stared for a moment at the trail of hair leading downwards and swallowed, then glanced up again. His mouth twitched and he stepped right in front of me.

'Why do I get the feeling that you're giving me brush off?' he asked, reaching out and fingering my hair lightly.

I tried to smile. 'I don't know. Perhaps it happens to you a lot?'

'Girls don't normally try and run out the door. They normally try and hang around for as long as possible.'

I bet they did. 'What can I say? I'm a busy person.'

His gaze heated up. 'Promise me that you'll call. I'm in meetings all day but I'll be free after six.'

I looked straight at him. 'I promise,' I lied.

'Good.' He bent his head until his breath was hot against my neck. 'I'll look forward to it,' he whispered.

I almost ran out of the room. I could swear he chuckled as the door closed behind me. So he was good looking, I told myself. And I could feel fizzy lust zipping through my system whenever I looked at him. It was merely a combination of the drugs and the fact that it had been too long since I'd had a man. He was a sexy guy and I wasn't immune. It didn't make me want to marry him or have his babies any more than he wanted that from me. I sighed. He certainly lived up to his reputation.

Locating my shoes at the far end of the sofa, I scooped them up along with my bag. There wasn't a peep from Bob so at least something was going my way. I clumped out to the front door, keeping one wary eye on Byron's bedroom. When I was sure he wasn't about to suddenly appear, I wrenched open the door and stood back, letting it slam shut. There was still no sound from the bedroom. Perfect. I tiptoed over to the silent unoccupied second bedroom and sneaked inside.

There was a gap underneath the bed. It would be a tight squeeze but I reckoned I could manage it if I had to. Helpfully, there were also several built-in wardrobes. It was nice to have options. Now all I had to do was wait and hope that Byron didn't plan to hold his meetings here in the suite. He had to leave sooner or later. I pinched the bridge of my nose and wished I'd thought to grab a glass of water before I pretended to leave. My mouth was as dry as a badger's arse. My breath probably smelled even worse.

If I closed the bedroom door completely, I wouldn't be able to see a thing. Whoever had crafted this room put a lot of effort into the details. I was certain, however, that it been ajar last night so, as long as I was careful, I could leave it that way and give myself a line of sight into the living room.

I experimented with the light, checking that my shadow wouldn't give me away if I stood in the corner, and peeked out. The chance of Byron wandering in here was slim. If he did, however, I wanted to be able to scoot under the bed without him noticing the flicker of movement.

Once I was satisfied with my position, I relaxed a little. Not a moment too soon either as I heard the door opening and Byron emerging. I squinted at him through the gap. He'd dressed casually in a pair of jogging trousers and tight T-shirt. It was as if he had to show off his pecs, even when he was alone. Poser.

He moved around the room, sometimes within my line of sight and sometimes not. After downing a glass of juice which looked so orange and so tasty that I was gagging to run out and snatch it from him, he reached into his pocket and pulled out a phone. He walked to the window and murmured into it. It was annoying that I couldn't hear what he was saying. I tensed, straining my ears, but no matter how hard I tried I couldn't catch more than a word or two.

Not long after he hung up, there was a sharp rap on the door. Byron strolled over and opened it.

'Morning. How are things?' asked another male voice. 'I thought you'd be done by now.'

'Things are good,' he answered. 'It's just a more delicate operation than I realised. I'm going to take my time. Come on. Let's head downstairs and see what Jamie has to say.'

I frowned. Delicate operation? That was an odd way to talk about getting your leg over. Not that I really cared. In fact, it probably wasn't anything to do with my little sleepover and was about the business he was in town for.

I nibbled my bottom lip. Was he here just for the Lia Saifire or was the jewel merely an added bonus? The part of me that had flirted with him the night before hoped the jewel's disappearance wouldn't cause him too many problems. The part of me that remembered what it was like to be eleven years old and dismissed by him hoped that it would.

I wasn't used to feeling this conflicted and I didn't like it.

After he left, I stayed where I was. It was important to wait for at least ten minutes. Speck used to tell a story about when he'd hung around hotels and, using a cleverly keyed master card that he'd developed himself, darted into the guest rooms when the occupants went down to breakfast. There were at least three occasions when he was almost caught. People are forgetful. They come back to see if they've left the iron on. Or they need their wallet or their phone or whatever. I had to allow for those sorts of memory lapses. It's not like this was my first snatch and grab; I was an experienced professional.

Once the allotted time had passed, I opened the door and snuck out. The suite was completely silent. Allowing myself a moment of luxury, I grabbed a glass, filled it with water from the tap and gulped it down. Damn, that was good. Then I squared my shoulders. It was time to get down to business.

Humming the theme tune to *The Guns of Navarone*, I went back into the main bedroom, making a beeline for the wardrobe. I pushed it open and knelt down, examining the small safe. I almost laughed aloud; it was a typical cheap hotel version. Breaking into this would be a piece of cake. The standard keypad lock would take me mere seconds to open. You'd think that a hotel as exclusive as this – and a suite as expensive as this – would have a better system. I tutted to myself. Served them right for taking so much care over the luxury fixtures and fittings and skimping on the important stuff.

I tried a few quick variations, just in case Byron had been daft enough to use an easy to remember number. When 0000 didn't work, nor 1234 or 4321, I pressed down on the 'lock' button until the LED display flashed. With my thumb, I jabbed in a series of nines and the safe buzzed. Hey presto. It really was that easy. I grinned. No crappy hotel safe was a match for me.

I reached inside. There were envelopes and papers and a slim, velvet-covered box. I took out the box and flipped it open. A dazzling necklace lay there, nestled against the black lining. Well, that was a nice little bonus. I lifted up one edge of it then I frowned. It was fake. The gems were nothing more than paste. I snorted. Some poor girl was going to be unpleasantly 'tricked' by good old Byron.

I tossed it back inside and squinted towards the back of the safe. Three seconds later I stood up and slammed my fist down on the top of it, making the contents inside jump.

No sodding way. Not again. The Lia Saifire wasn't inside here either.

I cursed, closed the safe door and paced round the bedroom. I'd been so sure that's where it would be. I took several deep breaths. It wasn't the end of the world; it just meant that Byron wasn't stupid enough to trust the safe. He'd either left the jewel in the main hotel safe downstairs - which would be a pain in the arse to get to but far from impossible - or it was somewhere else in the suite.

I pursed my lips and considered. If I were a Sidhe Clan heir with more money than sense, where would I keep a priceless gem? Under the bed, perhaps? I got down on the floor. Nope. Nothing there. Maybe in a cupboard. I checked every one I could find. No luck there either. Fridge? No. Under the sofa cushions? No. In the toilet cistern? No.

I spent a good thirty minutes exhausting every possibility. When I was certain the Lia Saifire wasn't anywhere I could access, I plonked myself down in the centre of the room to mull things over. It would take another twenty-four hours to access the main safe next to reception and I didn't want to waste that kind of time unless I absolutely had to.

Perhaps the wardrobe safe was a front and there was another one lurking somewhere, albeit better hidden? But how long could I waltz around here before Byron decided to come back?

I picked at a hangnail then grabbed my bag. It wasn't ideal but if I played my cards right I might able to wing it successfully. I slid out the letter opener and gave it a tap. When nothing happened immediately, I rubbed it against the fabric of my dress. There was an odd hiss followed by the familiar flash of blinding light and Bob appeared, standing on my leg.

'I was asleep,' he complained. 'You ignore me for days and then, when I finally decide to get some shut-eye, you force me to get up.'

Exasperated, I folded my arms. 'It was hardly days. It's been less than ten hours.'

His eyes narrowed. 'Are you sure?'

'Yup.'

'I just lose all track of time when I'm stuck in that thing.' He looked around, realising he was on my thigh and grinned. 'Hey girl. Nice legs!'

'Piss off,' I grunted.

He bent over, poking me experimentally. He was too tiny for it to hurt, but it was still irritating. 'Nice muscle tone, Uh Integrity. Wait a minute though. Weren't you wearing this before? Have you not been home yet? Girrrrl! You one bad lady.'

I willed myself not to react. 'Bob…' I said tiredly.

'Huh?' He glanced up as if confused. Then he shook himself as comprehension dawned and a look of pure glee transformed his face. 'You've finally come to your senses! You want your first wish!'

I drummed my fingers against my arm. 'Let's say I'm thinking about it. It's just…' I let my voice trail off.

Bob frowned. 'Just what?'

'It doesn't matter. I don't want to offend you. Go back to sleep.'

'No, no, no, no! You can't offend me. Tell Uncle Bob what the problem is.'

I fidgeted. 'How do I know you're any good? I mean, I know there'll be side effects from any wish I make but what if the wish doesn't work? I get all the nasty stuff to deal with and none of the benefits. I'd like to make a wish but I'm not sure I can trust you to be experienced enough.'

Bob's jaw dropped. He stared at me as if I were mad. 'Not experienced enough?' he shrieked. 'Not experienced enough?' His voice rose to an extraordinarily high pitch. Any choir would welcome that sort of soprano.

'Okay,' I said hastily, 'maybe you do have lots of experience. But you could be really rusty too. You said yourself that you lose track of time when you're stuck in the blade. Who knows how long it's been since you last did any wish fulfilment? I'm not sure I can take the risk.'

Bob was clearly aghast. 'I am a wish expert. In the world of wishes, there is none better than me!'

I shrugged. 'Prove it.'

'Fine,' he snapped. 'Ask for something.' He waved his little arms in the air. 'Make it something small, mind. I'm not giving away the big stuff for free.'

I blew air out through pursed lips. 'So asking you to cure a fatal disease would be a no-no, then?'

'You bet your cute arse it would be.'

'Hmm. Okay. How about you find an object? Lost and found has got to be pretty simple, right?'

He scoffed. 'Yeah, right. You ask for the Hope diamond as a test and then you're set for life.' He waggled his finger at me. 'No chance, sweet cheeks.'

'Hey, you don't need to retrieve the object. Just tell me where it is. If you don't think you can do even that though...'

'I can do that! Of course I can do that! What shall I search for?'

I tapped the corner of my mouth. 'There was something in the paper yesterday about a jewel. Some kind of sapphire, I think. Lia Saifire, perhaps?'

He clicked his fingers. 'Done!'

Placing two fingers on his temples, he closed his eyes and began to murmur. 'Shamamamamamama.'

'What on earth is that?'

He opened one eye and frowned. 'Don't interrupt me! I'm concentrating.'

I leaned back and kept my mouth shut, doing everything I could not to grin. After several seconds, he looked at me again. 'The Lia Saifire is in the possession of a young Sidhe man. He has dark hair, two adorable dimples in his chubby little cheeks and he's staying at the Astor Hotel in room number 907. Ta da!' His brow creased. 'Hold on. Where are we right now?'

'We're on the floor next to a coffee table.'

'The floor where?' Bob's eyes narrowed. 'Wait a minute. We're in the Astor Hotel too! You bitch! You tricked me! That's what you wanted to know all along!'

'Oops.'

'I hate you, Uh Integrity.'

'Sorry, Bob,' I said, obviously not sorry at all. 'Knock knock.'

Bob sniffed loudly. 'Who's there? Bitch.'

'Raoul.'

'Raoul who?'

I gave him a serious look. 'Raoul with the punches.'

'I hate you!' he howled.

'Bye Bob. Go back and catch up on your sleep.'

He waved his fists in the air. 'I'm going to pay you back, you know.'

'Yeah, yeah.' I nudged him gently with the tip of my finger. 'Go on. Off you go.'

He turned his back on me and folded his arms. 'I'm not talking to you.'

'I deserve that.'

'You're damn right you do.' Without another glance at me, he leapt back into the letter opener. I only just managed to shield my eyes in time. 'Sorry,'

I murmured again. 'Needs must though.'

I returned the blade to its sheath and considered what he'd told me. I knew exactly who he was referring to. What didn't make sense was why Byron had palmed off the jewel to one of his entourage rather than keeping it for himself. Unless it was a gift, of course. A pretty expensive gift, though.

I leaned back on my hands. It appeared I'd been attempting to seduce the wrong Sidhe. Oh well. It was a lady's prerogative to change her mind. I pushed away the flicker of disappointment. From the blush I'd received from my new target in the bar yesterday, he'd be far easier to manage than Byron. I just needed to shift gears slightly.

I got to my feet and yanked down my dress. As I was about to pull on my shoes and leave, I heard the buzz of voices right outside the door. Shite. I grabbed the shoes, my bag and the letter opener and made a dash for the spare bedroom. Byron's timing sucked.

Chapter Eight

I pushed myself into the corner of the room away from the door. In theory, I no longer needed to spy on Byron and find out what he was doing. but it was possible he was with his Sidhe mate who had the Lia Saifire. That would be useful to know. When I peered through the open gap, it certainly wasn't so I could catch another glimpse of the Moncrieffe heir. No sirree.

There was only one person with Byron and it wasn't Mr Dimples. It was some massive guy who was blocking my view. I wrinkled my nose. Come on. Get out of the way. I could hear Byron chatting about something to do with keys, which made next to no sense to me. The big guy shifted his weight. Jeez. He was the size of a freaking Wild Man. A second after that that thought, I smelled the cloves. No. Sodding. Way.

My heart hammering against my chest, I pulled back from the door and pressed against the wall. Why would the Wild Man enforcer be here with Byron? It wouldn't make sense unless he was working for him. Unless Byron himself was the moneylender who'd bought Taylor's loan. Several pieces slotted into place. I was a complete and utter fool. I thought I'd been manipulating him when all along he'd been the one manipulating me.

I thought of the letter I'd received demanding

my presence at the Sidhe court. The one that had made me ramp up my plans to leave Aberdeen. When I didn't answer, Byron must have put his own plans into action.

He dangled the cherry of the Lia Saifire in front of our eyes then yanked it away, ensuring at the same time that the jewel's whereabouts were well publicised. He found a weak spot with Taylor and bought his loan, then demanded immediate repayment - along with impossible interest - to force the issue. Who else but a Sidhe princeling could pull the police's strings and get Brochan and Speck arrested on nonsensical charges? Byron pretended to be into me while I pretended – sort of pretended – to be into him. He made me promise to come back tonight. All this was part of some elaborate plot to make me do as he wished and go to the Sidhe court. I still had no idea why but I didn't bloody care. The utter wanker. The total bastard. The…

'You can come out now, Integrity.'

I swore bitterly and flung open the door, glaring at him. 'You prick,' I hissed. 'You set me up.'

He linked his hands behind his head and grinned at me. 'You set me up too.'

I jabbed my finger at his chest. He was bloody lucky I hated violence because right now I was tempted to poke his eyeballs out. 'Why? Why go to all this trouble?'

'If you'd answered the first missive…'

'Missive? What are you? An eighteenth-century weirdo? Why not phone? Or show up at my door? If you'd talked to me in person…'

'You were already making plans to run off,' Byron said calmly. 'You wouldn't have listened. This way I got your attention.'

'My friends are in jail!' I shrieked. 'My mentor is hiding out in my flat under the impression that his throat is about to slit!' I glared at the Wild Man. 'Your henchman knocked me out!'

There was a rumble. 'Sorry about that,' the Wild Man said. 'I tried to be gentle but you're pretty fragile for a Sidhe.'

'It wasn't his fault,' Byron said. 'Candy was under orders.'

'Candy? That's his name?' I muttered under my breath. 'You're all a bunch of nutters.'

Byron swept a bow while I continued to glower. 'At your service, ma'am.'

'The champagne,' I accused. 'You knew it was spiked and you switched the glasses.'

'Hello? I'm a telekinesis expert, remember?'

I shook my head. All this bloody time… 'You can't keep me here,' I spat. 'This is a free country and I'm not eleven years old.'

'No. You're not that pathetic either.'

I narrowed my eyes. 'You remember who I am.'

He looked at me patiently. 'Integrity, how many other women are there with your colouring wandering the streets? Of course I know who you are. Everyone knows who you are.'

What did that mean? I cleared my throat. 'Everyone?'

'Your location was found less than forty-eight hours after you flitted from Bull Scrymgeour. Lots of people have been keeping tabs on you, not just me. We needed to know where you were because it we might possibly need you in the future.' His eyes gleamed. 'I must say, you've had a very interesting career.'

My nausea increased. 'Let me out of here.'

Byron stepped back. 'You're free to go at any time.'

'Just as well,' I huffed. I stalked past him, eyeing Candy in case he tried anything. Fortunately, the Wild Man didn't move a muscle. I placed my hand on the doorknob and tugged.

'There is just one thing,' Byron interjected.

I swung my head round. 'What?'

'Your mentor, whatever you want to call him, still owes me money.'

Shite. Well, I'd just find another way to solve that little problem. 'You'll get your money.' I opened the door.

'And your friends are still enjoying the very best that the prison service can offer.' He tutted. 'It would be a real shame if someone tipped the police off about all those thefts that have been occurring in the city. Your friends might never get out.'

I stared at the lift. It was right there, waiting for me. All I had to do was get in it and go home. I clenched my fists. 'What do you want?' I asked finally.

'Close the door, come inside, sit down and we can talk about it. I promise, it's really not that bad.'

Like I'd believe that. My shoulders slumped. So you can never escape your past after all. Fine. I'd listen to what he had to say then I'd take Bob and make whatever wishes were necessary to get myself and my adopted family out of this mess. Sod the consequences. Byron Moncrieffe might think he was holding all the cards but he didn't know everything.

I crossed my arms and stalked over to the sofa. I pushed myself into the far corner. The stupid hot pink dress immediately rode up my legs. I pulled down the hem and crossed my arms again. 'Speak then.'

'I did tell you,' Byron said, 'that I preferred it when I was in charge.' Rather than joining me, he ambled over to the fridge and reached inside for a bottle of water. 'Would you like a drink?'

'No,' I replied stiffly.

'Not even pink champagne?' His amusement was clear.

'Piss off.' Oh, what a brilliant rejoinder that was.

'Not just yet. Candy, if you'd be so kind…?'

'Sure, boss.' The huge Wild Man lumbered out, closing the door behind him.

Byron smiled. 'Alone again.'

I felt sick. This could not be happening. 'Spit it out,' I snapped. 'What do you really want?'

'You know, you were far more pleasant to talk

to last night.'

'Last night I didn't know that you were a scheming manipulative wanker who enjoys playing with innocent people's lives.'

His eyebrows shot up. 'Innocent? Is that what'd you call a group of thieves who between them are responsible for some of the biggest heists this century has seen?'

'It's 2016,' I said flatly. 'That's hardly much of a feat. And besides, you know exactly what I mean.'

He grabbed a chair, pulled it over and placed it in front of me before sitting down. 'You were quite prepared to steal from me when you thought I was innocent.' He ran his tongue across his lips. 'I can still taste you.'

Oh God. I hugged myself. 'Either tell me what it is you really want or I'm walking.'

'Tough words.'

I stared at him. He sighed, his amusement fleeing. 'It's not as sinister as you imagine. All you need to do is open a box.'

'Really?' I sneered. 'All the might of the Sidhe world behind you and that's something you can't manage on your own? They didn't cover box opening in Fey finishing school?'

He took a long swig of his water. 'It's a very special box.'

For a brief moment, a saucy sexual innuendo was on the tip of my tongue. I bit down very hard. No way was I going there. Not again. 'Go on,' I said grimly.

'On the wall behind you, there's a thermostat. It controls the temperature of this room so it's never too cold or too hot. It's really an extraordinary feat of technology when you think about it.'

I was going to get a lesson on thermodynamics now, was I? I resisted the urge to look round. 'And?' I asked, sounding as bored as I could.

'The Sidhe lands run on a similar concept except instead of temperature control, what we concern ourselves with is magic. Too little magic and systems start to fail. Too much magic and, well, kaboom. It's not pretty when that happens.' His mouth tightened and his eyes were momentarily distant and unfocused. 'The tidal surge down the Dee a couple of years ago? That was one of those occasions.'

I might have known. Hundreds of people died. Not Sidhe people though, of course. Poor people. Underclass people. *My* people. 'So the Clans are destructive and murderous as well as power hungry.'

His chin tipped up and I spotted a sudden flash of anger. 'A lot of my friends risked their lives that day to hold back the water.'

'Well they didn't do a very good job, did they?'

The way Byron's body tensed, I wondered whether he was about to punch me in the nose for that comment. I rather hoped he would. It would release some of the tension both of us were feeling.

'It might not have been broadcast in your neck of the woods, but Sidhe died too.'

I did what I could to ignore his haunted expression. 'My heart bleeds. Get to the point,' I snapped.

Byron straightened his shoulders. His green eyed gaze held mine until I felt trapped. 'Long ago, checks and balances were put into place to prevent any one Clan from gaining an overly advantageous hold on the flow of magic. The four strongest Clans were each granted a key, if you like, to the Foinse. Unless all four keys were used at once then the Foinse couldn't be touched.'

'Foinse meaning…'

He gave me a strange look. I was pretty certain it was along the lines of 'you're an absolute idiot for not already knowing this'. It was hardly my fault old Bull hadn't permitted me an education. And Sidhe lore wasn't exactly a concern of Taylor's. 'Source,' he said finally. 'The Foinse is the source of all Scottish magic. And it's failing.'

I could feel the corner of my mouth twitch in an uncontrollable spasm. It wasn't a particularly funny situation but it was still difficult not to laugh. Even I had enough scanty knowledge of Clan hierarchy to work out was wrong. Things might have changed in the last two or three decades but, before then, the top Clans had remained the same for five hundred years.

'Let me guess,' I said, 'you need access to this magical Foinse to solve the problem. The four Clans with these special keys are Moncrieffe, Kincaid, Darroch and,' I paused, 'drum roll, please, ladies and gentlemen…'

Byron nodded. 'Adair. And you are the sole remaining member of the Adair Clan.'

No wonder they'd been keeping tabs on me. I wondered what they'd have done if I had inadvertently walked out in front of a bus. It would have been *adios muchachos* and not just for me. Then my humour fled. No doubt this was the reason why I was shoved into the Bull's care, such as it was, instead of simply being smothered as a baby.

'So you're going to blackmail me into helping you open the Foinse. Like I give a shit whether the magic fails or not. In fact, seeing the Clans brought down might be worth my friends spending a bit of time in the slammer.' I tipped my head. 'Long term goals versus short term gains.'

Byron regarded me with a flat, emotionless expression. 'I was warned you'd be like this,' he said finally. 'Bitchy and uncaring. Last night I thought they'd got it wrong and you were actually a nice person. Clearly, I was wrong.'

I raised my eyebrows. 'They?'

'The Clan Chieftains. They don't normally agree on much but they agreed on you.'

'I haven't spoken to a single Sidhe in fifteen years. Whether your lot have been keeping tabs on me or not, none of you know anything about me. Don't presume that you know what I'm like or who I am,' I hissed. 'You have no idea.'

'And don't presume that keeping the magic stable in the Clan lands is purely to benefit the

Sidhe,' he shot back. 'That magic does many things which the Clan-less also benefit from.'

'Oh yeah?' I sneered. 'Like what?'

'That magic controls the Veil,' he said. 'The barrier that prevents the Fomori from entering the Highlands.'

I scowled at him. Okay, the Fomori were pretty scary demons who were better kept well away from us.

'That same magic keeps nature in check,' Byron continued in the patient, patronising tone you'd use when explaining something to a particularly stupid child. 'You want to build a factory? The magic adjusts itself so the environment isn't irreparably harmed.'

I didn't want to build a factory but I got his point.

Byron wasn't finished. 'You want more disasters like the Clyde surge? Only on a far greater scale?' He folded his arms. 'Then be my guest. Let your friends rot in jail. Let your mentor pay his debts by losing part of his soul. You'll also be letting all of Scotland suffer.'

Alright. Jeez, he'd made his point. 'You could have told me all this in the first place. The Lia Saifire ruse was unnecessary.'

'Would you have listened?'

Maybe. Okay, probably not. In fact no, I wouldn't have. The first ten years of my life ensured that the last person I'd listen to was a Sidhe.

'Fine,' I snapped. 'I'll do what you want.

Release Taylor from his debt though and let Speck and Brochan go.'

'That will happen when you've done what we require.'

My eyes flashed. 'You don't trust me.'

'You're a thief, Integrity. Why would I trust you?'

'It's not just my name. I've got more integrity in my little finger than the Sidhe will ever have. No matter who my father was.'

He shrugged. 'We'll have to agree to distrust each other then. We'll go to the Clan lands, you'll help us with the Foinse, then you can go back to your oh-so-wonderful criminal existence.'

I hated him. I really, really hated him. I stood up and, as he moved his head to watch me, his hair fell across his eyes. Damn it. I also still lusted after him. Awkward.

'First,' I said, as calmly as I could, 'I need a shower and a change of clothes. Second, I need to tell Taylor what is going on. Once I have achieved both those things, I will come and meet you.'

'I'm not letting you out of my sight.'

'Yes,' I said, 'you are. I will present myself at the Sidhe court this evening. Until then, you'll have to wait.'

And, with that, I stalked out.

Chapter Nine

Taylor couldn't stop shaking his head. 'All this time? They've been watching you all this time? How could we not have known?'

'I doubt they've been staking me out twenty-four hours a day. They probably just check on me from time to time.'

'But this is ridiculous! I'm a professional, Tegs. I should know when someone is watching me.'

I walked over to him and held his head in my hands. 'Stop jiggling your head around like that. It's making me nauseous.'

'Sorry. But to keep tabs like that… Do you think they were watching during the Scone job?'

I bit my lip. 'I don't know. Maybe. Whether they were watching or not, they didn't do anything to stop us. They've always chosen to take a hands-off approach.' I frowned. 'Until now, of course.'

'Do you think they'll leave you alone? After you help them reach this Fonzie thing?'

'Foinse,' I corrected him absently. 'And right now, I doubt it. I do this for them and then in a couple of years' time there'll be something else, then something else, then something else. I'll never be free.' I met his eyes. 'I'm sorry. It turns out that all this mess is my fault.'

'If I'd not gambled…'

'Brochan and Speck would still have been

rounded up. They'd still have found another way to get me to do what they want. Maybe it's better that they've forced the issue. The failure of the magic is a big deal and I should help out. It'll be disastrous for everyone if I don't. Now I know they're watching me, however, I'll do a better job of disappearing once I've fixed their problem for them.'

His eyes scoured me. 'You mean for good, don't you?'

I gave a helpless shrug. 'What choice is there?'

He ran his hands through his hair and I suddenly realised how old he looked. There were lines on his face and a pallor to his skin that went beyond grey hair.

'What if…?' He swallowed.

'Yes?' I prompted.

Taylor sighed. 'You said that the reason they didn't get rid of you when you were a kid was probably because they knew that they might need you for something like this. Once the Foinse is accessed, what if they decide that they don't need you again?'

'You mean they'll kill me once I've helped them open it?'

He nodded, trouble written all across his face.

'I've considered that,' I told him truthfully. 'I'm going to need several exit plans to ensure it doesn't happen.'

'Was what your father did really so bad that an entire Clan needed to be exterminated?'

It was a rhetorical question but I answered it

anyway. 'He was responsible for more than a thousand deaths. He exterminated Clan Adair himself. I'm not aware of more than that, though. I was a baby when it all went down and no one ever saw fit to tell me the salient details.' I smiled, although my smile was tinged with sadness. 'I was a nobody, remember?'

Taylor reached over and hugged me tight. 'You're not a nobody now.'

For a brief moment, I felt safe and secure but it was only temporary. I pulled away. 'I have to get going. There's a lot to do before I walk into the lions' den.' I met his eyes. 'Why did the lion lose at poker?'

Taylor didn't smile. 'I don't know.'

'Because he was playing against a cheetah.'

His eyes crinkled. Relief ran through me. That was more like the Taylor I knew and loved.

'Tegs, you're not going to…'

'I'm going to do whatever's necessary to keep myself and my family safe,' I said. 'No matter what.'

*

Wearing a far more sensible, if boring, black ensemble, I strolled onto the pavement, whistling a merry tune. I glanced up one way and down another. Two Sidhe were sitting in a car directly opposite, and there was a shadow in an alcove about fifty feet away. I pursed my lips. I could handle three of them. This was my territory, after all – not theirs.

I shoved my hands in my pockets and ambled

to my left. Keeping my pace measured and my steps short, I didn't stop anywhere but neither did I rush. Losing a tail was a game of patience and wit more than anything else.

I nodded to a few familiar faces, murmuring greetings. I didn't let anyone engage me in conversation but I needed my three followers to think I was relaxed and going about my business before handing myself over to them. That's why I made a beeline for the post office.

It was pension day so even though it was already after midday, the place was busy with people waiting to collect their money. Pensions weren't something that the Sidhe had to worry about, I thought sourly, as my gaze travelled the length of the waiting area. Everyone here was, unsurprisingly, Clan-less, from the short dwarf with wrinkles so deep you could probably hide coins in them to the stooped human in a headscarf.

Instead of joining the queue, I went to the side, pulled an envelope out of my pocket and scribbled out an address. I didn't have a stamp t but I didn't really need one. I simply walked over to the gap marked 'international mail' and dropped it in. I made a brief show of looking round anxiously in case anyone had noticed me, then left again.

At the corner, as I waited for the lights to change, I used the glass front of a nearby shop to scan behind me. As I expected, one of my followers – all of whom were now helpfully on foot – peeled off and entered the post office, no doubt to try and retrieve my letter. The post office didn't like people messing with their systems, even if those people were well-connected Sidhe, so it would take him some time to do it. One down. Two to go.

It was interesting to note that one of the remaining tails was Mr Dimples. I wondered whether he still had the Lia Saifire on him. There wasn't any noticeable bulge in his pockets but you never knew. Whether he had it or not, there was another pleasing bulge in his trousers that I enjoyed. Handsome and well-endowed. Well, well, well.

The moment the green man appeared, I crossed over, maintaining my earlier speed. This time, however, I lengthened my strides so I covered more ground more quickly. They would be expecting me to keep the same pace and it would take them a minute or two to realise that I was pulling away. It was a simple trick, but a good one. It was also well-timed as there was a set of crossroads ahead.

I checked my watch. 12.28pm. Perfect. I kept to the side of the pavement so my shoulder was almost brushing against the tall buildings on my left. A minute and a half later, I was at the MacReedy building just as the glass doors opened to let the vast secretarial department sprint out for lunch.

I hunched down, taking my battered baseball cap from my jacket pocket –it was the very same cap that Taylor gave me all those years ago – and jammed it on my head, tucking my hair underneath. Then I pushed my way through the crowd, zipped round the corner and ran.

Del's Coffee, a grubby dive of a place, was less than thirty feet away. I weaved my way in and out of the busy foot traffic and ducked inside. It might serve coffee that you'd be inclined to avoid if you didn't want to end up juddering for the rest of the day on a serious caffeine high but, with two exits, the place was ideal for me.

I sped through, throwing out a quick wave to the eponymous Del, the one-horned Bonnacon who ran the place.

'Hey, Integrity. Bit of a speed merchant today, ain't ya?'

'I only sell to friends,' I threw over my shoulder as I opened the door opposite and continued. I ran into a nearby pawnshop to check on my pursuers. Running around on the streets like a crazy person would ensure they caught up with me again; hiding was far smarter.

'You wanna buy something or not?'

I twisted round, spotting the shop owner behind the cage that protected him from his less savoury customers. He eyed me with a hard look that warned of trouble. His hand hovered somewhere beneath the counter. Either there was a gun or a panic button under there. Right now, I'd prefer the gun; I didn't want to attract any undue attention. I weighed up my choices and made a decision.

'Here,' I said, reaching into my pocket and pulling out a five-pound note. 'I'll be out of your hair in less than two minutes.'

His frown deepened. I cursed under my breath and took out another one. 'Will that do you?'

The owner didn't answer; he merely turned and hobbled away. That was an expensive sodding two minutes. Rather than dwell on it, I turned round to get a decent line of sight on Del's. It was just as well – I'd barely manoeuvred myself into position when Dimples burst out of the cafe, his head frantically turning from right to left. No prizes for guessing who he was looking for.

When the second tail didn't appear, I grinned. They must have split up to better their chances of finding me.

I crouched down, still keeping an eye on Byron's second-in-command. He couldn't seem to make up his mind which way to go. There was a chance that he'd try the pawnshop but he had plenty of other avenues to consider. My luck was in. He went right, jogging away from both the pawnshop and me. Now all I had to was to get out.

I stretched up to the bell hanging from the door, yanked it off and tossed it away. I didn't need it jangling; if Dimples heard it, he'd definitely turn around. Besides, ten quid for a dirty piece of junk like that? The shopkeeper was still getting a bargain.

If he heard what I'd done, he didn't come back out to investigate. Smart move on his part, I decided. I didn't fight but he didn't know that.

I sneaked back out into the street, shivering as a gust of wind whipped my hat straight off my head.

I lunged for it but it was too late. It flew away, tumbling down the quiet back street like a ball of tumbleweed in one of those old Western films. The ones where there was about to be a terrible shoot out.

That hat was an important part of my history and I didn't want to lose it. I gave a quick look to see if Dimples was still in play. His shoulders were slumped and he was trudging away, not turning round. I smiled smugly. He knew he'd lost me.

Staying light on my feet, I ran after him – or rather I ran after my hat. I just managed to snag it before there was another gust of wind. Giving the cap an affectionate pat, I put it back on and double-checked Dimples. He was oblivious to what was going on behind him. I did a little jig, causing a scurrying rat to pause and blink at me. I shrugged at it. 'You're right,' I whispered. 'It's time to go.'

I was just about to head off in the opposite direction when I noticed Dimples' backpack. There wasn't much of a bulge to it, which was probably why it hadn't registered before. I gnawed my bottom lip. The bag didn't fit with his tailored suit. It was a strange thing to carry unless... My smile grew wider. He still had the Lia Saifire with him.

In theory, snatching the jewel was now a waste of time. No matter what I did, Byron was going to hold me to my promise to open the Foinse. But it was a matter of professional pride; I wanted the arrogant playboy to know that he still wasn't completely in control.

I licked my lips. This was not the clever thing to do but it would be fun.

I jogged forward on the balls of my feet. If I could get close enough, I could probably swipe it. There was one seriously nervy moment when Dimples looked round. I was saved by a collection of mouldy cardboard boxes outside a door; I threw myself behind them, my heart hammering. When there was no shout or sound of feet thundering in my direction, I peered up. Dimples was blithely continuing on his way. Excellent.

When I got closer, I slowed my pace. One stretch of my arm and I'd be able to reach the backpack. I matched Dimples step for step so he wouldn't realise anyone was right behind him and eyed the bag. It was beyond ridiculous that the Lia Saifire would be in there. Firstly, taking it on a stake-out would be stupid. Secondly, leaving it in an unlocked backpack in this neighbourhood was dumber than surfing on Ben Nevis. There was no way the jewel was in there. I should have turned back round immediately and got on with what I was supposed to be doing. My fingers were itchy, however. I just couldn't help myself.

Pickpocketing is a hell of a lot easier than most people suppose. It just takes a delicate touch. Holding my breath, I reached forward and grabbed the edge of the zip, sliding it open two inches. Then I slipped my hand inside. My fingers brushed against something soft and velvet and I pulled it. Whatever it was, it was heavy. I pulled a bit harder, just as there was a sudden ring.

I froze, my hand still inside his backpack. He stopped, forcing me to stop as well, dug into his suit pocket and took out a shiny phone.

'Yeah,' he grunted.

I started tugging again, gently lifting the object towards the opening.

'No sign of her. Byron's going to be seriously pissed off.'

The velvet snagged on the edge of the zip. Shite, shite, shite. I was rusty. It had been a long time since I'd bothered with the sort of small ticket items you could get from this type of theft.

'We should double back. She might go back home.'

Just as I thought I was going to have to use my teeth, I managed to free the fabric and pull away. In my hand was a small black velvet bag, tied with a gold string. Whatever was inside, it was going to be valuable. Even if it wasn't the Lia Saifire, it was still satisfying. I carefully closed the zip again, something many pickpockets didn't bother with. Taking the time - and the risk - to do it meant it would be longer before he noticed that anything was amiss.

I sidestepped left just as Dimples went right and headed back the long way. The moment I was sure there was enough distance between us, I pressed myself against the wall until he'd vanished completely. Then I opened the bag. The deep-faceted blue of the Lia Saifire blinked up at me.

Crapadoodledo. Go me.

Chapter Ten

The small bar on the edge of St. Andrews Square was smoky and reeked of stale beer. I cast my eyes around, quickly alighting on Lexie who was sitting in the far corner, nursing some strange green concoction. It was so lurid in colour that I was briefly reminded of Byron's eyes. Ick. I didn't want to give him a single thought. Not unless it involved stripping him of all his wealth (and maybe his clothes too).

I slid into the seat opposite. 'Piss off,' Lexie grunted, without looking up.

'Hey,' I said softly. 'It's me.'

Her head jerked up and her face filled with relief. 'Integrity! Where the hell have you been? What's been going on? Why haven't you been in touch? Have you heard from Brochan or Speck? Do you know if I'm in danger? What about…'

'Whoa, whoa, whoa.' I raised my palms. 'Chill, Lex. Everything's good.'

She gazed at me like I was a total idiot. 'Good? Good? How can everything be good?'

I winced. 'Keep your voice down. You need to keep a low profile, remember?'

She subsided into a series of blue-tinged grumbles.

'That's better,' I said, like a disapproving teacher. 'How many of those have you had?'

She tapped her glass. 'These? I dunno. Half a dozen maybe.'

I eyed the drink with distaste. 'What's in it?'

'Crème de menthe, vodka and Amaretto. Want to try?'

Eurgh. 'No thanks.' I caught the attention of the bartender. 'Jug of coffee, please. And make it strong.'

'You're no fun. I'm drowning my sorrows. You should join me.'

'I have things to do. And so do you.'

'Yeah? Like what?'

I took out the velvet bag and threw it on the table. It clunked heavily against the wood. Lexie looked at it and then at me. She took another sip of her green monster before curiosity got the better of her. She picked up the bag and peered inside it.

I waited. When her jaw dropped and her eyes went wide, I grinned.

'How…?' she breathed.

'Long story. Taylor can fill you in on the details later.'

She shook her head with incredible vehemence. 'No way. You can ply me with all the coffee you like and give me as many priceless jewels as you can find but I'm not venturing out there again. I'm not going to prison, Tegs.'

About this, at least, I was confident. 'You're not going to go to prison,' I told her. 'They're no longer looking for you.'

'Yeah?' She did a good impression of one of

those disbelieving women you get on daytime chat shows when they're told their husbands have been cheating on them.

'Yes,' I replied firmly. 'It was me they were after and they've got me.'

Lexie blinked. 'Eh?'

'Like I said, Taylor will fill you in. What you two need to do is to get hold of the buyer and get rid of that.' I nodded towards the Lia Saifire. Recovering it had opened up a whole host of options. 'With the money, hire the meanest, nastiest lawyer in town. Get Speck and Brochan released, even if it's only on bail. Once that's done, you need to talk to Charlie.'

'Who?'

'My neighbour. He deals in a lot of black-market stuff. One of things which he professes to have is a device that will temporarily negate the barrier spells the Sidhe have put around the Clan areas. All four of you have to get to the Cruaich.'

Lexie's face paled. 'That's where the Sidhe court is.'

'Yup. Get there. Find somewhere to hide. Every night at midnight, set off our signal. I'll come and find you. If five nights pass and I don't come for you then get the hell out of there and don't look back.'

She stared at me. The bartender appeared out of nowhere and slammed the coffee jug down on the table between us. We both jumped.

'Got it?' I asked her softly.

She nodded. 'I'm not dreaming, am I? I don't think there's absinthe my drink but I could be mistaken. It's happened before…'

I pointed at the coffee and stood up. 'Drink that before you leave,' I instructed. 'All of it.'

*

Less than two hours later, I was standing in front of the gates leading to the Cruaich with a small pink suitcase in tow. As with many places in Scotland, it hadn't been easy to get here. So much for the joys of living in a rural location; not for the first time, I wished someone had invented the Star Trek transporters for real. Public transport was a pain in the arse.

I tugged at my case. I was hoping it wouldn't take long to do this Foinse business but it never hurt to come prepared. There weren't any guards on duty although, with the magical barrier in place, there really didn't need to be. I guessed that although the Sidhe knew the magic was failing, they weren't expecting it to happen today.

I took off my hat and ran my fingers through my hair, getting rid of any tangles. I'd swapped my trainers for a pair of high stiletto boots. I'd paid a cobbler to paint over the soles for me in lacquered hot pink. They weren't Christian Louboutin - they were better. Dressing to kill always made me more confident and I was going to need all the confidence I could muster. I'd even managed to paint my nails on the way here in the taxi and it took a steady hand to achieve that sort of art. The colour matched the shoes. Naturally. I was going to show all those Sidhe wankers – Byron included – that I wasn't afraid of them.

Just in case someone was watching, I tossed my hair disdainfully. The wind caught it and a halo of white flew up around my head. Even I had to admit it was impressive. Still looking like an avenging angel, with Mother Nature herself at my beck and call, I stepped through.

If I'd been here when I was a kid, I didn't remember it. Cruaich in Gaelic translates as 'hill'. What wasn't apparent from the other side of the barrier was the vast castle on top of that hill. The length of the driveway wasn't obvious either. I glanced down at my shoes. Maybe I should have worn my trainers after all. I shrugged. Well, I was here now. It wasn't the time to start rummaging through my bag.

I started walking. The trees here were different to the ones on the other side; their leaves were greener and their branches spread further. They were also considerably more gnarled, attesting to their age. A faint memory tugged at me as I strode upwards, one involving my far younger self clambering up a similar specimen to retrieve a particularly delicious-looking apple. As I recall, I fell long before I reached my goal and received a sharp scolding as a result. Not that getting a scolding was anything out of the ordinary for me.

Not back then.

I allowed the memories to flood over me. Almost every single one was unhappy and they bolstered my feelings of antipathy. The Sidhe weren't likely to convince me with their tales of 'oh, but we're saving the world' as long as I could remember how they'd treated one solitary orphan.

I was halfway up the drive, my expression grim and my heart hard, when I spotted someone. Unmistakably Sidhe. He came right out of the main gate, standing to one side as I approached. Whoever he was, he didn't appear to be doing anything other than watching me. Not long after, he was joined by another one. Then another and another and another.

By the time I'd gone another sixty steps, there must have been a hundred Sidhe watching me. None of them uttered a single word. It was seriously creepy. I could feel my stomach in knots. What exactly were they planning? I was no match for one well-trained Sidhe, let alone this number. However if they tried to rip me to shreds, they'd have no chance with the Foinse. If they were going to use words to intimidate me … well, I was sure I'd heard worse in my time. I stiffened my resolve. How bad could this be?

When I reached the first watcher, I made a point of refusing to look at him. There was a sudden movement and I tensed, waiting for the attack to come. There was nothing. The next Sidhe also moved, followed by the one after that. One by one, each of the watching Sidhe copied the next. At first I couldn't work it out; it was like some strange Fey Mexican wave. When I finally looked over and realised what they were doing, it hit me like a painful bolt in the chest. They were bowing. To me.

My heels clicked against the ground. Even I heard my steps falter. Then I picked up the pace again. They were probably just relieved I was coming to save their sorry arses. It didn't mean they wouldn't try and stab me in the back once I was done.

I'd almost reached the castle when another figure appeared. This one I knew. Byron was no longer wearing the casual T-shirt from our last encounter; instead he had on an elaborate floaty white shirt which was open at the neck. He'd foregone trousers for a traditional kilt in Moncrieffe colours. Irritatingly, it matched his eyes as if it had been designed just for him. The heavy tartan folds rippled in the gentle breeze. If he was trying to look like a cover model from a steamy historical romance, he was succeeding.

He pasted a smile on his face that belied his anger. When I stepped up to him and took his outstretched hand, he pulled me close and whispered in my ear. 'The Lia Saifire appears to have gone missing. You wouldn't know anything about that, would you?'

I grinned. 'Goodness. How very careless of you to lose such a priceless gem.'

Byron growled and released me. 'Miss Adair, if you'd like to follow me.'

I raised up my chin. 'Actually, it's Taylor.'

Something unfathomable crossed his eyes. 'Pardon?'

'Taylor,' I told him. 'My name is Integrity Taylor. Clan Adair is of no consequence to me.' I took Taylor's surname not long after I joined him. It meant far more than some defunct Sidhe Clan ever could.

Byron's green eyes darkened. 'These people are here because of the Adair name.'

'Despite what my father did?'

'Look a little closer. They're all lower-level Sidhe. You won't find many amongst the highborn bowing to you.' His tone was more sympathetic than taunting.

I looked back at the Sidhe who were still watching me and shrugged. 'Curiosity never killed anything except a couple of hours. They can rubberneck what they want.' Hell, despite the weird bowing thing, they were probably hoping I had horns sprouting from my head and a forked tongue. I was almost sorry to disappoint them.

Byron seemed to decide that engaging me in discussion about my name was pointless. He turned round and strode ahead. I gazed after him for a second then followed. Whatever was about to unfold within the depths of the Cruaich castle, it certainly wouldn't be dull.

Once inside, I was surprised at the interior. It wasn't as flash as I expected. It was grand, certainly, but more from a sense of ancient tradition than ostentatious wealth. Byron was moving well ahead of me but rather than quicken my step to keep up, I deliberately slowed my pace and drank in my surroundings.

A red carpet ran the length of the stone-flagged floor and the walls were draped with the different Clan tartans, most of which I was surprised to recognise. The Adair Clan colours, a clash of orange, blue and green as I recalled, were conspicuously absent. So much for making a big deal out of the Adair name, I thought sardonically.

There was a set of grand doors at the end of the carpet. Byron stopped at them and turned, impatiently tapping his foot as I ambled towards him. He didn't seem happy at my slow progress.

I was overtaken by a sense of mischief that I rarely indulged. I stopped and took out my phone. Byron's expression grew even more thunderous, especially when I took several selfies, flicking my hair and pouting at myself. I was taking inspiration from Lexie; she was very skilled at this sort of thing.

'Get a move on.'

'But, *Your Highness,* I want to record myself for posterity. There has to be some sort of record that I was here. Otherwise when you try to get rid of me once I've helped you reach the Foinse, I won't be able to prove that I was here.'

Byron blinked in astonishment. Interesting. Perhaps that wasn't the endgame after all – but I wasn't going to take any chances.

'I'm going to send this to a few friends,' I

chirped. 'So they know where I am.' I pressed the necessary buttons. My hairdresser would be *very* surprised when she checked her messages.

'Whatever you might think,' Byron said, his voice softening a touch, 'we are not going to hurt you.'

I met his eyes. 'I'll believe it when I see it.' I jerked my head at the doors. 'Aren't we going in?'

A muscle in his jaw throbbed. 'Just one thing first.' He dug into his pocket and pulled out an envelope. I recognised it immediately. It was good to know that my little diversion had worked. I wondered how hard it had been to retrieve the letter from the post office after I dropped it into international mail. 'Can you explain this?'

'Explain what?'

He slid out the glossy page that was folded inside the envelope and waved it in my direction. I'd torn it out of one of Taylor's girlie mags; it was a particularly graphic representation of a mocked-up Sidhe man performing fellatio on a rather well-endowed female troll.

'You know that intercepting mail is a serious offence?' I enquired, cocking my head.

'These immature little rebellions are pointless. They're only going to delay matters.'

I looked at him from under my eyelashes. The loss of the Lia Saifire and the pornographic post were really getting to him - probably because he wasn't as 'in charge' as he liked to be. Good.

'How long are these matters going to take?' I

asked.

'We'll head out for the Foinse straight after dawn. It takes about a day to get there. We'll arrive in the grove by midday Tuesday so if all goes to plan, you can be back home and sleeping in your own bed by Thursday night.' Something sparked in his eyes. 'If you wish, I can tuck you in.'

Byron was obviously irritated and was trying to intimidate me and put me in my place. I quashed down the lustful butterflies that sprang up in my stomach and licked my lips. I twirled my fingers through my hair and moved closer to him, brushing against his body. The answering tension in his muscles brought me deep satisfaction.

'Don't,' he growled.

I stepped back. 'Then stop trying to flirt with me. We both know that moment has passed.'

He looked like he was about to say something and thought better of it. 'Fine,' he snapped, 'come on then.'

Without further ado, Byron pushed open the large doors, revealing a vast room. Smack bang in the centre was a table, with a lot of well-dressed Sidhe sitting around it. Every head twisted in our direction while I sucked in a breath. I'd thought Byron was attractive but these guys were something else. Not a single blemish marred their skin and not one hair was out of place. It felt like I was walking into the pages of *Vanity Fair*.

A man at the far end of the table got to his feet. The simple gold band encircling his head signified his role and I immediately spotted the family resemblance. So this was Byron's father, the Sidhe Steward Aifric. He'd been the leader of the Clans for years. It had always seemed a rather pointless role – not just to me but to many Clan and Clan-less people. Each Clan head had his own agenda which almost never corresponded with anyone else's.

The general consensus was that the Steward was 'permitted' to make small decisions of matters of bureaucratic import and that he acted as a conduit to keep the others in check. Apart from the destruction of the Adair Clan, Aifric had done well to avoid outright war between any of the Sidhe groups. It didn't mean there wasn't still murder; it just meant there was less murder than if someone else had been in charge. Well, whatever he did, he wasn't *my* damned leader.

No doubt in deference to Aifric rather than me, the others also stood, gliding to their feet in smooth, practised movements.

Byron addressed them all. 'Good day to you all.' He paused for effect. 'I would like to present Integrity…' He paused again and shot me a quick look, 'Taylor.'

I felt an unexpected flash of gratitude that he'd used my chosen surname instead of Adair. The Sidhe Clan heads and royalty were taken aback and several threw startled glances in Aifric's direction. To the Steward's credit, he didn't blink.

'Well done, Byron,' he murmured.

There was a chorus of assent from around the

table.

'You did well to bring her in,' someone commented.

I balled up my fists. Yeah, go, Golden Boy. You brought the stupid Clan-less orphan in out of the cold. Let's not acknowledge her personally though. I pinned my mouth firmly closed. The tension of being around all these Sidhe wankers was getting to me. The last thing I needed was to snark out some comment that would put them on edge and make them hate me even more than they already did.

Aifric, dressed in a similar manner to Byron, approached me. Watch it, I projected silently. Get too close and I might bite.

He put his hands out, reaching for mine as if to clasp them. I stepped backwards and crossed my arms. I might be trying not to antagonise anyone but I wasn't the prodigal daughter returning home. I wanted it made clear that I was there under sufferance.

Despite the intake of breath from several of the other Sidhe, Aifric barely reacted. He gave me a flicker of a smile and a nod of acknowledgment, and returned his hands to his sides.

'It was good of you come. May I call you Integrity?'

'You may,' I replied formally. 'I didn't have much choice. I had to come.'

Aifric's facial features might be a match for Byron but his eyes were a brilliant blue rather than an emerald green. They fixed on me with surprising kindness. 'There is always a choice. We are glad that you are here.'

I wondered whether that was the royal 'we'. Judging by the dark expressions on some of the other courtiers' faces, they didn't share the sentiment. One gaze in particular caught my attention. When I recognised it as belonging to the Bull, I almost staggered backwards. I hadn't realised he'd risen to the position of Chieftain for the Scrymgeour Clan.

I felt the familiar feelings of inadequacy but I wasn't eleven years old any more, I reminded myself. I could do this.

'Explain to me exactly how this will work,' I said, in a clear voice that was free of tremor.

'A delegation will ride out tomorrow.'

I choked. Ride? As in horses? Shite.

Aifric didn't notice my reaction but I was certain that Byron did. I could almost feel the amusement emanating from him.

'It will take just over a day to reach the Foinse. It's not an easy journey and the rural location requires old-fashioned transport. There will be two representatives from Kincaid, Moncrieffe, Darroch, as well as you. Kincaid's key opens the path. Our key – the Moncrieffe key – opens the cavern. Darroch's key opens the bridge and your key opens the final barrier to the box, within which the Foinse resides.'

I nodded, trying to look wise. 'And the key looks like…?'

There was a snort from the table. I was pretty certain it came from the Bull but I couldn't be sure. Aifric barely reacted but I could swear his shoulders stiffened. 'The key is you. The humans call it DNA. We are less prosaic. We call it your soul.'

Oh. That made a kind of sense. 'No problem.'

Aifric smiled benignly. 'All you have to do is whisper your true name and the key will work. The difficult part will be getting to the Foinse. Once you're at the site, it will be easy.'

I stared at him. A tiny furrow crossed his brow. 'Is something wrong?'

'The, um, true name part.'

He nodded. 'I can understand why you'd be worried about that. No-one will hear you say it. Every representative will be respectful. You have my word.'

'She'd better be respectful back,' someone muttered. 'If she learns one of the others' true names then…'

Byron strolled over to the red-haired grumbler. He didn't touch her or speak to her; he simply stood behind her chair. She immediately fell silent. Damn. That was some power. What exactly did he do for his father? Was he some kind of enforcer? I knew of a few Clan-less gangs that had people like that in their ranks. They didn't tend to last very long.

I shook myself. Whatever Byron's role, it didn't alter the issue confronting all of us.

I cleared my throat. 'This probably isn't the best time to bring this up but I should mention it as it has a bearing on your plan.'

Aifric appeared confused. 'Go on.'

'I, er, don't have a true name.'

You could have heard a pin drop in the room.

'Say that again?'

I licked my lips and repeated myself. 'I don't have a true name. I never received one.'

It started slowly. Aifric's cheeks flushed pink then, second by second, they grew darker until his entire face was a mottled purple. His blue eyes turned icy. 'What is the meaning of this?'

I stepped back. It wasn't my fault. If any of them had stopped to think about it, they'd have realised. All the same a shudder of fear ran through me. What would he do now?

Byron returned to his spot next to me. Surprisingly, he wrapped his hand round my upper arm and squeezed it reassuringly. By the look on his father's face, however, that wasn't going to help.

'How can you not have your name?' He turned to the table of astonished SIdhe, fixed on the Bull and raised his voice. 'How can she not have her name?'

The Bull's eyes darted around in terror and I realised for the first time that the man who was such a focus for my nightmares when I was a child was actually rather unremarkable. He was morbidly obese, which detracted slightly from his Sidhe good looks and poise, but he wasn't the monster that I remembered. Whether age had diminished him or whether it was simply that I was no longer a child, I found that I could look at the Bull and feel nothing more than vague disdain. I was neither scared nor angry nor vengeful. I had won.

'She was eleven years old when she ran away,' he stammered. 'It wasn't my responsibility.'

'*She* was your responsibility!' Aifric thundered.

Byron's grip round my arm tightened.

'We agreed to leave her be,' the Bull began.

'Enough!'

'If she doesn't have her true name, then she didn't receive her Gift,' the moany red-haired Sidhe interjected. 'That's why she didn't…' The woman's voice trailed away as Aifric's icy blue gaze turned on her.

I frowned. Didn't what?

'Byron,' Aifric snapped, 'you will attend to this immediately.'

He bowed. 'Of course.'

'We will have to delay the journey to the Foinse.' Aifric stroked his chin. His voice dropped. 'When was the last time one of us waited until adulthood to receive our name?'

Silence answered him. He scowled.

'It might make the fever worse,' a stunning blond hulk of a man muttered.

'It could be a week before she can travel,' someone else agreed.

Excuse me? Fever? I crossed my arms and glared, expecting someone to explain.

Aifric shook his head in irritation. 'Either way, we are forced to wait.' He looked at Byron again.

'Make the arrangements.'

A haughty-looking man with a hooked nose cleared his throat. 'Is the Adair grove still standing?'

Several of the Sidhe exchanged nervous glances. I spotted a few shrugs and one or two head shakes.

'Even if it's still there,' Aifric stated, 'we don't have time to travel there. We're going to lose enough days as it is. We have no clue when the Foinse is going to give out. It might be days or it might be months but we can't afford to wait. She can use the Cruaich grove.'

There was a collective intake of breath. 'That's reserved for Clan heirs,' the ginger woman complained.

Aifric appeared unimpressed. 'She's the heir to the Adair Clan.'

She wanted nothing to do with the Adair Clan. I decided, however, that this was a good time to keep my mouth shut. Sometimes you learn more by listening. It wasn't a habit I practised very often but I held my tongue – at least until I had a better grasp of this situation.

'You can't let her in there!' someone burst out. 'What if she desecrates the ground?'

'It's sacred,' another agreed. 'Not for the likes of her.'

I almost laughed. It was amusing that they thought I would soil their precious grove simply by my presence. Not for the likes of me, indeed. Had I wandered into the pages of a Victorian novel?

Byron growled, 'She's not going to desecrate the grove. She's here, isn't she? She's going to help us with the Foinse. She's hardly some marauding brute out to destroy us all. She's not her father.'

I was rather touched by Byron's interjection. I noticed that he failed to mention that I was here because he'd blackmailed me. Or that I was a criminal.

'She will use the grove here,' Aifric boomed, his expression thunderous. 'And I will hear no more on the matter.' He glared at every single person. Most – but not all – dropped their eyes.

Still piqued, he sniffed loudly, gathered up his robes and swept out of the room. The remaining Sidhe looked at me and I looked at Byron. I wasn't going to damage their damn grove. I was more concerned about myself than a bunch of old trees.

'Fever?'

Byron looked at me with a new light in his eyes but ignored my question. 'All those thefts. I was sure you had to have…' He shook himself. 'You're more impressive than you realise.'

My earlier amusement dissipated, replaced by tingling wariness. I didn't understand what was going on but I definitely didn't like it.

Chapter Eleven

It was with some relief that Byron escorted me out. 'Naming ceremonies typically take place at midday,' he told me. 'They go more smoothly when the sun is at its peak so you'll need to hang around here until then.'

'What was that ginger woman going to say?' I asked. 'What didn't I do because I've not received my gift? And what the hell is this about a fever?'

'You have to understand, Integrity, that this has never happened before. All Sidhe receive their true names when they turn thirteen. This is new territory for all of us.'

'You didn't answer my questions,' I pointed out.

'I don't know what she was going to say,' he admitted.

There was a husky interruption from the side. 'Byron, you're back! I was hoping you'd come up to my rooms and visit.'

My hackles rose. I craned my neck round, stiffening when my worst fears were confirmed. Tipsania. What was she doing here?

She sauntered up to Byron and hooked her arm round his neck, planting a kiss on his lips. He shifted awkwardly, extricating himself from her grasp.

'Hi Tipsy.' He gestured to me. 'I'm sure you

remember Integrity.'

'Who?' She glanced at me, pretending to be surprised. It was a ridiculous display. Considering how many Sidhe had watched my approach to the castle, she had to know about my presence. This show with Byron was probably for my benefit. 'Oh,' she said, her lips curling. 'It's you. So that's what you're calling yourself these days.'

I refused to be cowed. 'Hello Tipsy. How wonderful it is to see you again. It's like meeting my long-lost sister after years apart.'

She almost choked. This was more fun than I thought it would be. 'Yeah,' she muttered unconvincingly, turning away and focusing her attention back on the hapless man. 'Thank you so much for my present. It's beautiful.' She touched her neck. Hanging against her alabaster skin was the bright emerald necklace I'd found in Byron's hotel safe. The fake one. 'I love that you gave me emeralds,' she gushed. 'The colour matches your eyes perfectly. Every time I wear it, I'll think of you.'

My eyebrows flew up. So these two were involved? Given what I remembered of her nature, it was hardly surprising. Tipsania had always had an uncanny knack of getting what she wanted. I almost felt sorry for Byron. Almost.

'It must have been really expensive,' she continued, kissing him again.

I let out a tiny snort. Byron's eyes flashed at me in warning. I shrugged. It wasn't my fault he was pulling the wool over her eyes with some bits of pretty glass.

'I'm glad you like it,' he told her. 'But it wasn't expensive. It's...'

'Darling! That's so like you to downplay things. You know,' she said with a wink, 'I like emerald rings too.' She held up her hand, rubbing her thumb against her marriage finger. Well, well, well. Byron's flirtation with me had been all about the manipulation; I doubted that he was the marrying kind. He certainly hadn't appeared unhappy when the giggly Sidhe girl came onto him. Maybe good old Tipsy was prepared to agree to an open marriage.

Byron coughed. 'I need to take Integrity up to her room. I'll come and find you later, alright?'

She beamed. 'I'll look forward to it.'

Taking my elbow, he led me away. Once we were out of earshot, I couldn't help myself. 'You and Tipsy, eh? How long has that been going on?'

'It's complicated,' he grunted. 'And I'm sorry you had to bump into her like that. I know she wasn't very nice to you when you were a kid.'

Wasn't very nice? That was an understatement. 'You weren't very nice to me either, Byron.'

He didn't look at me. 'No,' he said after a long pause. 'I don't suppose I was.'

We lapsed into silence. I still wanted answers to my questions about the naming but I sensed this wasn't the right time. He'd shoved his hands into his pockets and was looking particularly grim. I'd find someone else to explain - Byron apparently had far weightier things to worry about.

He deposited me in a small suite of rooms in the high reaches of the castle without saying another single word. It wasn't until he was preparing to leave that he grunted that someone would come to help me settle in. Whatever that entailed.

Still, I was finally getting some much-needed solitude. I looked around the rooms approvingly. While I was betting that the other Sidhe were housed in far more luxurious quarters, the simple elegance here pleased me. Until I sat down on the bed; it was rock hard. I tried bouncing up and down and received nothing more than a sore arse for my efforts. I snorted. Well, it wasn't like I was here to sleep.

Checking the door and the corridor and satisfied that I was well and truly alone, I opened my bag and pulled out the letter opener. I had been rather mean to Bob the last time we talked and I needed him on my side. Especially now. Steeling myself for some grovelling, I unsheathed the blade and gave it a good rub.

Bob appeared with the now-familiar flash of light. That was a start at least. He was, however, clearly put out. I received a petulant grimace before he turned his back on me, sat down and crossed his legs and his arms.

'Come on, Bob,' I soothed. 'Don't be like that.'

He didn't answer.

'I didn't mean to hurt your feelings before or to take advantage of you. I won't do it again. I promise.'

When he still refused to look at me, I reached out with my little finger and gave him the gentlest poke. 'You know how you were impressed with the luxury of the last place? Wait until you see where we are now.'

His body jerked. I was getting somewhere.

'It's not as opulent,' I continued, 'but it's certainly exciting. You must be bored being stuck in that knife all the time. Now you can do something more interesting.'

He muttered a few words under his breath. I leaned forward, not quite catching them. 'What was that?'

'Dagger. It's not a knife. It's not for buttering bread. It's a dagger. In fact,' he said, 'from now on you will only refer to it as a sword. Or a scimitar. Yes. Call it a scimitar.'

I pressed my lips together, forcing myself not to laugh. The letter opener was about as far removed from a scimitar as I was from a troll. If that was all it took to appease him, though, I could manage it.

'Scimitar, then. It must be boring inside the scimitar.'

'It's not so bad. I have *Deep Space Nine* to keep me company.'

I whistled. 'The boxset?'

'The entire boxset. Frankly, you're interrupting my viewing.'

Sitting down with a slab of chocolate and some classic sci-fi sounded incredibly appealing and I was genuinely envious. Unfortunately, I didn't have time to see if it was within his powers to lend it to me. How did he even get it inside the knife? Distracting questions swirled around my head before I tamped them down and got back to business.

'You've still not asked where we are,' I said, dangling the carrot in front of him again.

He sniffed. 'I don't need you to tell me. I'm perfectly capable of working it out for myself. I'm a vastly powerful magical being, remember? I…' He halted in mid-flow. Then he stood up and slowly spun round, his expression full of awe. 'The Cruaich? We're at the Cruaich? Girlfriend!'

I grinned. 'See? I knew you wouldn't be disappointed.'

He bounced up and down. 'I thought you were some crappy minor Sidhe with no powers. But you've brought me to the Sidhe Court. I've never been to the SIdhe Court before. Are the hallways really paved in gold?'

'Er, not exactly.'

'Oh.' He seemed disappointed. 'But I bet all the plates are encrusted with diamonds, right? I like diamonds.'

'I have a fondness for shiny, sparkly things myself,' I confided. 'But I've not been given anything to eat so I can't tell you what the kitchenware is like.'

His expression was eager. 'Find out. You must find out.'

'I will do my best.'

My earlier rudeness apparently forgotten, Bob leapt onto the palm of my hand, belly-flopping and linking his fingers underneath his chin. 'So, why are we here?'

'Something to do with the Foinse and the flow of magic. It's running out or broken. I'm going to help open it so it can be…' I hesitated. Actually, I was bit unclear about what was going to happen once it had been accessed. Rebooted, perhaps?

'What?' He sprang up, the very picture of alarm. 'The Foinse is failing? Uh Integrity, that can't happen! You can't let it happen!'

I regarded him thoughtfully. It hadn't occurred to me that the Foinse would regulate Bob's magic too. I supposed it really did affect everyone after all. 'I'm certainly going to do my best,' I told him, meaning it. 'The thing is, before I can help the other Sidhe to open it up, I need to receive my true name. I left the Clans and the Sidhe before I was thirteen so I never went through the ceremony and I have no idea what to expect.'

'You don't know?' He rolled his eyes. '*Everyone* knows what happens during the naming ceremony. You get your true name. And usually a magical Gift too.'

'Yes, that part I'm aware of. But how does the ceremony work?'

'You're the Sidhe,' he blustered. 'You should

know.'

I sighed. 'You don't know anything about it either, do you?'

His shoulders drooped. 'No,' he admitted. 'Not a scooby.'

Shite. 'There was something about a fever,' I said, worried at the thought that I might get sick. 'I'm going to need you to stick close,' I told him. 'I might need to use one of those wishes after all.'

'Don't tease me, Uh Integrity,' he moaned. 'I know you're one of those stubborn types.'

There was a sharp knock at the door. I looked meaningfully at Bob and he snapped off a salute, hopping back into the blade with another blinding flash. He gave me a little wave from inside then vanished.

Cautiously opening the door a fraction, I gazed out. Well, well, well. It was none other than Dimples himself.

'Hey!' I said cheerfully. 'Good to see you again!'

He threw me a look that was dirtier than the magazine picture I had shoved into the envelope and pretended to post. Okay, he was going to hold a grudge. That was a shame.

'I'm here to ask if everything is to your satisfaction.'

He wouldn't even look me in the eyes. He was probably being made to do this as a punishment for losing the Lia Saifire. I should feel guilty but he shouldn't have been so naïve as to carry it around with him in the seediest part of Aberdeen.

'The bed's going to feel like I'm doing penance for my sins,' I said cheerfully. 'But other than that, I'm all good.'

'Great.' His expression wasn't thrilled. 'I'll leave you in peace then.'

'So I can rest?' I punned. 'But I'm too young to die!' He gazed at me blankly. 'Rest in peace,' I tried to explain.

'Is that supposed to be a joke?'

'Obviously not a very good one,' I muttered. 'What's your name, anyway?' I didn't think he'd warm to me very much if I went around calling him Dimples.

He grunted in response. 'Jamie.'

'I'm Integrity.' I stuck out my hand for him to shake. He eyed it like it was a venomous snake. 'Maybe we could start over, Jamie. I feel like we got off on the wrong foot.'

'I got into a lot of trouble because of you. You stole from me.'

'You mean the Lia Saifire? Byron mentioned something about that. What makes you think that was me?'

He threw me a doleful glance. 'I'm not a complete idiot.'

I bit my tongue, waving my hand instead. He took it reluctantly, his grip tight and painful. I squeaked and pulled away. 'While you're here, Jamie, do you think you could tell me a little about this true name ceremony thing?'

His lip curled. 'You don't know?'

Would I be asking if I did? 'No,' I replied pleasantly.

Jamie sighed as if a huge burden had been placed on his shoulders. The sigh was followed by a strange burble. I blinked at him. 'Are you feeling alright?'

The burble deepened. Jamie's eyes widened and he stared at something behind my shoulder. Ha. I wasn't going to fall for the old 'look behind you' trick. I was smarter than that. Or at least I thought I was until something coiled round my waist and dragged me backwards.

'What the hell?' I shrieked.

Jamie tried to back away but as I was dealing with the tentacle round my waist, another one snapped up round his wrist and dragged him inside the room. My fingers scrabbled, trying to loosen the damn thing's grip. It wasn't dry to the touch, despite its scales; it was slimy and wet, making it even more difficult for me to get a decent hold on it.

'Tell me,' I gasped, as I was flung against the far wall, 'that you have a useful gift like telekinesis.'

'Psychometry.' He karate-chopped the tentacle that encircled his wrist. All he succeeded in doing was pissing it off because another tentacle appeared from nowhere and grabbed his other arm. 'It means,' he said, as he squirmed desperately, 'that I can tell you this is a stoor worm. From the North Sea. It's just a baby.'

What kind of a worm has tentacles? This was not good. 'If it's from the sea, then how the hell did it get here?'

'Don't know,' he muttered as he was thrown up into the air then slammed down onto the stone floor with a painful thud.

'Is this normal?' By which I meant: is someone likely to work out what's going on and come and rescue us?

'No!' He was face down so his answer was muffled.

'Is it because of the Foinse?'

There was another muffled grunt that sounded like another no. The tentacle round my waist tightened until pain shot through me. If this wasn't a result of the magic failing then it had to be because someone had conjured it up. Someone who wanted me dead. There was no way I was going to allow that to happen. Death by sea monster while three hundred miles inland was not the way I wanted to go.

Another tentacle whipped out, this time aiming for my throat. I lashed out with my feet, doing everything I could to kick it away. The squeeze around my waist was bad enough but if the worm latched onto my neck it would be *adios muchachos*. My feet flailed, jabbing at the slimy thing. I managed to keep my body clear of it but that enraged the thing even more.

There was a strange, high-pitched noise. I didn't speak sea monster but I guessed it was something along the lines of 'screw you'.

Abandoning me for the time being, the lashing

tentacle snaked towards Jamie's squirming body instead, wrapping itself round his legs and starting to drag him out of my line of sight and towards the window. Panicking, I stretched up to grab the light fitting in the ceiling so I could turn and get a better look. My fingers just managed to curl round the hanging wire so I could spin round. I could already feel the electric cord stretching - it would break in seconds. I had enough time, however, to see what the stoor worm actually was.

Jamie said this was a mere baby; I dreaded to think what the fully grown version looked like. Half of its body hung out of the open window. The other half was a monstrous size, filling the room. I counted six tentacles - but they weren't what really bothered me. It was the gaping mouth lined with sharp yellow teeth and the vast, dark, sightless eyes which struck terror in my heart. We had no chance.

I swung my legs back and forth, trying to gain some momentum. The worm responded by squeezing harder until my breath was coming in gasps and I felt as if my intestines were about to rise up through my gullet. The pain grew more intense and I was afraid I was going to black out. I forced myself alert. Once I had built up enough energy, I dived down and grabbed one of Jamie's white-knuckled hands. His head rose and he stared at me in stark fear.

'Hang on,' I grunted, adjusting my grip so I wouldn't lose him. Then I swung back, yanking hard.

Like a toy caught between two toddlers, Jamie's body was now being pulled in both directions. His mouth opened in a silent scream. The stoor worm let out a strange whine again and loosened its hold slightly. Jamie was no longer being pulled in the direction of its cavernous mouth but it wouldn't be long before it happened again.

I cast around. There had to be something here I could use as a weapon. Bob's knofie – scimitar – was on the floor but it was well out of reach. If I could grab one of the pillows on the hard bed I could smack the stoor worm round the head – but unless the worm was allergic to feathers, that wasn't going to help.

Growing more and more angry, the stoor worm threw out another tentacle. It smashed against the side of my head, making my senses reel. There was no way out of this, not without asking for help.

'What do we do?' Jamie shrieked.

'The scimitar,' I gasped. 'Throw me the sodding scimitar.' I couldn't reach it from up here in the air but if Jamie could grab it I could summon Bob. Yes, there would be dangerous consequences but the alternative right now was either being squashed to death or chomped on.

Jamie was baffled. 'Scimitar?'

'Letter opener! Throw me the letter opener!'

His head swung round until his eyes alighted on the little knife. 'It's too small. It's not going to do anything,' he yelled as the stoor worm's jaws snapped forward, narrowly missing him.

'Just do it!'

He stretched out, taking the hilt and flinging it upwards. Unfortunately he timed it badly and the knife bounced into another swiping tentacle. Instead of flying up to me, it went out of the other window.

'Bob!' I screamed as the silver flashed in the failing sunlight. The genie didn't answer.

He had told me that I couldn't rid myself of him and that, like a bad penny, he'd always turn up again. I had the sneaking suspicion that this would be all over for both Jamie and me by the time that happened. I cursed, just as there was another tug round my waist. The stoor worm had apparently decided I was the tastier one and was pulling me towards its mouth.

I stared down the thing's throat. Dark saliva glistened from within. I swallowed my fear and tried to reach the light fitting again. This time I was too far away.

The dim recesses of my brain registered how stupid all this was. Who got eaten by a sea monster when they were up a mountain? It'd go down in history. I wondered if the person who'd used magic to bring the damn thing here knew about the Foinse. They had to. But didn't they realise that by killing me they were damning everyone else too?

The stoor worm whined, then made several clicks. It was probably telling me that I was going to make a bloody tasty snack. Wait a minute…

'How good is your psychometry?' My words

came out garbled but I think Jamie got the gist.

'I'm one of the best.'

'Can you use to it learn the language? To communicate?' The tentacle round my waist tightened and I winced in pain.

'And say what? Please don't eat us?'

'No. Say there's a river. The River Tay's near here, right? It leads to the sea. Use your psychometry to glean enough words to tell this thing that it can get back home. We didn't bring it here but we can help it escape.'

For what seemed like an eternity there was absolute silence, not just from Jamie but from the stoor worm as well. It pulled its tentacle towards its horror of a mouth again. Now my toes were only inches away from those teeth.

Jamie screeched then he clicked. The stoor worm's jaws opened wider and I knew it was about to bite. I squeezed my eyes shut while Jamie whined. My life should have been flashing in front of my eyes right about now but all I could think about was how pointless all this was. I held my breath. Hopefully death would come quickly.

Nothing happened. There was a series of clicks from the worm but unless my adrenaline had truly kicked in to the point where I could feel zero pain, it wasn't actually eating me. I lifted up one eyelid. The worm's blind eyes were turned in Jamie's direction. It hissed and spat. Jamie whined once more then I fell to the ground with a heavy thump as the worm released its hold on me. It withdrew every tentacle, lifted its head up in sea-monster acknowledgement and a heartbeat later it slithered out of the window and vanished.

I stared at the spot it had just vacated. Pushing away the urge to scream, I scrambled to my feet and lurched to the window. The stoor worm was already on the ground, its body snaking with incredible speed towards the Tay. A few Sidhe standing around far below shrieked, but the worm paid them no attention. Before I could draw another breath, it was out of sight.

Jamie shook his head in disbelief. 'It worked. I've never used my Gift before to learn another tongue. I thought what I had was useless unless it involved archaeology or analysing a murder weapon.'

I refrained from telling him that I had had the same thought. Psychometry generally meant you could touch an object and learn its history because the object's energy field would transfer knowledge to someone gifted enough to understand it. Using psychometry to communicate with a sea monster had seemed like the longest of long shots.

I looked at him as he got to his feet. 'I thought I was a goner,' I told him, honestly, my heart still rattling around my ribcage.

He nodded. 'Me too. How did you know it would leave like that?'

'Because it didn't want to be here either. Someone used their Gift to drag it here from whichever sea depths it came from. It was angry and scared so it attacked us.'

He held my gaze. 'I can't believe we're still alive.'

I fervently agreed. 'We make a good team.' Without thinking, I reached over and gave him a tight hug. His arms wrapped round my body, holding me close. He smelled really good.

He sucked in a breath and pulled back slightly, looking into my eyes. 'I'm shaking,' he muttered.

'Adrenaline,' I said, more breathily than I'd intended.

We stared at each other then his gaze dropped to my mouth. I licked my lips and he groaned. A second later we were kissing, a frantic 'seize the moment' kind of action that left us both gasping for air. His mouth pressed hard on mine, stealing away my breath.

'This is a mistake,' he told me as he curled one hand round my head and the other round my waist.

'Textbook,' I agreed.

My fingers fumbled with his shirt, undoing the buttons and pulling his shirt free. He grabbed my top, virtually ripping it off me and running his hands up and down my bare skin.

'We should stop.'

'Mmm.'

His mouth trailed down towards my collarbone. I felt the damp sheen of sweat but I had no idea whether it was from him or from me.

'You smell like worm.'

I sniffed and grinned. 'So do you.'

His fingers tugged at the waistband of my jeans, then dipped below. Coherent thought fled. This had nothing to do with Jamie and me and everything to do with the consuming desire to remind ourselves that we were alive. I fumbled with his trousers, getting the zip caught in the fabric and cursing. Giving up, I knelt down and yanked. There was a loud rip. Within moments we were naked, clinging to each other and falling backwards onto the hard floor. His expression was tense and filled with concentration but, as our bodies rose to meet each other, he began to relax.

It was fast and unromantic but, sod it, it was fulfilling.

Drenched in sweat, we collapsed against the wall. 'Shit,' he swore. 'I'm sorry, I didn't mean to…'

I touched his cheek. 'I wanted it too. Don't apologise.'

Then the door opened. Both Jamie and I froze, our heads turning guiltily towards the interloper. Byron. Of course it was.

His expression was impenetrable as he stared at us with granite-flecked eyes. Jamie sprang up, snatching his clothes to cover himself. I considered doing the same but I wasn't going to let Byron make me feel ashamed for doing what had felt so natural. It wasn't like I'd committed adultery. If he wanted to judge, he could go ahead. Besides, he'd already seen me virtually naked.

'There were reports of a disturbance,' he bit out. 'Except now I can see it wasn't a disturbance at all.'

Jamie flushed. 'There was a monster. It tried to eat us,' he said quickly, in a vain effort to explain away our actions.

'You should go,' Byron snapped. 'I want to talk to her alone.'

I was tempted to say to Jamie that he should tell Byron to piss off. Judging by the expression on his face, however, it probably wouldn't help. With his bundle of clothes still clutched to his body, he darted out of the door.

I got to my feet, deciding to brazen it out. 'Don't you knock?' I enquired.

Byron bent down, grabbed my discarded top and flung it at me. 'Cover yourself.'

I caught it but made no move to put it back on. 'If you're embarrassed, you are free to leave.'

He hissed through his teeth, 'Is this a ploy to get back at me for Tipsania? Are you trying to make me jealous?'

I blinked. Seriously? 'No. It had nothing to do with you.'

Byron snorted. 'Sort yourself out. When you're decent, I'll be waiting in the library.'

Like I was supposed to know where that was. He spun round and stalked out before I could ask him for directions. I glared at his retreating back. God, this place was even worse than I'd thought.

Chapter Twelve

After dousing myself with water and scrubbing my skin clean of slime, gunk and Jamie's lingering scent, I went in search of Bob. Byron's glowering face could wait.

I ignored the many Sidhe who stared at me with unchecked fascination and limped downstairs. It was painful to breathe; I could swear that the damned worm had broken one of my ribs. Whatever, I was going to have some brightly coloured bruises. Going by the looks I was getting, there was a good chance several of them would be on my face.

I glared at a few of the less subtle Sidhe and they backed off. I also scanned every face for signs of disappointment that I was still alive. One of these wankers had summoned the stoor worm. Unfortunately, if my would-be executioner was one of these guys, he or she was a damned good actor.

I'd just reached the front doors and was about to step outside when there was an alarmed shout. 'Chieftain Adair! You can't leave! Not yet.'

I turned, sucking in a breath as my body complained at the sudden movement. 'It's Taylor, not Adair. Whoever my parents were, the Adair Clan is dead.'

The Sidhe who'd addressed me was an older woman with a lined face and less than pristine clothes that marked her as a lower-class Sidhe. She caught up with me. 'You should be proud of that name,' she scolded. 'Pride is important. Like lions. Lions are strong. They're the kings of the jungle. That's why they live in prides.'

I raised my eyebrows. I'd been accosted by a mad woman. 'Why should I be proud? Everyone treats me like I'm a leper because of that name.'

She shook her head. 'They're just too scared to come and talk to you.' She grabbed my shirt and started pulling, as if she wanted to drag me back inside. 'The Adairs are legends in their own right.'

'*Were* legends,' I said flatly, shaking her off. 'But thank you for your words.' I supposed the least I could do was to be polite. I turned to go.

'Where are you going? Don't leave! We need you.'

'I'm not leaving,' I said through gritted teeth. 'I'm going for a walk.'

Her eyes rolled in an alarming fashion. 'Walk the walk and talk the talk! Let me get you an escort at least.'

I shuffled away from her. 'I think I can manage to walk on my own.' Besides, the only person in the entire castle who I trusted at that moment was Jamie. He was the only one who couldn't have set the damn stoor worm on me.

'I knew your parents,' the old woman burst out desperately, her frizzy hair trembling with the effect of her outburst. 'Mummy and Daddy. Mother and Father. Mum and Dad. Mere and Pere. Ma and Pa.'

Her voice trailed off.

I looked at her. When I was growing up in the Bull's demesne, I heard my father mentioned a lot. No one ever breathed a word about my mother. The woman beamed at my sudden interest. 'I can tell you all about them,' she said. She flapped her arms. 'Chat chat chat!'

Something inside me hardened. Whoever my mother was, she was dead now. And I'd had it drummed into me that my father was a villainous prick who sacrificed hundreds of lives simply because it had suited him. People said the apple didn't fall far from the tree. Well, I didn't want to be anywhere near it. Anyway, this woman was clearly nuts.

'No, thanks,' I said curtly, trying to ignore the way her face fell.

I shoved my hands in my pockets and strode away, glad that she didn't try and stop me. It was already dusk, with the sky the colour of murky purple in the way you only ever see in the Highlands. I sucked in a breath, got my bearings, and marched round the castle walls. My posture and frown made it clear to anyone watching that I wanted no further part in small talk about my heritage or even the damned weather.

I found Bob's 'scimitar' in a clump of dandelions by the far west corner. Glancing up, I could still see the trail of slime left by the stoor worm. I shook myself, still incredulous that I'd escaped, then reached down, grimacing in pain, and grabbed the hilt.

Checking that no-one was watching me, I rubbed the blade.

Bob squinted up. 'This isn't a good time,' he declared. 'Sisko's in trouble and I'm not sure he's going to make it.'

'Oooh, *The Visitor*? The episode where he's come unstuck in time and his son is trying to save him? That's a good one.'

'I know.' He glared. 'Can I get back to watching it?'

'Perhaps you need to put away the boxed set and start paying more attention. I almost died half an hour ago.'

'Hmm?' Bob drummed his fingers impatiently against the ground. 'Do you think his son will save him?' His mouth pursed. 'No, wait. Don't tell me. I don't want to know.' He cupped his hands round his ears. 'Tralalalalala. I'm not listening.'

I sighed and waited. It took him a moment or two. He blinked and dropped his arms. 'Wait a minute. You just about died?'

'Stoor worm.'

Bob's puzzlement grew. 'We're still at the Cruaich.'

'I know.'

'How stupid do you think I am, Uh Integrity?' he said, affecting hurt. 'Stoor worms live in the bottom of the ocean.'

'I know.'

He leaned forward and sniffed. 'Soap,' he

declared. 'Definitely not stoor worm. Soap and,' he paused, 'sex.' He lifted his eyebrows admiringly. 'Fast work.'

I gazed at him, exasperated. 'I'm not lying. There really was a stoor worm. Someone must have conjured it to try and get rid of me.'

Bob shrugged. 'So they failed. Better luck next time!'

I narrowed my eyes. 'You want me dead?'

He threw up his hands. 'My raison d'être, Uh Integrity, is wishes. First there was the banker who was too stupid to realise what he had right in front of him, and now there's you who's a stubborn as a mule and refuses to ask for anything in case I'm trying to cheat her. The best thing I can hope for is that you drop dead as quickly as possible so I can move on.' His expression was defiant but also slightly nervous.

'That's my point, Bob,' I told him. 'I wanted to ask for a wish. I would have made a wish. But you were thrown out of the window so I couldn't.'

'Why did you throw me out of the window?'

'I didn't.'

'Because you know if you want to make a wish, I have to be in the room to hear it,' he said. 'I have unbelievable magical powers which you can only dream of but they don't work if I can't hear you.'

I folded my arms. 'Bob,' I said, in the sternest tone imaginable, 'I need you to pay attention. You told me you will find your way back to me if I try and throw you away.'

'Yes, it's true. Because I am a supreme being with powers that...'

'...that I can only dream of. Yes, I got that part. Well, listen, Bob. I'm not going to throw you away. In fact, I'm going to make sure you stay very, very close to me.'

'Ooh! Uh Integrity, I had no idea! You're rather large and lumbering compared to me but you're not bad looking, I suppose. We could work something out.' He waggled his eyebrows.

Good grief. 'I'm going to keep you very close because it appears that someone is trying to kill me,' I said with patience that was wearing thin. 'And, despite my best intentions, I might be forced to make a wish to survive. Which means that until I say otherwise, you need to pay attention at all times. If we get separated, you need to jump back to me as soon as you can.'

'Is that a wish?' he asked eagerly.

'No. But if you want me to use up any of your wishes, then this is the best shot you've got.'

Bob's bottom lip jutted out. 'But Sisko...'

'My next of kin is a man named Taylor. He's human. He won't recognise you for what you are.' I stroked the blade. 'He will, however, appreciate this very fine silver and melt it down to make something more bankable.'

Bob was aghast. 'He wouldn't dare.'

'He wouldn't know. So,' I said, 'my death will not help you. The only chance you've got of me asking for any wishes is when my back is against the wall and I have no choice. So pay sodding attention.'

I thought for a moment that I'd gone too far and that Bob would relapse into a sulk. Instead, he shrugged cheerfully. 'Okay.'

'Good,' I muttered.

'Can I just watch the end of the episode first?'

I considered. 'Very well. But only because it's a really good one and I don't want to have to listen to you talk about it for days to come. Once it's done, you're frosty and alert at all times. Got it?'

'Got it, Uh Integrity.' He winked. 'We're going to make a great team.'

I sighed. I really hoped that it wasn't going to be long before Lexie showed up with the others. Between now and then, I probably needed to learn some patience. Like immediately.

*

'What do you call it,' I asked Byron when I eventually found the library and his stiff-backed form staring out a window, 'when worms take over the world?'

He didn't answer.

'Global worming,' I informed him.

He turned and faced me, his brows drawn together. The hair which normally fell so artlessly across his forehead had somehow formed a cute little curl. It was difficult to resist the urge to brush it away.

His eyes searched my face. I wondered what exactly he was looking for. 'Jamie told me what happened,' he said finally.

'He tried to tell you when you barged into my room,' I reminded him. 'You just didn't seem to be in the mood to listen.'

'The Foinse must be failing faster than we'd thought,' he said, ignoring my pointed comment.

'You're kidding?' I scoffed. 'You think it's because the magic is draining away from your safe little Sidhe world that a sea monster suddenly appeared from hundreds of miles away? In my bedroom? I gave you more credit than that, Byron. Either someone wants the Foinse to break down, or their desire to rid the world of me is stronger than their desire to see the magic safe.'

'No-one would dare,' he growled. 'You have guest privileges.'

'Oh yeah? Because I'm pretty sure someone just did dare. If you don't believe me, go have a look outside. The stoor worm left a lovely snail trail all the way down your wall.'

His jaw worked. 'I'll have a guard put on you.'

The last thing I wanted was to be watched twenty-four-seven. 'I don't need a guard. I need you to make sure that whoever is behind this is stopped.'

'Investigations have already begun,' he said stiffly.

'Good. Now tell me what you want.'

He took a step closer so I had to crane my neck to look up at him. His voice dropped until it was both silky and dangerous. 'Did he make you scream?'

'The worm? Of course I bloody well screamed.'

Byron's emerald eyes glittered. 'No. Did Jamie make you scream?'

I swallowed and stared at him, my tongue suddenly unable to form any words.

'I could make you scream,' he continued. He reached over and brushed my bare arm with the tip of his index finger.

I jerked away and Byron laughed.

'Is that why you summoned me here? To measure your sexual prowess against your mate's?'

He watched me with amusement. I decided I preferred glowering Byron. 'No. We need to go over the arrangements for tomorrow and the naming ceremony.'

I felt an odd mixture of relief and disappointment. 'Well, good. Go on, then.' I crossed my arms firmly across my chest. Just in case. Of course I received a sharp jab of pain in my ribs when I did so. It was a struggle to stay composed.

'Normally, the ceremony would take place on your Clan ground,' Byron explained.

'I don't have a Clan.'

He didn't rise to the bait. 'Just so. Besides, after your father's untimely demise, the Adair grounds were salted. It'd be a miracle if the sacred grove is still standing.'

'You guys don't mess around, do you?' I asked, feeling faintly sick at the wanton destruction and the thoroughness with which the Adairs had been treated.

He looked as if he knew what I was thinking. 'It was before my time. And tempers were running high.'

'I'll bet.'

'The grove here at the Cruaich will serve just as well,' he continued, as if I'd not spoken. 'Every Clan is represented here.'

'Even the murderous Adairs?'

He held my gaze. 'Even them.'

'Fine. So what do I have to do?'

'You enter alone.' He pulled out a scroll and tossed it in my direction. 'You read this aloud, asking your ancestors to guide you. Then you'll receive your true name. Your Gift should emerge within a few days.'

'You've got more than one Gift. Maybe I will have too.'

'Maybe. I only have two. Your father had three.'

I was surprised. Three Gifts? I'd known he was powerful. I just hadn't realised by how much.

'Of course,' Byron continued, 'you might not get any. Your body might not be able to handle the shock as it's already in the full bloom of adulthood. Your system might just reject it.'

Such a scenario would probably the best for everyone. I didn't need a Gift to open the Foinse. Perhaps whoever had tried to kill me would back off if I were essentially powerless.

'I know you have telekinesis,' I said. 'What's your other Gift?'

'Do you care?' he asked softly.

I guessed not. I shook myself and changed the subject. 'That's why there's a fever,' I mused. 'It's the body fighting against the Gift.'

Byron gave me an approving nod. 'Indeed.'

'It'd be better if that didn't happen. Then we can leave for the Foinse immediately.' My tone was decisive. I ignored Byron's sharp look .

'The onset of the fever happens almost immediately,' he admitted. 'You'll know you're getting sick before you leave the grove. The sicker you are, the stronger your Gift. Because I received two, I was ill for a fortnight. It wasn't … pleasant.'

That sounded like a considerable understatement. Great. I didn't need a temperature and sweats to add to my already aching body. I sighed. 'There was something else I wanted to ask.'

'You wanted to know what Rebekah meant.'

'Rebekah is the ginger nut?'

He stiffened slightly. 'She wouldn't take kindly to being called that but, yes, that's her. There have been many Sidhe who wondered why you didn't come back to take revenge for what happened to your Clan.'

These guys were all about knee-jerk reactions. Maybe I should try harder to borrow Bob's DS9 box set and force them all to sit down and watch it. They might learn something from Commander Sisko. 'I suppose I might have once taken revenge on the Bull for making my childhood so miserable. But I'd be more likely to thank him than punch him. If he hadn't been such a wanker, I might not have left when I did. Then I'd never have met my real family. The ones who count.' My eyes narrowed accusingly. 'The ones who you're messing with.'

Byron cocked his head, gazing at me as if he were trying to work me out. 'You should never have been placed with him. My father made a mistake, even if he had the best intentions.'

I didn't want to discuss the past. It was, after all, the past. 'From what I was told, what happened to my Clan was my father's fault. And I can't take revenge on a dead guy.'

Byron stepped back and ran a hand through his hair. 'You're not your father,' he said.

I searched his face. He was telling the truth. Unlike most of the other highborn Sidhe in this place, neither he nor Jamie seemed to care whose daughter I was.

'Sir? Byron?' someone interrupted. 'You're wanted in the grand hall.'

Both of us turned. It was a nervous-looking pixie who was doing everything he could to avoid eye contact with me. Interesting. Perhaps these people really were afraid of me. I could use that.

'On my way,' Byron grunted. He gave me a final glance. 'I'll escort you to the grove tomorrow. Until then, try and avoid having sex with anyone else. We don't need half the castle in love with you.'

I grinned. 'Why ever not?'

Byron rolled his eyes. 'By the way, it's pyrokinesis.'

Puzzled, I stared at him. 'What is?'

'My second Gift.' He touched me lightly on the shoulder and walked out. The pixie ran.

I watched them go, then dropped my head and examined my shoes. I didn't like the idea of being able to call up fire. Certainly it would have its uses but in this day and age it would be used far more for destruction than anything else. I shivered and thought about Byron's other comments. Whenever I got answers, I also ended up with more questions. I hadn't come here to learn about myself, however. I didn't need new revelations or an emotional growth spurt. I was happy the way I was.

I lifted my chin up and spotted a pretty feather in an inkwell on a table nearby. I picked it up, then whistled. I couldn't be entirely sure but this looked like it came from the wings of a unicorn. It was priceless. The damned beasts were so hard to catch unawares that unless you were an unblemished virgin, you'd no hope of getting close to one. I grinned to myself. Charlie would give me a good price for it. I shoved it down my top. It tickled my skin but I wasn't going far. I was Integrity Taylor, thief extraordinaire after all - not Integrity Adair, Clan princess.

Chapter Thirteen

I took one last critical glance in the mirror. It was just as well as I'd arrived at the Cruaich well prepared. The hot pink scarf went very well with my black jumpsuit. Topped off with diamante-encrusted sunglasses, I decided I looked more like a footballer's wife than a shady Sidhe. It wasn't a bad effort but I didn't want any of these royal idiots getting the wrong idea and thinking I was a glittery pushover so I also attached my trusty utility belt with my thievery gadgets. Ha! Let them make of that what they would.

'We need to go now, Integrity,' Byron drawled from the doorway.

I tapped the scimitar nestled securely in my inner pocket where it would be safely out of sight. 'You ready for this, Bob?'

There was the tiniest vibration in response. The genie had kept me up half the night with his plans to find an astronaut for his next owner and blast off in a spaceship. I'd let him babble on. It might keep him more focused for the next few days if he felt like he had plans for the future that didn't involve stubborn Sidhe naysayers.

'Coming!' I called, before stepping out to meet Byron. The second I did, I was tempted to duck back into the bathroom and change my clothes. The formal finery he was wearing put me to shame.

'You look nice,' he told me politely.

Damned by faint praise. 'Well, you look like an over-dressed duck,' I told him, pretending not to notice the way his shirt moulded itself to his torso.

He lifted an eyebrow. 'Are you suggesting that I'm fowl?'

I stared at him. 'Did you just make a joke?'

He grinned. 'It seems like it's the best way to get your attention.'

Slightly nonplussed, I let him take my arm and lead me out. It was a long way down to the ground floor. Several Sidhe minions and other Clan workers dipped in curtseys and bows as we passed.

'It must get kind of irritating,' I muttered, 'having people do that all the time.'

He gave a short bark of a laugh. 'They're not doing it for my benefit.'

I bristled. 'Well, they're certainly not doing it for mine. Most of you lot hate me. And one of you is trying to kill me.'

'I've not found any evidence of a plot against you. And nobody hates you.'

We passed by Tipsania, who was wearing an alarmingly low-cut gown. 'Interior, how *are* you?'

I gritted my teeth. 'It's Integrity.'

'Oh!' she simpered. 'I'm so sorry. I'm just awful with names.'

'Alright,' Byron conceded once she was behind us, '*most* people don't hate you.'

'I don't know why her knickers are in such a twist. She's got the perfect life. At least in her eyes, anyway. I'm the lowlife crim without a true name.'

'Not everything is as it seems,' he replied cryptically. 'Not even you.'

When we eventually made it outside, the older woman who'd stopped me before was in front of us. She swooped down in another low curtsey and said, in a clear voice, 'Chieftain Adair.' Unfortunately her words were followed by a high-pitched cackle that made her appear even crazier .

I stiffened. There was a murmur from the cluster of Sidhe around us and I spotted several dirty looks. It confirmed that all those who despised me openly were high born. I chewed this over silently as Byron and I continued on our way.

The last person we encountered before the grove was Jamie. His cheeks reddened rather adorably but he did give me a small grin.

'Hi,' I said softly.

He raised a hand in acknowledgment. Feeling Byron's gaze, I smiled tightly and walked on.

'Jamie is a good man,' he told me quietly. 'I'd hate to think you were toying with him.'

Actually, I felt a bit sorry for Jamie. He'd probably been chewed out by Byron and was suffused with embarrassment when he saw me. Well, two could play the cryptic game. 'As you said, Byron dear, not everything is as it seems.'

Without waiting for his reaction, I strode ahead, halting only when I reached the edge of the grove. I peered inside. There was a path and there were a lot of trees but I couldn't make out much else.

'You know,' I said to Byron as he reached my side, 'when I was four or five, I made the mistake of stumbling into the Scrymgeour grove. I didn't get very far. It was probably only a few metres. The reactions I got though?' I whistled and shook my head. 'You'd think I'd tried to commit murder.'

He squeezed my fingers. 'That was wrong,' he said simply. 'The groves are holy places to us all but you were only a child.'

I stared in, emotions warring inside me. Trepidation was winning. 'Are you going to come with me?'

'No.' He released my hand. 'Only one person should enter at any time. It makes it less confusing for the ancestors.'

'But whose ancestors will I meet?' I whispered.

Byron didn't answer. From here on in, I really was on my own. I reached for Bob's scimitar and handed it over. Byron looked confused. 'You're giving me a letter opener?'

It was safer not to get into a discussion about what it actually was. Not with Bob listening in. 'Just hold onto it for me, will you? It has, um, sentimental value.'

Despite my concerns that someone was out to get me, I couldn't risk Bob hearing my true name. There was no telling what he'd do with that kind of power. And even if Byron tried to clean the blade, Bob wouldn't appear. Until I used up my wishes – or died – I was Bob's owner. Besides, the sacred groves were places of peace. It would be sacrilege for someone to attack me here.

Byron nodded, watching as I squared my shoulders. With a deep breath, I crossed into the grove and focused on logical thinking rather than my twisty emotions. Truth be told, I was hoping that my true name would be something manageable. My knowledge of formal Sidhe language was scanty; it was just as well it was only used in ceremonial settings and for legal documents, or I'd be stumbling around here without a clue about what was being said around me.

If I received a complicated Sidhe name, I'd be as likely to forget it as to make the mistake of letting someone else know what it was so they could attain absolute power over me. One syllable might be okay: 'Pink' would be cool if someone hadn't already nabbed that name. Two syllables could work. If my true name turned out to be 'Danger', I could have a lot of fun. I imagined meeting someone for the first time. 'Hi. I'm Integrity and Danger is my middle name.' The best part would be no one would ever twig I was telling them the truth. It'd be a great in-joke. Unfortunately it was more likely that I'd end up with Poo Madra Na Cathrach Ar Mo Brog or something equally dim-witted and unpronounceable.

I ducked my head to avoid some low lying branches. I thought the trees lining the driveway on the way up here were unusual, but they were nothing compared to these. None of them possessed a single leaf but all the same they were stunningly beautiful. The branches and trunks were a soft silver, gleaming in the weak midday sunshine. I glanced back; I couldn't make out Byron's figure. Despite the lack of foliage, these trees did a damn good job of concealment.

I was surprised at how nervous I was feeling. I'd been a part of some seriously ambitious heists in the past and never felt more than the faintest trickle of nerves. In those scenarios, however, I was always well prepared. Right now I had no idea what to expect. By the time I reached the small clearing in the centre of the grove, with its gurgling fountain and paved stone circle, I was shaking.

'Okay,' I said aloud, balling up my fists, 'I'm here.' I pulled out the scroll Byron had given me and began to read, my tongue stumbling over some of the words. I felt beyond awkward. Once I was done, I took a deep breath and looked up. Nothing happened. Now what?

There was a whisper from right behind me. I spun round, expecting to see someone but there were only trees. The branches hung overhead, gnarled twigs reaching out towards me like ancient fingers. I shivered and turned back just as there was another strange whisper. I took a deep breath.

'You're going to have to speak up,' I called out. 'I can't hear you.'

The whispers increased in volume, although what they were saying remained incomprehensible. I squeezed my eyes shut and tried to identify the words. Their sibilantic hush made that impossible until they all abruptly fell silent and one clear musical voice of no distinguishable gender spoke, freezing my bones.

'Adair.'

A strange image flitted through my head of a young man in old-fashioned dress. He had brilliant white hair and violet eyes. He was also wielding a sword, swinging it with unrestrained violence about his head. His eyes turned in my direction and I gasped involuntarily as he heaved the sword towards me.

Then he was replaced by another man of similar build and colouring. Then another and another and another. The images came so thick and fast that I felt dizzy. The only thing that seemed to change was the mode of clothing. I cried out, willing them to slow down. There were too many and it was all too quick. Nausea filled my stomach. I couldn't take any more. It had to stop. It had to…

Another man appeared. This time he wasn't alone; he was pressing his cheek against the rounded stomach of a heavily pregnant woman. Both of them looked at me and smiled and, unable to help myself, I smiled back. There was tenderness in their expressions - and unfathomable, immeasurable love. Even though I knew they were only in my head, I still reached out. I wanted to touch them.

The woman held out one graceful hand. If I stretched I might be able to grasp hold of her fingers. The moment I tried, however, she began to choke. Blood trickled from her mouth and she collapsed. The man roared in helpless, silent agony as she slid from his arms to the ground. His eyes filled with an anguish that turned to rage. I stepped back as he stretched out his arms and howled at the heavens. He seemed to be struggling with some terrible inner turmoil. In the past I might have made fun of the phrase 'gnashing their teeth and renting their clothes' but it suddenly made sense. I desperately wanted to help him, to soothe him in some way, but I had no idea how. His body writhed and his eyes bulged. Then, like a cloud passing, it was over. His eyes were clear as he turned to me.

'Layoch,' he said before vanishing entirely.

I fell to my knees. There was a wetness on my cheeks. It took me a moment or two to realise it was tears.

Chapter Fourteen

It took some time before I could pull myself together enough to get to my feet and start walking back. I was confused by what I'd seen and my thoughts were in free fall, tumbling one after the other as I tried to make sense of it all.

The one thing I knew was for certain was that I hated my true name. Layoch? I mean, come on. It sounded like it belonged to a boy. Had Daddy Dearest been wishing for a son? If so, maybe it was just as well he'd not stuck around long enough to meet me.

The journey back seemed longer. Perhaps it was because of the kerfuffle going on inside my head. Despite my sniffy attitude towards my true name, I kept seeing the expression in my parents' eyes as they looked at me. It was haunting - and not in a particularly good way. My father didn't looked like an evil murderer. He looked like a man grieving.

I was so focused on the recurring images that I didn't notice the root jutting out from the ground until it was too late. The tip of my toes caught it and I went flying to the ground with a heavy thump, receiving a mouthful of dirt in the process. It was the only reason I didn't scream aloud in pain. Who knew that a cracked rib could hurt so much?

I choked. 'Nice move, Integrity,' I scolded myself. Between tripping up over a pile of clothes in my own flat and a tree here, I was starting to think I was developing some serious coordination problems. I'd need to get Taylor to put me through my paces when I got back to Aberdeen. I didn't want my new colleagues at mountain rescue thinking I was as unbalanced and tottery as Bambi.

I pushed myself up gingerly, dusting the debris off my scarf with a hiss of irritation. Then there was a far louder hiss and something flew past my head in a rush of heat, almost blistering my skin.

There was a loud crash, followed by a strange sizzle. I glanced back into the clearing and gaped when I saw one of the trees behind me ablaze. There was another hiss. This time I paid more attention. I ducked down, covering my head in my arms as a genuine, honest-to-goodness fireball blazed past, slamming into another tree and immediately engulfing it in flames.

Pyrokinetics, I thought. That's Byron's second gift. I cursed myself for a fool for beginning to trust him and rolled to my right, away from the path and the danger. I move just in time. A third fireball appeared, flying much lower this time. If I'd stayed where I was, I would have been toast.

'Man's house is on fire,' I muttered to myself, still rolling, although now I was away from the path it was harder to avoid the trees and, with every move, my ribs yelled up at me to stop. 'He calls up the fire brigade and asks for help. "How do we get there?" asks the fireman. The man frowned. "Don't you still have those big red trucks?"'

My shoulder crashed into one of the solid tree trunks and I yelped in pain again. No more fireballs appeared to be on their way; not surprising really. If I'd been standing up on the path - which I should have been - they'd have hit me already. Unless they were sentient fireballs that could weave in and out of trees, now I was in the dense wood I wouldn't be hit. I got to my feet and stared at the blaze.

It might have been only three trees that had been struck but the ferocity of the flames licking at the dry branches meant that more of them were catching fire. Before my very eyes, the flames danced, attacking another one, blackening the bark and crackling with intensity. In less than five minutes the entire grove would be alight. The entire sacred grove that was so special some of the Sidhe thought I shouldn't be allowed inside to taint it.

Cursing loudly, I uncoiled my scarf and ran towards the nearest tree, using it to whip at the flames and contain the fire. My movements were curtailed by my previous injuries and I couldn't move as fast as I normally did. When I managed to stamp out one section of burning wood, another started up at the side of me. I ran from tree to tree and branch to branch, doing what I could. Shite, shite, shite.

With no water and no help, I was fighting a losing battle. Screw my stupid true name: I should have brought Bob along after all. Instead I'd thrown him into the hands of the man who might end up being my greatest enemy. Yet again, it was damned good luck that I was still alive. If I had died and Bob's wishes were passed along to Byron - the villain - then goodness knows what might have happened.

I continued to fling myself from tree to tree, fighting the fire. The heat was tremendous and it was getting harder and harder to reach the flames, let alone douse them. Soon I'd have to abandon the grove altogether if I wanted to save myself. The sacred grove was screwed.

Making one last effort, I let out a war whoop and threw myself towards the flames, praying that the velocity of my body would do something to stamp them out. Before I reached them, however, something knocked into me and I was shoved aside rudely. I blinked teary eyes against the now billowing smoke, my mouth dropping open when I realised who it was.

'Stay the hell back, Tegs!' Brochan shouted. 'I've got this!'

He raised both his hands. I was beyond glad to see him but I wasn't sure what he could do to help. He might be a merman but, as the stoor worm had already attested, we were a long way from the sea. The sea that Brochan was terrified of.

I tried to rush forward to help but I was beaten back. The fire was too strong. I stumbled backwards, unable to do anything more than watch as Brochan grasped at air as if he were pulling it down. The atmosphere felt heavy and unnatural and I jumped as thunder rolled across the sky.

Brochan didn't react; he simply continued to yank at the air.

And then I felt it. One little drop splashed on my cheek. I gasped as hope sprang anew. The drop turned to a drizzle. Before I could blink again, it became a deluge.

The rain sizzled on the fire, steam flying up as the weaker flames were extinguished. More and more water fell until Brochan and I, and all the trees around us, were soaking wet.

I ran over and wrapped my arms around him. 'You did it!' I croaked. 'How did you do it? Thank God, Brochan. This place is important.' It really was. After what I'd experienced in the clearing, I was no longer the blithe and dismissive person I was before I'd entered.

'I'm a merman, Tegs, you know that. It's a simple matter of the water cycle.'

His face was wan and drawn and I realised that it wasn't a 'simple matter' at all. 'Thank you,' I said into his ear. 'Thank you.'

'Someone's really got it in for you.'

'You can say that again.'

'Someone's really…'

I smirked. 'Yeah, yeah. Come on. Let's get out of here before they try again.'

Foregoing the path in order to keep ourselves safe – and Brochan's presence hidden – we tramped through the trees while he filled me in on his news. It was slow going because I was hurting all over now, but at least it allowed Brochan plenty of time to cover all the details.

As the trumped-up charges against both him and Speck were entirely false, it wasn't difficult to get them released. Of course, the sizeable wad from the sale of the Lia Saifire had helped. Money talks. Taylor had stayed behind in Aberdeen to ensure there was no further fall-out while the rest of the gang vamoosed over here.

'You had no problem getting through the magical barrier?' I enquired, stepping over loose bracken.

'Your friend came through.'

I snorted. 'Charlie? He's not what I'd call a friend. He does have his uses, though.' I shot Brochan a curious, albeit grateful, look. 'How did you know I was in the grove?'

He shrugged. 'We have got ourselves a prime piece of real estate. Some disused tower towards the east side. It's got great views. We were able to watch you walking with that Sidhe guy then entering the spooky forest.'

'It's a grove.'

'Whatever it is, it's not natural. Even from our vantage point we couldn't see anything. It's all obscured by these damn trees.' He poked one as if scolding it for existing.

I was puzzled. 'Then how did you know I was in trouble?'

'I didn't. We only knew you were alone. It seemed like the perfect opportunity to come and talk to you.' He looked troubled. 'It's just as well I did.'

I nodded fervently. 'Amen to that.'

Going by what Byron had said, only one person was ever allowed into the grove at any one time. I wondered if that was merely tradition or if Brochan had gained access because he wasn't Sidhe. Either way it gave me an edge on all these Fey wankers. Doing the unexpected and the unthinkable seemed to be the only way I'd have of surviving this stint.

'The smartest move is for all of us to lie low. It's not ideal and I know you're hoping for a fresh start in Oban but we've talked it over and, if it's okay with you, we might come and join you. Just temporarily,' Brochan added hastily. 'We don't want to cramp your style or anything.'

I laughed, then regretted it when my ribs complained again. 'You lot are hardly going to cramp my style. I'm more likely to get extra cool points for having you with me.'

Brochan grinned, relieved. 'Now we've got the money to sort out Taylor's debts and we're out of jail, we can all skedaddle. Is there anything you need to fetch before we leave?'

I sighed. Skedaddling was incredibly tempting. Unfortunately I had to choose another path. 'I can't go,' I told him reluctantly. I explained about the Foinse.

'I'm not sure if you were paying attention, Tegs, but one of those people who's so desperate for you to stick around and save them, just tried to kill you. Do you really care if the magic fails? I understand things will be bad for a lot of people for a while but maybe you need to think long term. If this weakens the Clans' hold, it might end up being a good thing.'

'Where's the line, though? Is one death enough to shove the Sidhe into oblivion? Is one hundred?' I ran my hand through my hair. 'A million? Because that might be what it takes.'

Brochan was silent for a moment before replying. 'It's not up to you to save the world, Tegs.'

I bit my lip. 'Actually, in this scenario it might be.' What I left unsaid was that the trippy images I'd just experienced had made me wonder if I'd done the right thing by abandoning my Sidhe heritage. Maybe I was going to stick around here until I had a better grasp on all this Adair shite.

More light started filtering in through the trees. It was clear we were reaching the edge of the grove. I halted and gazed out. 'You should go. You and Lexie and Speck. You should all leave. Go to Oban. I already have a deposit down on a house. Use it.'

'Do you really think we'd abandon you here? No chance. We're family, remember? We'll stay and do whatever we can to help you out. With this Foinse thing and,' he paused, 'whatever happens after that.'

Brochan was one shrewd merman. Swallowing the lump in my throat, I whispered, 'Thank you.'

He beamed. 'So what's the plan?'

I considered. 'There's the guy who walked me down here. One of his Sidhe Gifts is pyrokinesis.'

Brochan whistled. 'So you think it was him who

chucked those fireballs at you?'

My mouth thinned into a grim line. 'Possibly.'

'How many gifts does he have?'

'Just the two. Which is two more than me. I don't need any freaky Sidhe magic though. What I have to find out is if he wants me dead. If he does, then I need to know.' I pushed away the surge of dismay I felt at saying those words out loud. Our childhood encounter notwithstanding, I'd known Byron for all of three days; I knew him no better than he knew me. Why he'd gone to such an effort to bring me here to simply kill me didn't quite fit; neither did the fact that he wouldn't benefit in any way from the Foinse failing. But fireballs after his announcement of being gifted in pyrokinesis? I couldn't shake off my suspicion.

Brochan threw me a sidelong glance. 'Forgive me if I'm mistaken but aren't Sidhe supposed to get their Gift when they get their true name? If you just received your name, then...'

I interrupted him. 'I feel fine.' Apart from a cracked rib and singed eyebrows. 'Apparently Sidhe also get sick. Something to do with their physical body accepting the Gift. I reckon that because I'm an adult that time has passed.' I grinned at him. 'It's a good thing. It makes me more human than Sidhe.'

'If you say so.'

I punched him on the arm. 'I do.'

He smirked. 'So you're going to confront this guy?'

'Nah. I'll do a little reconnoitring first. The

others were prepared to delay the journey to the Foinse if I got ill. I'll pretend I am so that I've got enough time to find out what's going on.' I thought of Bob and my mouth turned down. 'He also has something of mine that I want to get back.'

'Sounds good,' he said approvingly. 'We can help with all that.'

My eyes gleamed. 'You can. There are enough other species and races around here that you three can probably wander around the Cruaich more easily than I can.'

'What do you need us to do?'

I met his eyes. 'Find out what really happened to the Adair Clan.'

Brochan sucked in a breath. 'Are you sure?'

I nodded. 'I am.'

'Okay. We'll use the signal to get in touch with you once we have something.'

I shook my head. 'No. I have a better way.' Expect the unexpected. 'You can summon me. Layoch. My true name is Layoch.'

Brochan's jaw dropped. 'You shouldn't have told me that, Tegs. If I know your name then…'

I waved an airy hand in the air. 'Yeah, yeah. You can obtain absolute power over me. I already trust you with my life, Brochan. Lexie and Speck too. The least I can do is trust you with one sodding word.'

'The Sidhe never reveal their true names. Not even to their families.'

'They can't trust each other,' I said simply.

'You're still taking a big risk.'

I smiled. 'No, I'm not.'

He squeezed my shoulder. 'Do you know what it means?'

'My name? No. It has a meaning?'

'You should brush up on your Gaelic,' he scolded. 'It translates as "warrior".'

I gaped. 'You're kidding me.'

He lifted one shoulder in apology.

'Oh, well,' I dismissed. 'I've not lived up to Sidhe expectations so far. I'm certainly not going to live up to that name. Not unless it's an X-Box warrior anyway.'

Brochan turned and gazed back out of the grove. 'Well, if you're not going to fight your way back to the castle, how do you suggest we slip out of here unnoticed? The last thing we need are more fireballs being flung your way.'

'Not to mention it's better if we're not seen together,' I agreed. 'Er…'

'Pssst!'

Both Brochan and I jumped. 'What the hell was that?'

'Over here!'

We exchanged glances then peered in the direction of the hushed whisper. As soon as I realised who was speaking, my shoulders relaxed. 'It's her,' I said, thoughtfully. 'That's good.'

Brochan watched the old woman as she continued to beckon. 'Who is she?'

'Apparently she used to know my parents. She

might have insights into Clan Adair.'

'Can we trust her?'

'No,' I said cheerfully. 'We can't trust anyone here. She also seems to have a touch of crazy about her. But she might still help us out.' And with that, I stepped out from under the cover of the grove and joined her.

'What happened? I saw smoke.' She shivered. 'Burny, burny. There were reports of fire…'

'Everything's fine. Can you do me a favour? Can you help my friend get to the tower over there?'

She didn't take her eyes off me but she nodded. 'There's only supposed to be one person in the grove at any time. Grove for one and one for grove.'

'So much for that then,' I said.

'I can help you too, Chieftain. We can use the back way. If you go to the fork instead of the spoon and turn right, you'll be on the servants' path. No-one will bother you there.'

I frowned. 'I'm not a chieftain. Thank you for the information about the path though. I'll use it.'

'I can come with you if you want,' she added eagerly.

'It'll be better if you stick with Brochan. I don't want you drawing attention to yourself by being seen with me.'

She looked like she wanted to argue. I placed my hand on her arm in what I hoped was a reassuring manner. 'I'll be fine.'

'Yes, Chieftain.'

I sighed, exasperated. 'My name is Integrity.'

'Yes, Chieftain.'

I obviously wasn't getting anywhere with this. Brochan looked amused. 'What's your name?' I asked her.

'Lily Macquarrie. Macquarrie Lily.'

Ah. That explained a lot. 'Pretty name,' I said aloud.

'Thank you, Chieftain!' she beamed.

'Lily, before you go, could you point out Byron Moncrieffe's room to me?'

Startled, she jerked her hand up towards the castle. 'It's next to the flagged tower. The fourth window down.'

I made a mental note. 'Excellent.'

'He's a good man,' Lily said, with a hint of anxiety. 'Not like some of the others.'

He was good at putting on an act, at least. I didn't want to upset her so I refrained from commenting.

'We should go now.' She pointed to her left. 'We can take that path, sir. We won't bump into anyone that way.' She dipped a curtsey, displaying odd-coloured stockings. One was striped black and white while the other was adorned with flowers. The effect was rather kooky and cool.

'Let's do it,' Brochan said. He gave me a meaningful glance. 'I'll see you soon.'

'Call me and I'll come.'

'You won't have any choice,' he grumbled. 'Toodle pip.'

Chapter Fifteen

As soon as Lily and Brochan vanished from view, I started making my own ascent to the castle. I quickly reached the fork in the path and turned right. As Lily had promised, other than a few scurrying figures, none of whom were Sidhe but all of whom were laden with goods, it was empty. No one stopped me and no one bothered me. They apparently had their own problems to worry about.

Soon I was high enough to see the commotion going on in front of the grove. A large group had assembled there and there appeared to be a lot of hand wringing and shouting. Excellent. The more arguments, the better. It would give me more time to do some real investigating.

I turned my back on the anxious cluster below and jogged up to the castle walls. At least their imposing height would provide me with some cover. While I reckoned the castle's interior might be quiet enough for me to skulk through the corridors, the tower I was aiming for was hidden from view thanks to the curving edges of the castle walls to the right. I fancied a bit of exercise.

Using Lily's directions, I skirted round until I was directly below Byron's room. No doubt he'd still be down with the others at the grove. With any luck, he'd think I was a burnt-out corpse. I'd never get a better chance to sneak into his room than this.

Craning my neck up, I examined the stonework. It helped that the castle was old because there were plenty of footholds. Unfortunately a lot of the stone was worn and weathered; I'd have to be careful to avoid the smoother patches. I grinned at my foresight in bringing my toolkit and sprung up.

Despite my aching body, I was surprisingly fast. It was considerably easier scaling up this sort of surface than glass. I found several cracks wide enough to wedge my fingertips in. Only once was I forced to unclip my old ice-pick and jam it between two bricks to avoid sliding back down. All the same, Byron's room was higher than our entry point at the bank had been, so I was sweating by the time I hooked my leg over his window ledge and pulled myself in.

I was surprised to see that Byron's rooms were smaller than mine. They were very clean and tidy but there wasn't room to swing a cat. Maybe it was some sort of show of humility. If he could be the Steward's son and not demand the grandest suite in the castle, then other Clans couldn't complain about him getting preferential treatment. No wonder he'd gone all out at the Astor Hotel. I bet he spent as little time here as possible. Byron probably lived in palatial luxury back on Moncrieffe lands.

Ignoring his lingering scent, I made a beeline for his bed and checked underneath the mattress and the frame. I found a chewed-up pen lid and little else. I stood up again and stepped over to the chair where a pile of folded clothing lay. Carefully examining each item, I discovered nothing interesting. Perhaps Byron was too clever to leave anything incriminating behind. It was annoying, however, that there weren't even any jewels or money that I could nab. There wasn't even a crappy safe to crack.

After running through all the items in the bathroom, including checking the shampoo to see if it had a false bottom, I returned to the bedroom and sat on the end of the bed. I could play the seduction game again but I doubted he'd fall for it after walking in on Jamie and me. I wasn't entirely sure I could stay in control in that kind of situation either. I needed to be sneakier.

I might have failed miserably at hiding out and spying on Byron at the Astor but if he really thought I was dead, he wouldn't be expecting me here.

I sniffed my armpits. After my climb, I was definitely on the whiffy side. Not wanting my own smell to give me away, I grabbed his bottle of (surprisingly cheap) aftershave and daubed myself with it. I rather liked it. Maybe I'd keep it. Without thinking, I stuffed the bottle into one of my pockets. Then I smoothed down the sheets to remove all traces of my presence and scooted under the bed. I rather hoped he'd take his time returning. I could do with a little nap.

I was dozing off when the door slammed open. I just managed to stop myself from banging my head painfully as I jerked up. Close call.

'Fuck!' There was another bang. It was

definitely Byron. He thumped something else. 'Fuck, fuck, fuck!'

Was he upset because he'd realised there wasn't a body - charred or otherwise - inside the grove and I'd escaped? Or was he upset because he thought I was dead and he now had no way of restoring the Foinse?

I watched his feet stomp about, up one way and down another, over and over again. Considering the size of the room, I thought he'd get dizzy after a few turns but he just kept stomping and turning.

Eventually - and scant seconds before I thought I was going to go insane from watching his feet - there was a hesitant knock on the door. Byron flung it open with such force that it banged against the wall. If the castle hadn't been made of stone, the ensuing vibrations would have been felt floors below.

'What?' he snapped.

I twisted my head, peering at the new set of shoes which had appeared. I was still trying to work out who they belonged to when the nervous cough enlightened me.

'The Steward asked me to inform you…'

'Of what?' There was a strained urgency to Byron's voice.

Jamie dropped the formality. I was glad. Regardless of what else was going on here, it didn't seem fair for him to lose one of his friends just because of a quick shag based on post-traumatic desire. 'Byron,' he said, 'she's not there. Integrity's not in the grove.'

Shite. I needed to see the expression on Byron's face to be able tell whether he was pleased at this news or not.

After what seemed like an eternity, he finally spoke. 'You're sure?'

'Yes. She must have got out another way. She's not in her room – we've already checked. I mean,' Jamie backtracked, 'Brody checked. Not me. I didn't go inside. I…'

'It's fine, Jamie. But if she's not in her room then where the fuck is she? Whoever did this might have hold of her. I should have taken that story about the worm more seriously.' He thumped something again as overwhelming, unmitigated relief flooded through me. It hadn't been him after all. 'Fuck! I told her!'

'Uh, told her what?'

He groaned. 'That my second gift is pyrokinesis. No wonder she's run.'

'I'm sure she wouldn't think that you had done all that though.'

Oh, you'd be surprised, Jamie.

Byron sighed. 'Why would she trust me? I blackmailed her into coming here. I escorted her to the grove where someone threw fire at her. What if she's hurt? If she's hiding somewhere we might not find her in time.' His voice was growing in both sound and desperation. That was nice. I could feel myself relaxing.

'The Foinse isn't dead yet,' Jamie answered,

obviously doing his best to be reassuring. 'It could be months before all the magic leaks out. We'll find her in time.'

I rolled my eyes. Of course. It wasn't my life that was important; it was making sure the Foinse survived another thousand years that was the issue. I didn't know why that stung. I didn't want the magic to fail or gazillions of people to die. Even if someone else apparently did.

'We'd better,' came the growly rejoinder. I shivered. I was glad that Byron wasn't the evil mastermind I'd suspected but I was still disturbed that he had such an effect on me. A husky rasp like that made me think of our encounter in his hotel room, with him underneath my legs, pinned so that I could… I mentally slapped myself. Enough of that.

Jamie coughed. 'There is something else.'

Silence stretched out. I didn't think it was possible for the nervous tension to ratchet up any further but I was wrong; I could virtually feel the air crackle. I was half tempted to leap out and grab Jamie by his lapels, shove my nails into his cute little dimples and demand that he get on with it.

'Go on,' Byron said grimly.

Yes, Jamie, get on with it.

'The police were forced to let her two partners in crime go.'

Byron hissed. 'We knew that was going to happen sooner or later.'

'Not this soon, though. I still have evidence of that last job they pulled. I could make an anonymous tip.'

I seethed. So much for our night of passion, Jamie. Or hour of passion. Okay, ten minutes of passion. Brochan, Speck and Lexie might be safely tucked away around the corner but they'd want to return to their own world sooner or later. If Byron made that an impossibility, I'd ruin him - whether he was concerned about my wellbeing or not.

'No,' Byron answered. 'We've gone past that point now. It was a means to an end. But how did they get out so quickly? I thought we'd have a couple of days at least.'

Jamie coughed again. Uh oh. Here we go. 'There was a barrister. He petitioned the courts.'

'Where did the money come from to pay him?' Jamie didn't answer. I heard a heavy sigh. 'Let me guess,' Byron said tiredly. 'The Lia Saifire.'

'It was sold for a considerable amount to a warlock over in Fort William.'

There was another loud thump. 'Fucking hell.'

I frowned. He was taking the loss very badly. Did the sapphire have powers that I'd not been aware of? But why use it as bait if it were so precious? Surely the Moncrieffe Clan could have rustled up some non-magical gems to use. Something wasn't adding up.

'Does my father know?'

'Not yet,' Jamie said.

Byron sighed. 'Come on then. You can watch me be the bearer of yet more bad tidings.'

I stayed where I was until I was certain both of

them had left the room. Then I scooted out from underneath the bed. Well, well, well. Byron had been correct: – all was most definitely not as it seemed.

*

I slid out of the room, taking extra care in case anyone spotted me. I didn't want to be caught sidling out of Byron's rooms. Thus far, the lower class Sidhe and the servants had appeared to be on my side, but that didn't mean I was going to take unnecessary risks.

I stayed as low as possible until I was well away from Byron's wing of the castle. As I walked, I pinched my cheeks; hopefully I could make them red enough to give the illusion on oncoming fever. The moment I emerged out onto a busier corridor, I straightened my back, allowed my features to form into a hard mask and marched towards the round-tabled room where I'd encountered Aifric and the rest of the Sidhe royal wankers.

Several people gaped at me along the way. I glared at them, satisfied when most of them scuttled away. When I reached the room, I slammed open the door and glowered. The light from behind me was strong, silhouetting my form. Aifric, Byron and Jamie were there and they had to shade their eyes to work out it was me. I rather liked that effect. I'd have to time grand entrances like this more often.

'What gives?' I snarled. 'I thought the grove was supposed to be sacred. Now you're all trying to kill me instead. I've got a banging headache, I don't feel well and I'm in a really shitty mood. Where did those fireballs come from?'

Aifric recovered his voice first although I noted that both Byron and Jamie looked relieved. Yeah, yeah. I was still around to save all their sorry arses. Hurray.

'I'm glad you're alright, Ms Taylor.'

It was a shame he didn't address me as chieftain; that would have been even more fun. 'No thanks to any of you. Who is doing this? Who's trying to murder me? That's two attacks in less than twenty-four hours!'

Aifric's expression was grim. 'I can assure you that we're working on it.'

'Working on it? You're going to have to try a damn sight harder than that. Who has more than one Gift around here? Pyrokinesis and summoning? Who can do both?'

Aifric exchanged a look with his son. 'No one that we know of. We have our best people working through the magical register though. We will find them.'

I tilted up my chin. 'You'd better hope it's before I end up getting fried. Where will you all be then?'

'We will put a guard on your rooms.'

'No, you sodding won't. How can I trust your guards? They might be in on the plot.'

He stiffened. 'Our people are loyal.'

'When someone stops trying to murder me, I might believe that.' I swept an imperious gaze across the lot of them. 'I don't feel well,' I declared. 'I'm going to lie down. Give me back my letter opener.'

Jamie and Aifric both gave me strange looks but Byron dug into his pocket and handed it over. I felt considerably more secure with Bob back with me. As soon as I'd tucked the knife away, I held a hand to my forehead and frowned.

'You have a fever.' Byron's voice was quiet.

Yes, Golden Boy. I have a very bad fever. Spread that little titbit around so everyone thinks I'm about to receive some terrible Gift that'll put yours to shame.

'It better not last long,' I grumbled aloud. 'The faster we can start travelling to the Foinse, the faster I can escape this hell hole.'

'I'll have some chicken soup sent up to your room. That usually helps.'

My eyes narrowed in disgust. 'I thought you guys had been keeping an eye on me. Don't you know I'm vegetarian?' I had no idea where that came from. I loved bacon. I must have been trying to goad poor Aifric Moncrieffe into more grovelling.

'I'm sure we can arrange something that will suit your tastes,' he said without a trace of a grovel. Oh well.

I harrumphed loudly and spun round, adding a wobble for good measure. Then I stalked out.

My grand exit wasn't as dramatic as my entrance. Mainly because I'd barely gone three steps before Byron caught up with me and grabbed my elbow. 'Are you okay?' he demanded.

'Do I look okay?' I snarled back. 'I'm amazed I have any eyebrows left after that fiery demonstration.'

He gazed at me, his face impassive. 'How did you get out of the grove without anyone noticing?'

A slightly crazy Macquarrie woman. I sniffed. 'It's not my fault if you weren't paying attention.'

Something sparked in his eyes but he sensibly held his tongue. 'You should take up the offer of the guards,' he said instead. 'Whatever you might think, the Moncrieffes are not trying to hurt you.'

'I'll believe that when I see it.'

He ran a hand through his bronzed hair. Damn that stupid curl for still being there. 'I know you think that it was me because my second Gift is pyrokinesis. It wasn't me, though, Integrity. I promise you that. I wouldn't have gone to all the trouble of bringing you here simply to try and kill you. I could have done that when you were sleeping in my arms.'

I stiffened. This time it wasn't an act. Why did he have to bring *that* up again? 'I know it wasn't you,' I said with an air of affected insouciance. 'You're not the type.'

'You didn't suspect me?' He was watching my reaction very carefully.

'No,' I lied. 'I'm good at reading people.'

Byron looked relieved. 'I'm pleased.'

'Now I really do have to go and lie down.'

'I'll escort you.'

I looked him over. It would take a brave evil mastermind to try and kill me when the Steward's son was around. He could easily get caught in the crossfire. 'Fine,' I snapped. 'Lead the way.'

Byron took my arm. I must have been doing a better job of acting sick than I'd realised. He leaned in towards me and sniffed. 'You smell … interesting.'

Shite. I'd forgotten that I'd thrown his aftershave all over my skin. 'What can I say?' I shrugged. 'I meant it before when I said you smelled delicious so I bought some of that aftershave to use myself.'

Something flitted across his face and he dropped his voice. 'I like that you want to smell like me. It's as if you've been rubbing yourself all over my body like a cat.'

I pushed away the image of me doing just that. It certainly hadn't taken him long to get over the trauma of my 'death'. 'It's the smell of the aftershave I like. Not you.'

He grinned. 'And here was me thinking you were a girly girl with all of your hot pink attire.'

A girly girl? I liked Hello Kitty and hot pink and sparkly nail polish. But pigeonholing me was unfair; I also liked science fiction and scaling high walls without a rope. Why did men always think you were either a tomboy or a princess? It was possible to be both.

Byron must have sensed my antagonism. 'It doesn't mean I think you're a pushover,' he breathed. 'Far from it.'

His voice had changed into that husky rasp again. It was sooo time to back away. 'Considering I've survived being eaten by a giant sea worm and being barbecued like a marshmallow, I'd say that was a given,' I said stiffly. And with that, we walked in silence back to my room.

Chapter Sixteen

I might not have known much about the Sidhe but people were predictable. It was pretty much a given that Aifric would place an unobtrusive guard on my rooms. He couldn't afford to have me killed off by whichever renegade Sidhe was doing all this shit - not before I'd fixed his Foinse. With that in mind, I slipped out soon after Byron dropped me off - and before any guards could take their places.

I couldn't wait around for Brochan to use my true name to bring me to him. I wasn't sure how long I could carry off this fever business. When it was all over, I'd also need to pretend that I had gained some stupid Gift. I had no idea how I'd manage that. Still, I still felt chipper, despite my near-death experiences; I was certain that my words to Brochan were going to prove true and I was going to escape any divine presents.

I found all three of them huddled round a table in a room near the top of the tower Brochan had pointed out. Lexie and Speck sprang up, barrelling into me with outstretched arms.

'You're safe!' Lexie exclaimed. 'Brochan told us what happened. How can these idiots want you to save them when they're trying to kill you at the same time?'

'Because you said it, Lex,' Speck added, giving me a warm hug. 'They're idiots.'

Lexie raised her blue eyebrows. 'Are you actually agreeing with me for once?'

'Even a stopped clock is right twice a day,' he said.

She frowned at him before turning back to me. 'You wouldn't believe the bounty we've managed to get while we've been here. These Fey planks just leave stuff lying around all over the place. Look!' She pointed to a collection on the table: there was all manner of jewellery, coins and fripperies.

I gave an approving nod. 'Nice work. Take care who you target, though. It might be better to leave the Moncrieffes alone.'

Even Brochan looked surprised at that. 'Why?'

'Byron Moncrieffe is stepping out with Tipsania Scrymgeour. He gave her a beautiful emerald necklace made entirely out of glass.'

Speck's eyes gleamed. 'A man after my own heart.'

'Not only that,' I continued, 'but he seemed very worked up at the loss of the Lia Saifire. I think the Moncrieffes are broke.'

Lexie's mouth dropped open. 'No shit. There's not been the faintest whisper of that anywhere on the streets.'

I shrugged, picking up one of the gold coins and weighing it in my hand. 'They'd want to keep it quiet. Aifric Moncrieffe might have been the Steward for the last three decades but if he can't keep his own finances in check, the other Clans might toss him out.'

'What goes around comes around,' Speck shrugged. 'Although it explains why his son's shagging Tipsy Scrymgeour. Her Clan is loaded.'

Brochan was watching me carefully. 'I'm guessing that since you're not encouraging us to help ruin them, Byron Moncrieffe isn't responsible for the attacks.'

'He's not. And sometimes better the devil you know. Aifric Moncrieffe is a known quantity. If someone else took his place as Steward, things might get better – or they might get a whole lot worse. Until I have a better understanding of Sidhe politics, we're best not exacerbating his situation.'

Both Lexie and Speck shot glances in Brochan's direction. 'I told you,' he said smugly. 'She wants to stick around.'

'And be a Sidhe?' Lexie whispered. She stared back at me. 'Really? I thought you hated them.'

'I do hate them. But there's more to the story about my parents than I realised. I want to stick around and find out what. If my father wasn't the murdering bastard that everyone has made him out to be…'

Lexie smirked. 'Hell hath no fury like an angry Integrity.'

I grinned. 'Indeed.'

Speck gnawed on his lip. 'Aren't you worried about whoever is really trying to kill you?'

I met his eyes. 'Frankly, I was expecting it. I get enough looks that could kill when I wander around the castle. A lot of the highborn Sidhe really don't like me. And they've not even spoken to me. I've laid the groundwork for them to believe that I'll have at least one gift emerge in the next few days. I've also made a big show of being angry rather than scared. It might buy me some time.'

Speck wasn't ready to let it go. 'That's all very well, but shouldn't you be scared? I'm terrified and no one even knows I'm here.'

'I have a secret weapon,' I said simply. I pulled the scimitar out of my pocket and laid it down.

'You're going to read their mail?'

'It's not a letter opener.'

Lexie frowned. 'It looks like a letter opener.'

'It's a scimitar.'

'Tegs, I love you to bits but that's not a scimitar.'

I placed my finger to my lips, encouraging her to be silent. 'Watch.' I slid the blade out of the sheath but, before I could rub it, there was a painful flash of light. All four of us moaned in sudden pain, covering our eyes.

'Bob,' I complained, 'I'd not summoned you yet.'

'Jeez Louise. You tell me to pay attention in case you need me at the drop of a hat then you fling me off to some Sidhe dude who stomps around and shouts a lot and you're annoyed because I'm listening in and ready to appear when you want me to.'

He had a point. 'Okay, okay. But it's nice to have some warning before you do the flashing thing.'

He smirked. 'Flashing? I can do flashing if that's what you want.' He began to unbuckle his tiny belt.

'No! That's quite alright.'

'It's larger than you'd think.' He winked at me. 'Size does matter.'

I gritted my teeth while the others slowly pulled their hands away from their eyes and gaped.

'What is that?' Speck asked, recoiling. 'I don't like little people. They give me the creeps.'

Bob stuck out his tongue.

'He's so cute though!' Lexie interjected, jabbing Speck in the ribs. It must have been painful because he exhaled loudly and threw her a dirty look.

'I prefer handsome,' Bob said. 'Or stud-like. Magnificent will also do. Cute suggests kittens and puppies.' He shuddered. 'That's not me.'

Brochan, still staring, let out a massive sneeze that startled us all. 'Genie,' he said flatly.

'How did you know?'

'I'm allergic.' He took out an embossed handkerchief and rubbed his nose.

Bob jumped up and down. 'You're allergic to genies? That's awesome! Let me get closer! Can I make you sneeze on command?'

'Bob,' I said warningly, 'that's enough of that.'

'Uh Integrity, you're no fun.'

'So you keep saying.'

Lexie's brow knitted together. 'Tegs, you've not made a wish, have you? Because that could be related to all the attempts on your life.'

'No,' I said cheerfully. 'Those are all Sidhe and nothing to do with Bob. Up till now there have been no wishes.'

The pixie looked relieved but Speck's eyes narrowed suspiciously. 'Up till now?'

I beckoned all three of them over. We got into a huddle, our backs turned on Bob. 'I know what the side effects are,' I whispered. 'But they're always related to the wishes themselves.'

Speck nodded. 'I heard there was a guy in Fife who came across a genie. He wanted everyone to like him so he wished he could hear everything that was said about him. The genie turned him invisible and he was never heard of again.'

'If he was never heard of again,' Lexie pointed out, tossing her hair, 'how did anyone ever hear the story of the wish? Although there was that woman who wished to be younger and ended up trapped in the body of a baby. That was real.'

Speck scowled at her. 'Why is your story real and mine isn't?'

Brochan rolled his eyes. 'Enough. Either way, wishes always go wrong. This is a bad idea, Tegs. You can't trust genies.'

'I can still hear you, you know,' Bob piped up from behind. 'I'm not deaf. I'm not evil either.'

'I know all that,' I told them, ignoring Bob. 'It's why I've not asked for anything yet, despite what's happened.' I didn't bother mentioning that I would have tried when the stoor worm attacked if I'd had the chance. Under that kind of pressure, I could really have messed things up. It was better not to dwell on it.

'So why now?'

'Because I'm going to wish for knowledge. If I phrase it properly, it won't screw things up.'

'Tegs,' Speck said seriously, 'if you wish to know who wants you dead, you might end up with a long list of people. It'll drive you insane.'

Brochan nodded in agreement. 'Any time anyone's thought they'd like to kill you might count. You'll never trust anyone again.'

I tilted my head. 'Are you three saying that you've thought in the past that you wanted to kill me?'

Lexie wouldn't quite meet my eyes. 'Not seriously.'

'Yeah,' Speck added, 'not like we'd *actually* kill you. Just more the fleeting thought that we'd like to rip your head off and flay your skin.'

'I thought you liked me!'

Brochan tutted. 'We do like you. We love you. But sometimes…'

'Sometimes what?'

Speck shifted his weight. 'Those jokes are really annoying.' He looked relieved to have said it.

'Yeah,' Lexie bobbed her head. 'They're so cheesy.'

'And you tell them *all* the time,' Brochan added.

I looked at him. 'You too? You feel this way?'

He shrugged. 'The thought might have crossed

my mind once or twice. It's not any different to the way I've wanted to kill Lexie for singing all the time.'

She glared at him.

'I can't believe this,' I said, shaking my head. 'You could have mentioned before that you didn't like my jokes.'

'Would you have stopped telling them?' Speck asked hopefully.

I frowned. 'Don't be silly. I'd have told more so that you could get a wider range of them. What do you call it when you tell a joke in the shower?'

Speck stared at Brochan. 'Please make her stop.'

'A clean joke!'

Lexie groaned. 'That's the worst one I've heard in a long time.'

'Oh yeah?' I said, putting my hands on my hips. 'Well, expect a lot more from now on, darling.'

Bob coughed. 'Helloooo? I'm still here, you know.'

I turned round. 'Bob,' I began.

'Tegs, don't.'

I held up my finger. 'I've got this.'

Bob smacked his palms together in glee. 'Yes, Uh Integrity? I think I'm going to cream my pants in anticipation.'

Speck winced. 'Don't. Just … don't.'

'I wish…' Brochan interrupted with three loud successive sneezes. Speck and Lexie jumped nervously but I stayed on track. 'I wish to know who's responsible for trying to kill me with the stoor worm and the fireballs.' I smiled to myself. As wishes went, that was pretty much perfect. I'd kept things as simple and specific as possible.

Bob beamed. He snapped his fingers. 'Uh Integrity, your wish is granted.'

There was a strange buzzing in the air. My muscles felt tight and tingly, then it was like I was being pulled. Pulled very painfully. Oh shite. 'No!' I yelled as I realised what was happening. 'I want to know! Not see! Bob!'

He shook his head sadly, 'Sorry Uh Integrity. The wishes do what the wishes want to do.'

I braced myself. This could be very, very bad. With one final sharp tug on every molecule in my body, my vision went blurry. Blinking hard to keep as much control of my senses as possible, I clenched my fists. At least I'd know what it felt like to be teleported before I ended up in a bodybag, I thought dully.

When my eyes focused and I saw the stunned face of the Bull staring at me, I groaned. I might have known.

'You … you…' he stammered. 'Your gift is teleportation?'

I squashed down my terror and smiled nastily. It was time to lie for my life. 'One of them. I have several. I am Clan Adair, after all.'

The Bull swallowed. All I could think was 'oh shite'.

Chapter Seventeen

It took the Bull less time to recover from my sudden appearance than I anticipated. He flung back his head and roared. It was a deafening sound. If his intention was to scare me, it worked. When his eyes fell on a point beyond my shoulder, however, I realised he'd done it for a different reason. Behind me was a door. He was calling for back up.

Assuming that he had Clan members close by, I wasted no time. To the right there was an oak table. It wasn't huge but it might buy me some time. I grabbed the edge of it and tipped it so it fell heavily against the door. For good measure, I also gave the lock a hefty kick, splintering it to help jam it. It was a move Taylor had me practise for weeks on end until I'd got it right - goodness knows how many doors we'd gone through. He'd insisted that it was important in case I ever found myself cornered during a heist and needed some breathing space to work out an escape route. At the time, I'd stubbornly declared that I'd never approach a job without having numerous escape routes and I'd never be stupid enough to let myself get cornered. Now I was seriously grateful for that training.

Unfortunately my preoccupation with the door gave the Bull time to attack. He came at me from behind, swinging a heavy sword. I heard the whisper as it flew through the air and just managed to duck in time, leaping away a heartbeat afterwards. He didn't manage to hit me but there was an odd buzzing in my ear that didn't sound right. I shook my head in a bid to clear it and focused on the Bull.

'Now that's a weapon,' I said. I showed him my bare palms. 'I'm not here to fight though. In fact, I'm a pacifist. I don't do violence.'

'Oh yeah?' he sneered. 'Then what's that in your pocket?'

Rather than take my eyes off him, I raised one hand to check. It was Bob's sodding letter opener. No doubt he'd come along for the ride in the hope that the mess created by my first wish would make me ask for a second.

'This is a letter opener,' I told the Bull. Screw Bob's delicate ego. 'It's not much good for anything. I keep it handy for urgent letters. I'd forgotten I had it.'

There were several shouts from the other side of the door, followed by a series of loud thumps. The Bull bared his teeth. 'You've got about five minutes before you're surrounded. Whatever you're going to do, you'd better do it fast,' he said.

He swung the sword again, his muscles straining. Sadly for him, he'd clearly fallen out of shape over the last twenty years and those muscles were encased in far too much fat. He'd made the classic error of using a weapon that was too unwieldy for him to manage. It was easy to avoid his blow and scoot to the other side of the room.

I pursed my lips. He'd kept me at such an arm's length when I was a kid that I'd never known what his Gift was. Judging by the fact that he was obviously biding his time until his Clan came to rescue him, I bet it was something fairly useless. Of course, that knowledge would only help me until his goons arrived.

'You didn't do the actual conjuring, did you?' If he possessed that kind of Gift, he'd already have used it here.

'Unlike you, I have a loyal Clan bursting at the seams with talented people. They did what I asked.'

I felt a slight twinge. It'd be handy to have people around who jumped to your every demand, even if it was attempted murder. 'Why are you trying to kill me?'

'You know why.'

Er, no. 'If I die,' I said, circling away in case he decided to take another heavy-handed swipe, 'then you'll never be able to open the Foinse.'

His lip curled. 'The Foinse is already doomed.'

I blinked. He didn't even think it was worth trying to kickstart it? 'You'll lose all your magic. The Sidhe will lose their standing. Not to mention it might mean hundreds of thousands of deaths.'

'The Scrymgeours are prepared. Any Clan worth its salt is prepared. This has been on the cards for a long time.'

'You're rich,' I said quietly. 'As rich as Croesus. You're going to make sure that your Clan survives because you can pay for the protection you'll need.'

There was a flicker of acknowledgment in his dark eyes. 'You might even be happy,' I continued. 'If other Clans are decimated then you'll rise up even further in the ranks.'

'You have no idea what it's like,' he hissed. 'I've got bodyguards outside my door because you can never be sure what the others are going to do. You think I was a bastard to you? Well, think again. I'm nothing compared to some of these bloodthirsty pricks.'

I had the odd sensation that he was telling the truth. Or at least that he believed what he was saying. 'I don't see your bodyguards right now,' I pointed out.

'They'll be here. Do your worst, Adair.'

I just kept circling. Even if had the skills or the desire, getting into a fight wouldn't help me. I had to be smarter. If I could keep him talking, perhaps I'd find a weak spot. 'That's why you could fling those fireballs at the grove,' I realised. 'If the Clans are doomed then it doesn't matter if the sacred ground is destroyed too.'

His face twisted. 'I don't need the other Clans on my back right now. You were going to be alone. I didn't want anyone to get hurt.'

I lifted an eyebrow. 'Other than me. Why do you hate me? Even as a child, you hated me.'

'Black,' he spat.

'Come again?'

'Your aura is black. It always has been. Even when you were a babe in arms, it was black.'

'That's your gift,' I breathed. Wow. That was pretty awesome. You'd know as much about your enemy as they did about themselves. Another strange wave of nausea hit me but I swallowed it down. 'You read auras. What does black mean?'

He shifted his grip on the sword. Even from here, I could tell that his palms were sweaty. He was as likely to drop it on the ground as he was to strike me with it. 'Evil. It has to be. No-one else has an aura like yours. I see greens, blues, reds. Every hue under the sun. You're the only person, Sidhe or troll or damned kookaburra, who's got black. No wonder you hang around with the dirty Clan-less.'

I was taken aback by the venom in his voice. Was that why I'd been treated so badly when I was his ward? Because everyone thought I was evil? I didn't feel evil. I was a thief, sure; I wasn't always on the right side of the law. But pure, unadulterated evil? I was confident that if my soul truly was like that, then I'd know it. Hell, I'd probably revel in it. That's what evil people did.

'Your father was evil,' the Bull spat. 'And you're evil.'

'I thought you said I was the only person you'd ever seen with a black aura?'

'His was close enough. Dark grey.'

'Have you seen a lot of those?' I was genuinely curious.

'What are you trying to do? Are you going to kill me or talk me to death?'

'I could tell you a few jokes,' I suggested.

He stared at me as if I were insane. Right now, he probably wasn't far off the mark. I was trapped in a room with the man who'd caused virtually every nightmare I'd ever had, and half his Clan were trying to break down the door. If anything was likely to make crazy, then this would be it.

The continued banging on the door finally had some effect. Whoever was on the other side had kicked hard enough to make some headway. Now there was little more than the table between me and several vicious Scrymgeour goons.

Panicking, I pulled out the letter opener and sprang towards the Bull. He was three times my size – it was no wonder how he'd earned his name. If I could put the blade to his throat, however, the rest of his Clan might back off. It was unlikely but I was desperate.

'You think that's going to work?' he sneered.

No, not really. I kicked upwards, knocking the sword out of his hands. It fell to the ground with a clatter.

'You made a mistake coming here, girlie. It's a shame you won't live long enough to regret it.'

'Believe me,' I grunted, shoving the letter opener towards his throat and grabbing him from behind, 'I'd rather be falling out of the sky than here with you.'

The door burst open and a number of grim-faced Sidhe piled in, a few of whom I recognised. Before I could say so much as boo, however, my body was yanked backwards.

'Teleporta...' the Bull started to yell. Except his shout was swallowed up in the billowing wind. We were no longer in his quarters. Sodding hell: we were falling through the sky.

My stomach lurched. Bob. I kept my grip on the Bull but I was losing control of my body. We twisted and tumbled through the air. The ground seemed a long way down. As I spun one way, I could just make out the dot of the castle below. It might look far away but it wouldn't take us very long to go splat.

'What the hell have you done?' the Bull yelled. Instead of pulling away from me, his hands frantically scrabbled forward, latching onto my shoulders. 'Get us out of here!'

'Bob!' I screamed. 'You wanker!'

There was the inevitable flash of light. I heard a curse from the Bull, before the genie appeared in front of my face.

'Hi, Uh Integrity!' The little shit had a parachute strapped to his back.

'First you send me to him and now you do this?'

He shook his head. 'Nah, sweet cheeks. I didn't do this. You didn't say "I wish".' He gave me a salute. 'I'm here at your service if you need me, though.' A tiny furrow lit his brow. 'You must have ... never mind. I seem to be stuck here with you.'

He spoke the truth. I switched my attention to the Bull, who was gaping at Bob. 'What are you?' he whispered.

'None of your sodding business,' I snapped, trying to time to stretch my body in the way I'd seen free fallers do on television. 'I thought you said your Gift was aura reading?'

'It is! This is down to you, you Adair bitch!'

Huh. I jerked my head down. The castle was getting bigger. Maybe I had received a Gift after all: I really could do teleportation. Pretty cool. I grinned to myself.

'What are you smiling at, you freak?' he yelled. 'We're going to die!'

I released my grip on him. His eyes widened in terror. 'Don't do that! Hold on to me!' He clutched at me in desperation, his fingers white-knuckled.

'You tried to kill me,' I said calmly. Now that I was in control, I was starting to enjoy myself. My hair was flying up behind me like Superman's cape - or so I imagined. Unfortunately the gusting wind was making my eyes water. My ear was still buzzing irritatingly. Next time I tried this, I'd remember to bring goggles - and perhaps ear plugs as well. Bob perched on my elbow, grinning manically.

'I'm sorry,' the Bull babbled. 'But it was only a matter of time before you came after me for what I did.'

'Tell me. Tell me what you did.'

'I'm going to die,' he moaned. 'Tipsania will be all alone. She's just a kid. She's not going to manage.'

No. I was just a kid when he'd treated me like

shit. Now we were all adults. I glanced down at the castle again. As this was my first skydive, it was difficult to estimate how much time we had before we reached the ground. It didn't look like it would be long.

Almost casually, I reached over to the Bull's left hand and eased it away from my body. He clawed it back but I twisted away. With only one set of fingers linked to me, the Bull's terror was growing.

'There's no time,' I said sadly. 'I'm going to have go. It's a shame because I really wanted answers.'

'No. No. Don't go.' His eyes pleaded with me.

'Give me your true name and I'll take you back with me.'

His face went pale. 'I can't do that.'

I shrugged, which isn't easy to do in midair. 'Your choice.' I turned my attention to his right hand, prying off one finger.

'You said you were a pacifist. This is murder.'

I considered. 'It's more manslaughter than murder. I didn't intend for this to happen. You just came along for the ride.'

'You're going to rot in hell.'

'Probably.' I pointed down. 'Hey, look! I can see sheep!' I pried off another of his fingers. They were remarkably fat and squat; clearly he wasn't a piano player. 'Before I go, do you want to know what the hardest part of skydiving is?' The Bull stared. My grin widened. 'The ground.'

'Alright! It's Cul-Chain. My true name is Cul-

Chain.'

A wave of power filled me. It wasn't just an emotional reaction, I felt a physical surge as well. 'Let's test that, shall we?'

'There's no time!'

'I'm off,' Bob announced, breaking into our conversation. I'd almost forgotten he was there. He pulled his parachute cord and jerked upwards. 'I'll catch up with you later, Uh Integrity!'

I looked down. The ground was getting dangerously close. 'Let go of me, Cul-chain,' I ordered.

The Bull released his grip. Crapadoodle – it worked. I lunged forward and grabbed him again, while he closed his eyes and muttered a prayer. I'd have to hope that the first time wasn't simply a fluke. 'The library,' I said aloud.

For one heart-stopping moment, nothing happened. Then I felt the tug. Both the Bull and I fell onto the hard, stone floor, smack bang in front of a grey-haired Sidhe who was so astonished he dropped the pile of books he was carrying right on top of us. Ouch.

I picked myself up and pushed off the books. Stretching a hand down to the Bull, I offered to hclp him up. He screwed up his face. 'Piss off.'

'You could be a little more polite,' I told him. 'Especially as you've sworn fealty to me now.'

'I've done no such thing.'

I turned my head, addressing the older Sidhe who was still staring at us. 'Leave us.'

He didn't need telling twice. He pivoted on his heel and ran off.

'Cul-chain,' I said in the most dulcet tone I could manage, 'be more polite.'

The Bull's expression tightened. He bowed, however. 'Yes, Miss Adair.'

'Taylor,' I said. 'Until Clan Adair is resurrected, call me Miss Taylor.'

He bowed again. I clapped my hands. I could get used to this.

'How did you do it?' he asked. 'How did you do the teleportation?'

'Beats me,' I shrugged. 'I'll let you into a secret – I didn't think I'd get any Gifts. When I didn't get a fever, I was sure of it.'

'That's not what I meant.' There was a dangerous glow in the back of his eyes. The Bull still hated me probably more than ever now. But his fear was greater than his hatred. With my knowledge of his true name, he'd do whatever I asked even if that meant slitting his own throat. 'How did you bring me along with you?'

I frowned. 'Eh?'

'I know other Sidhe who can teleport but they can only bring themselves and the clothes they are wearing. They can't even hold a cupcake and bring it with them.'

No wonder he didn't seem concerned when I grabbed hold of him in his room. Thanks to Bob's machinations, the Bull already believed I could teleport before I did so – but he didn't think I could include him on the trip. Interesting. 'You will tell no one about this.'

The Bull nodded. Then there was a tiny twitch at the side of his mouth.

I smiled. 'I almost forget. It's like Simon says, isn't it? I have to say your name to force you to do my bidding. Cul-chain.' I rolled the word around my mouth like a tasty treat. 'You will tell no one about this. And you will order your Clan to keep quiet too.'

He snarled. He also said, 'Yes, Miss Taylor.'

I circled round him. 'Let's start at the beginning, shall we? Why did I become your ward?'

'Aifric commanded my Chieftain. I either agreed to take you in or lost several key lands to the north.'

I rubbed my chin. 'But why you?'

He looked defiant. 'I'm the Bull.'

'I don't understand.'

He set his jaw. 'Your mother was engaged to me.' I sucked in an astounded breath. He ignored it. 'But because I am the Bull, she grew unhappy and left. I assume he thought that because you were her child, I would take good care of you.' He looked at me. 'I swore to keep you alive.'

'Because you're the Bull, she split up with you?' I asked, puzzled. He rolled his eyes at the same moment I realised what he meant. 'Ohhh. You're not called the Bull because you're a big guy. It's because you think of yourself as a stud.' I looked at his body derisively.

'I was younger then,' he spat. 'I was a different man.'

He'd have to have been very different for anyone to want to shag him. I stared at him in mock horror. 'My goodness! You could have been my real father after all!'

He hawked up a ball of phlegm. Before he could do anything with it, I wagged my finger. 'I don't think so, Cul-chain.'

He swallowed it back down. Eurgh.

'So,' I said, 'you wanted to kill me because of my aura. And because you want the Foinse to fail. Is that correct, Cul-chain?'

Yes,' he mumbled.

'Speak up.' I nudged him gently with my toe. 'Is that correct?'

He cleared his throat. 'Yes.'

'Was my father really evil?'

'Yes.' His gaze was unwavering.

'If I asked any other highborn Sidhe, would I get the same answer?'

'Yes.'

'What about the lower classes?'

He looked away. 'They're naïve.'

'Why do they think differently?'

'He manipulated them. There are stories suggesting that it wasn't him. Or that he was possessed by a demon.' His expression made it clear how unlikely he thought that was.

'Very well. From now on, Cul-chain, you will not seek to harm me. You will ensure no-one in your Clan seeks to harm me. In fact, you will not seek to harm anyone.' I smiled. 'I wasn't lying. I really am a pacifist. I might have an imaginative interpretation of the word but I'd never have let you fall.'

His eyes spat fire. 'Evil bitch.'

I shrugged. 'Evil bitch who's now your boss.' Not that I thought he needed reminding. 'You may leave now.'

He turned tail and ran. As I watched him go, my hard demeanour softened to something more genuine and far more troubled because from the moment, the Bull told me his true name, I'd been able to see a strange halo round him. It was a sickly yellow and it followed him as he spun out of the library door. The aura of the grey-haired man who dropped the pile of books was more of a chocolate-brown colour.

I had no way of interpreting what each hue meant but apparently I could add aura reading to teleportation as one of my gifts. It was a damn shame it wouldn't be of any use without a colour chart.

Chapter Eighteen

The faint buzzing in my ear still hadn't gone away. It was incredibly annoying. I tried scratching and slapping at it but they had no effect. It was as if I had a bee trapped inside my ear canal. I wondered if one had flown in during my little skydiving adventure but I'd been too high up for bees - and the buzzing had started before then anyway. Odd.

Bob winked into existence. He'd managed to lose the parachute but he still had a smug smirk plastered over his face.

'You waste of space, genie,' I hissed. 'You almost got me killed.'

He raised his eyes to the heavens. 'Come on, Uh Integrity. You knew there would be consequences. You told me about them often enough. Besides, it all turned out well in the end, didn't it? You discovered your Gift and you got the nasty old Bull to tell you his true name. Now you own two people.'

I gritted my teeth. 'I don't "own" anyone.'

'Monsieur Scrymgeour and I would beg to differ.'

I scratched at my ear again. Damn, that sound was annoying.

'That's your friends,' Bob told me cheerfully. 'I told them it probably wouldn't work.'

My brow furrowed. 'What do you mean?'

'They're trying to summon you with your true name but they're not Sidhe. They can probably bend you to their will if you're in the same room as them and you can hear them. But from a distance?' He shrugged. 'It's never going to be a strong enough call.'

'Well, that's stupid,' I said irritably. 'If they'd summoned me back straightaway then your little game would have been null and void.'

'As I've already said, you have benefited immeasurably from my,' he sketched air quotes, ' "little game". Don't be a sore winner.'

'They'll be worried. I should get back.'

Bob beamed. 'You're right. They *are* worried.'

I started running out of the library. I had to get back to Lexie, Speck and Brochan as quickly as possible before they did something rash.

'What are you doing?' Bob shouted after me.

What did he think I was doing? I cursed under my breath then smacked into a hard body. Slightly dazed, I pulled back. Byron. The shimmer around him was a deep purple. It should have clashed with his bronze hair but instead it made him appear more regal and charismatic. Great. That was all I needed.

He caught my arm and gave me a funny look. 'I thought you were feeling sick and lying down in your room.'

Shite. 'Er, I was. But now I feel better.' I gave a disarming smile. 'I can't tell what gift I have yet, though.' I might have more reason to trust him but that didn't mean I was going to volunteer information.

His eyes suspiciously. 'How did you get past the...'

I raised my eyebrows. 'The guards that I asked you not to post but you did anyway?'

He sighed. 'Someone's trying to kill you, Integrity. You shouldn't be flippant about these matters.'

'Not until the Foinse is safe and sound anyway, right?'

A strange expression crossed his face. 'Right,' he muttered.

'Actually, I was coming to find you,' I said. 'That's why I was in the library. You asked me to meet you there before, so I thought it might be where you liked to hang out.' I gave myself an imaginary pat on the back. Nice little side step I did there.

'What do you need?'

I grinned. 'As I'm clearly hale and hearty, we can get on with the crusade to the Foinse. The sooner we fix it the better, don't you think?'

I still hadn't allayed his suspicions. He folded his arms and gazed at me. 'Are you sure you're up to the journey?'

I beamed. 'I can't wait. Let me rush upstairs and grab my things and I'll be ready to go.'

The furrow in Byron's brow deepened. I caught sight of Jamie and Tipsania hovering in the back and gave them an enthusiastic wave. 'We're going to the Foinse,' I bellowed out. 'Do you want to come? We could take a picnic.'

Jamie threw a nervous glance at Byron then looked embarrassed again, while Tipsania wrinkled her nose irritably. I wondered whether her father would tell her what had transpired between us; somehow I doubted it. The Bull wouldn't want to look weak in front of anyone, even if they were his closest family or loyal Clan members.

It was interesting that Tipsania's aura was a pretty pink, with some flecks of scarlet. How come I was the evil black-aura woman and she got pink?

'They can't come,' Byron muttered. 'Only two representatives from each Clan are going to travel to the Foinse.'

'Why two?'

He didn't meet my eyes. 'It's an auspicious number.'

'Really,' I said flatly. 'Or is it because you need an heir and a spare?'

'Accidents happen.'

'Is that what we're calling murder these days?' I asked, although there was a lightness behind my words. Byron might not be aware of it but there was little chance of any further mishaps now I'd sorted out the Bull. But it still didn't seem fair that I was the only one without a buddy. 'There's only me from Clan Adair,' I said, pointing out the bleeding obvious. 'Does that mean I can nominate someone to come with me?'

Byron's gaze flickered towards Jamie. 'I'll talk

to my father. But even if he agrees, you can't bring someone who's in the Kincaid, Darroch or Moncrieffe Clans because they will be already be represented.'

I shrugged. 'Suits me. Jamie can be one of the Moncrieffe reps.' I winked at him. The corners of his mouth tugged up in a quick answering smile. He was still very cute, especially when he put his dimples on show like that.

Byron's jaw tightened. 'No, he can't. Both my father and I will be travelling for Moncrieffe.'

I was surprised at that. Byron's attendance made sense; he had, after all, been one of the few Sidhe I'd had proper contact with and I doubted that the other Clan reps would be keen to chew the fat with me during our journey. However, I'd assumed that the Steward would delegate the journey to someone else. He must be a hands-on kind of leader.

Tipsania was looking bored. 'He's made things very awkward for the other Clans. Now they all have to send their Chieftains so they don't lose face.'

'As they should,' Byron replied. 'This is a matter of some importance.'

'So I've heard,' she said sarcastically.

His expression softened. 'Sorry. It's been a long week.'

Tell me about it. 'Can we get this show on the road?' I interrupted.

'I'll inform the others. Despite your sudden desire to get going, we won't leave until first light tomorrow. By the time everyone gets their gear together, it'll already be too late today.'

I remained cheerful. 'More time for me to hang around the Cruaich and get to know the Sidhe, then. What fun.'

Tipsania rolled her eyes. 'Byron, baby, will you come with me to the garden? I need some fresh air.'

'It would be my pleasure.' It was interesting that his expression told an entirely different tale. He was going to have to work on his acting ability if he planned to make an alliance with the Scrymgeours through Tipsania to solve the Moncrieffes' financial woes. Although, looking at the way she hooked her arm round his and gazed adoringly up at him, that might not be too hard.

I watched them go. Jamie said reluctantly, 'I have to, um, I have to go too.'

I smiled at him. 'Okay.'

Byron's head turned for a moment, as if he were checking up on his mate. Perhaps he was worried I'd jump on Jamie and rip his clothes off right here and now. But as soon as Jamie walked off in the opposite direction, Byron returned his attention to Tipsania.

'You like him,' Bob said coyly into my ear.

I jumped. He was perched on my shoulder like a damn parrot. 'Don't sneak up on me like that!'

'Why? Are you worried I'll catch you drooling?'

'For Jamie Moncrieffe?' I considered it. 'His dimples are rather alluring.'

'Not him,' Bob purred. 'The other one.'

I stiffened. 'Just because I might find Byron Moncrieffe sexually attractive, along with his friend,' I added quickly, 'does not mean that I drool. Besides, as you can see, he's already taken.'

'I don't see no ring.'

'Watch this space.' I started to stride away again.

'Uh Integrity! Stop!'

'I have to find the others,' I said. 'They probably think I'm dead by now.'

The genie looked exasperated. 'So why are you taking the long way around?'

'What do you mean?'

Bob stood on his tiptoes and smacked me on the side of my head. 'Hello? Teleportation?'

Oh. I'd completely forgotten. I grinned. 'Thanks, Bob.'

He tsked. A faint shadow crossed his face while I snapped my fingers and declared in a deep voice, 'The tower.'

'You don't have to do that with your hand, you know.'

'I know but I think it adds a little something to the effect,' I said, as I felt myself being tugged away. It really was a handy Gift to have.

*

Lexie, Speck and Brochan were relieved to see me. Once again I enjoyed several hugs. 'We're making a habit of this,' I joked.

'We didn't know what had happened to you!' Lexie burst out. 'That wanky genie…'

I sighed. 'It wasn't his fault. But I certainly won't be asking for any more wishes any time soon.'

'What happened, Tegs?' Brochan asked. 'Who was it?'

'It was the Bull all along. I should have suspected him from the start. I guess there are so many people around here who seem to hate me that he was too obvious.' I explained to the three of them what had happened.

Speck's face turned green. 'Heights. I hate heights.'

'It was kind of fun once I realised I wasn't going to hit the ground.'

'What colour is my aura?' Lexie asked eagerly.

'Orange. It's very bright,' I admitted.

She folded her arms. 'Orange? That's awful!'

I blinked. 'Why?'

'Orange and blue don't go together at all. Now I'll have to re-think my entire wardrobe! Not to mention dying my hair.' She shook her head. 'All this time I've been clashing.'

'I wouldn't worry about it, Lex. I don't think there's anyone except the Bull and me who can see it.'

She pouted. 'That's two people too many.'

'What am I?'

I turned to Speck. 'Dark blue. And Brochan is…'

He held up his hands. 'I don't want to know.' He paused. 'Tegs, have you thought about how you came to have this Gift?'

I frowned. 'What do you mean?'

'It's a bit of a coincidence, isn't it? You take the Bull's true name and now you have the same Gift as him?'

'I've never heard of that happening,' I said slowly. 'But it does seem to make a kind of sense.'

'Let's face it, you could write down everything all four of us know about the Sidhe and it probably wouldn't fit on the back of a stamp. Maybe it's not just the true names that have power. Maybe if give away your true name, you also give away part of that power.'

'I'm sure the Bull would have realised if his Gift had been diminished.' I nibbled my lip. 'What happened with Bob...' My voice trailed away.

Speck scratched his chin. 'What do you mean?'

'Teleportation. It wasn't until after Bob had teleported me to the Bull that I could suddenly teleport myself. And others, too. The Bull seemed to think it was strange that I could bring him along with me.'

'You think you absorbed some of the genie's magic too?' Lexie's eyes were round. 'That's so cool!'

Speck nodded. 'Osmosis.' When he received a funny look from Lexie, he scowled at her. 'What? Just because I paid attention in school when you were too busy partying...' She thumped him and he let out a small screech. 'Stop doing that! You know I don't respond well to pain.'

Brochan gazed at the pair of them with an expression of long-standing sufferance. Then he turned back to me. 'Maybe the Gift you received is one of learning. You learn what other people can do.' He drew in a breath. 'It would make you incredibly powerful, Tegs.'

'I can think of a few Sidhe who wouldn't be very happy about that.' I shrugged. 'I didn't learn pyrokinesis, and those fireballs were flung at me after I received my true name.'

'That was immediately afterwards. Maybe you weren't ready.'

I shrugged. 'Unless someone else uses their Gift on me, it's not a theory we can test. I'm certainly not about to ask for anything else from Bob.'

Lexie gasped. 'What if you caught wish-granting from him?'

'You make it sound like a disease,' I grunted. 'And I don't think that would be possible. Wishes are specific to genies. Teleportation, however…'

'Hello darlings!' Bob sang. 'My ears were burning so I knew you were talking about me.'

I stared at him suspiciously while Brochan sneezed. 'Why did it take you so long to get here?'

'I was in the library doing some research.' He reached up to the tips of his ears; tiny flickers of flame were dancing around them. 'Scorchio!' he hissed.

'Your ears are burning,' Speck said in wonder.

Bob threw him a scathing look. 'I already said that.'

We glanced at each other. 'Ear we go,' I grinned.

Everyone groaned. Bob settled down on the back of a chair and pulled off his shoes. He started to examine his toes, picking out miniscule bits of fluff.

Lexie turned away. 'That's disgusting.'

'You'd probably like to know what I discovered in the library,' he said, holding up a greenish ball to the light before chucking it over his shoulder with a shrug. Speck jumped back about a metre.

No-one said anything. 'Oh come on,' Bob complained. 'Aren't you going to ask me?'

I exchanged a look with Brochan. 'Go on then,' I said finally. 'What did you find out?'

'Well,' he huffed, 'if you don't want to know…'

I rolled my eyes. 'I do.' It was probably some pointless fact about genies' feet, which was why we were being subjected to this display of toe picking.

'To all intents and purposes,' Bob declared, 'the Adair Clan doesn't exist.' He pulled his socks and shoes back on and stood up, looking around as if he were expecting applause.

'We know that,' I told him. 'It's hardly news.'

'You misunderstand me. There's no record of the Adairs. Some books have pages ripped out of them. Others just have a blank space. I am certain that you could scour every piece of paper in that place and you wouldn't find a single mention of them. Isn't that curious?'

I paused. 'They're being wiped from history.' I licked my lips. '*I'm* being wiped from history.'

Brochan pursed his lips. 'Very few cultures do that. Most prefer to remember their mistakes so they don't repeat them.' He gestured towards me. 'And the Adair Clan is, in effect, still here. Erasing you doesn't make sense.'

'Why would someone do that?'

'Because in a generation or two, it'll be like they never existed,' Speck answered.

'I've seen it happen before,' Bob said knowledgably. 'The Timentuns, for example.'

'Who?' Lexie asked.

He snapped his fingers. 'Exactly!'

They all looked at me. 'It does make it more likely that there'll be another attempt on my life once the Foinse is sorted,' I said thoughtfully. 'Rubbing out the past is a big deal. I wonder what they're all so scared of.'

'More bad jokes,' Bob said cheerfully.

I stuck out my tongue at him, then softened my expression. 'Thank you,' I told him. 'You didn't have to do that. Look around the library, I mean.'

He blushed. 'Against my better judgment, I like you, Uh Integrity. This is the most fun I've had in a thousand years.'

'So what's the plan?' Speck asked.

I ran my hands through my hair. 'I travel to the Foinse with the others. I might be able to glean some information during the journey. Aifric

Moncrieffe is going and there's no way that de doesn't know that the Adair Clan is being deliberately forgotten. Perhaps I can find out why.'

'You're going to have to make a run for it once the Foinse is opened,' Brochan said grimly. 'It might have only been the Bull who was trying to kill you before but that could change when you've done your duty.'

I nodded. 'Yep. Teleportation makes escape pretty simple though.' I pointed to Speck. 'Can you go back to Aberdeen and talk to Taylor? He knows a lot of people who've been around for a long time. See what the Clan-less know about the Adairs.'

'He probably already knows, Tegs,' Speck answered. 'You might have wanted to abandon everything to do with your family and the Sidhe, but I bet that he looked into what happened.'

He was probably right. And if Taylor had never discussed it with me, it was probably because what he'd unearthed wasn't good. I had to stop pretending it wasn't part of me. I'd take the news, whether it was good or bad.

'Brochan, it's a lot to ask, but do you think you can find a way to get to the old Adair lands? It's almost three decades since they were used but…'

'I'll do it. There might be traces there of things that can help.'

'I can use the teleportation thing to get you there,' I began.

He shook his head. 'No. I can use the journey to help me. There'll be some tired travellers along the way who might be more loose-lipped than the people around here.' He looked at me warningly. 'Rely on those Gifts too much and who knows what you'll miss.'

He had a point. It wasn't just teleportation. I could spend hours trying to work out what one person's aura meant instead of paying attention to more reliable indicators like body language and tone of voice.

Lexie bounced up and down. 'What can I do?'

'Eavesdrop. Everywhere. Sneak around here and find out what's really going on with all these highborn Sidhe wankers. Not just in terms of the Foinse and the Adairs, but everything.'

She beamed. 'Gotcha.'

'And me?' Bob piped up. 'You've still got two wishes, you know. You ask for the Adair Clan to be restored to their rightful position and…'

'No. No more wishes,' I said.

He pouted. 'I'd be better at eavesdropping than her.'

Lexie looked like she was about to slam her palm down and squash Bob like a bug. 'I think she'll do fine,' I replied drily. 'You're coming with me. You can be another pair of eyes. An honorary Clan member.' My eyes gleamed. 'For the first time in twenty-six years, the Adair Clan entourage will outnumber the others. There'll be three of us for two of them.'

'Three?' Brochan asked. 'Who's the third person going to be?' He looked at my face and groaned.

'No. Not her. She's nuts.'

I grinned at him and winked. Right now, she was the only Sidhe apart from possibly Jamie whom I trusted.

Chapter Nineteen

The Sidhe were sticklers for punctuality. I'd slept surprisingly well on the hard bed and the pain in my ribs was far more manageable now I'd had some rest. It was a struggle to get up and drag myself down to meet the rest of my merry band at dawn, even though I was usually a morning person.

They were waiting, several with scowls on their faces. It clearly galled a lot of them that they'd had to come to an Adair for help– and that they'd been forced to delay the trip because of me. For my part, I waved happily at them. Lily and Aifric smiled back. Byron glared at me suspiciously for a moment before relaxing into a small smile. The others simply glowered.

'Chieftain! You honour me with your request,' Lily sang.

'I can't believe the Macquarries let her come,' the younger of the two Kincaids muttered.

'That's because they're all crazy,' I heard the Darroch Chieftain reply. Even though she was agreeing with Kincaid, she still received a nasty look for butting in on the conversation. Interesting. Maybe they all hated each other as much as they hated me.

One by one, they mounted their horses. Even Lily sprang up onto a pretty white mare. 'No bells,' she said sadly. 'I like bells. Ding a ling a ling a ling!'

Byron leaned over to me. 'She wanted them tied into the mane,' he informed me. 'Along with multi-coloured ribbons.'

I shrugged. 'What's wrong with that?' If I could get a nice docile horse with hot-pink fripperies attached to its mane, maybe this riding business wouldn't be so bad.

Byron frowned. 'You haven't forgotten how serious this mission is, have you?'

'Hey,' I said lightly, 'I chose to accept it. It would have been a shame if you chose to self-destruct ten seconds after delivering it, though.'

'Huh?'

'*Mission Impossible*?'

Aifric and his horse trotted over. 'This mission is far from impossible, Ms. Taylor. Don't be so anxious.'

Good grief. Pop culture references were clearly going to be lost on this lot.

'Mount up, Integrity,' Byron said. 'We don't want to waste time.'

He pointed at a red-faced man who was struggling to keep hold the reins of a massive black stallion. It bucked and snorted. Even the other horses seemed terrified of getting too near to it.

My mouth dropped open. 'You have to be kidding me.'

He smirked. 'Psych,' he whispered. 'He's mine. That one's yours.' He pointed at a chubby mare. It had a vacant expression in its eyes and what appeared to be the chewed remnants of a straw hat hanging out of its mouth. 'Ethan Hawke might not agree but I thought Barbie would be a better fit.'

I raised my eyebrows. 'Barbie?' And Ethan Hawke? Byron wasn't that removed from the rest of the world after all.

His amusement increased. 'She likes hot pink too.'

I gazed doubtfully at Barbie. Judging by her expression and her lack of interest in the world around her, I was going to have a hard time getting her to keep up with the others. I wondered if Byron had deliberately picked her to make me look like a fool. Then I dismissed the idea. He was conniving, sure, but generally he was a decent guy.

I walked over and patted Barbie's neck nervously. She ignored me. Maybe that was a good thing. I stepped back and eyed her saddle. I could climb up tall buildings without a rope; surely, I could get on top of a horse. I put one foot into the stirrup and pulled myself over. Barbie didn't so much as twitch.

'Yee-ha!' I yelled, lifting a hand in the air as if I were on a bucking bronco.

The Kincaid wanker sniggered, throwing me such a derisive look that I stiffened. I formed my fingers into a gun and mimed shooting him. His amusement was immediately replaced by stark fear. I smiled coldly. Yeah, buster; it was probably not the best move in the world to piss off the mass murderer's daughter.

As I adjusted my weight, out of the corner of

my eye I spotted Byron approaching the black beast. The stallion visibly relaxed, allowing him to stroke his mane. With one lithe movement, Byron sprung up. I eyed his thigh muscles as they tightened round the horse's girth then coughed slightly when he glanced round, grinning as he caught me staring. Oops. I willed the horse to buck him off but although it had appeared to be a deranged beast, now it stood as docile than Barbie.

Aifric moved to the front of the pack and turned to address us. From my position, I had to crane my neck to look up at him although his aura, a vivid scarlet, remained visible. 'You should all be proud of yourselves,' he intoned. 'What we do will secure the Clans for generations to come. Your children's children will thank you.'

My shoulders tightened. I wasn't doing this to 'secure' the damn Clans. Aifric seemed to sense my thoughts and continued. 'By ensuring the safety of the Foinse, we will save countless lives, both Clan and Clan-less.'

That was better. I noticed the two Darroch reps nudge each other at the mention of the Clan-less. I narrowed my eyes at them. Unfortunately they didn't notice.

'We will return victorious,' Aifric boomed. 'Because for the Sidhe, there is no other way.' He gazed at us meaningfully then, with a flourish, turned his horse round and took off.

The others followed in his wake. I tried to remember what I was supposed to do to get Barbie to move. I squeezed my legs together but nothing happened; she simply kept on chewing. I gripped the reins. 'Giddy up!' She swung her head round as if vaguely curious, blinked once, and returned to chewing.

I gritted my teeth. This couldn't be that hard. 'Come on, girl,' I whispered. 'You can do this.' Even Lily was managing her horse perfectly. If I didn't get Barbie to get a wiggle on, the others would disappear out of sight.

The red-faced man who'd been holding Byron's horse walked over. I opened my mouth to ask him what on earth I was supposed to do to get her going. He didn't say a word, just smacked Barbie on her rump. Startled, she burst forward into a canter. I was so unprepared for the sudden movement that I almost fell off backwards. Hanging on for dear life, I bellowed out a thank you. I don't know whether he replied; I was concentrating too hard on not falling off. Barbie might not look like much compared to the others but, given the right incentive, she really could move.

I followed the others for some distance before we caught up. Aifric still led the way but Byron was at the rear. As soon as Barbie reached him, she started eyeing the stallion's backside in a manner that had me very worried. She trotted up and gave him a nudge. The stallion was unimpressed, whipping his head round and giving a good imitation of a horsey glare. Before she could try it again, I tugged her reins. She swung her head round at me as if to ask what on earth was wrong with me.

I shrugged. 'Sorry, Barbs,' I told her. 'I don't think messing with the monster is a good idea.'

Byron, turned his head and frowned.

'I didn't mean *you,*' I explained. 'You're not a monster.' I thought about it. 'Well, you're a blackmailing monster. And a manipulative monster. But…'

'Integrity,' he sighed. 'I thought we were past all this. What kept you, anyway? Were you admiring the scenery?'

'I have a dozy mare,' I pointed out. 'You have a stallion.'

Byron slowed down until we were neck and neck and looked at me critically. 'You need to relax,' he instructed. 'Sit back in the saddle. You're not a jockey and this isn't the Grand National. You've been hanging around with your old mentor for too long.'

'You mean instead of spending more time with stand-up guys, like the Darroch women who can't even pretend to care about the lives of the Clan-less?' Byron opened his mouth to answer but I didn't give him a chance. 'Or with the Kincaids who think it's okay to sneer openly at another Clan? You lot spend all this time telling the world that you're better than everyone else when you all hate each other, snipe at each other and apparently go around trying to kill each other.'

His jaw tightened. 'I'll admit,' he said stiffly,

'that there are some Sidhe who need to learn both manners and humility. And Sidhe politics can be … bloody. But we are not bad people, Integrity.'

'Neither are the Clan-less.'

'Point taken.'

I sniffed. Well, good. Rather than continue spelling out the flaws of the Sidhe, I focused on something less controversial. 'The Foinse?' I said, a question in my tone.

'What about it?'

'How do you know it's failing? The magic is still working, right? I've almost died twice as proof of that.'

Byron considered my question. 'You'd know if you spent more time on Clan lands,' he said. 'The magic is easier to sense here so it's easier to notice changes. You're aware of the change in atmosphere before a storm?'

I nodded. 'Sure.'

'Well, it's a similar kind of thing with the magic. We can feel a difference. Few people have been affected so far but it's definitely there.' His face took on a tight, brooding expression. 'There are always lulls with the Foinse, moments when it's harder to get a handle on our Gifts, or when things don't work as they should.'

I absorbed this. 'And when we reach it and open it, then what?'

'The representatives here aren't just along because of their Clan blood.' Byron nodded towards Aifric. 'My father is better at telekinesis than I am.

He will able to fine tune anything that isn't working. The Darroch woman – not Mali the Chieftain but the younger one – she's an expert in dowsing. If there's a blockage somewhere, she'll be able to locate it.'

'Ah,' I said knowledgably, 'so it's like plumbing then.'

Byron looked amused. 'Sort of.'

'And the Kincaids?'

'Both of them are Gifted in precognition.'

I started. 'Telling the future?'

'Not quite as obviously as that. They get glimpses of a future that might be. Which is another one of the reasons that we knew the Foinse was failing.'

'So if we can fix it, they'll get glimpses that tell them everything will be okay?'

'In theory. Precognition isn't an easy Gift to manage.'

I could well imagine. I resolved to keep well away from the pair of them. Not just because they were snooty Sidhe but because seeing the future was about the creepiest thing I could imagine. If Brochan's theory about me learning others Gifts was correct, then I had to avoid them like the plague. Half the fun of life was not knowing what came next.

'What do you know about my father's Gifts?' I asked, dropping my voice slightly so that the others wouldn't hear. 'You said there were three.'

He looked away.

'Byron?' I prodded.

He sighed. 'I don't know much. You have to remember I was only seven when all that happened.'

Not to mention that there was a conspiracy to get the world to forget the Adairs ever existed. 'I know,' I said aloud, crossing my fingers and making a quick decision to twist the truth wherever possible. 'But as we suspected I didn't receive a Gift from the grove and I'm curious about what his were.'

'I heard it said that one of them was soul punching.' He still wouldn't meet my eyes.

Whatever that was, it didn't sound good. 'What is that?' I asked quietly.

A muscle twitched in his jaw. 'It's the ability to reach inside a person and kill them. Their soul is attacked and, well, they die.'

I absorbed this information. 'Is that what happened to everyone in the Adair Clan? He … punched their souls?'

Byron nodded. 'For what it's worth, I don't think you're like that.'

'You don't think I'm like a mass murderer? Well, that's comforting.'

'I didn't mean it like that.'

I bit my lip. 'I know.' I took a deep breath. 'I heard a story that my father was possessed by a demon. That it wasn't him at all.'

'Apart from one incident when I was a kid, there haven't been demons this side of the Veil in five hundred years. I'm sorry, Integrity. I realise you don't want to think ill of him.'

'I never even met him,' I said. 'I don't know what to think.' I knew what I saw in the grove, though.

Without warning, Byron released one of his reins and took my hand. He squeezed it tightly. Rather than making me feel comforted, the action made me flinch. I tried to force myself to relax. Byron meant well, after all. He pressed his thumb into my palm, drawing small concentric circles. My eyes shot up. He watched me intently, making my mouth dry. It was getting damned difficult to think with any semblance of coherence.

'There's something I want you to know,' he said awkwardly.

I forgot to breathe altogether. 'Yes?'

'That day. When we first met and you were just a kid.'

I stiffened, desire fleeing as quickly as it had arrived. 'The day you called me pathetic.'

He winced. 'Yes.' His fingers tightened round mine again as if he were worried I would escape. 'I knew that things were difficult for you living with the Scyrmgeours.'

'Difficult?' I tried to pull away but his grip was too strong. 'I wasn't even given a name, Byron. I was just a thing. The Bull's hounds were treated like kings compared to me.'

'If I'd been nice to you that day in front of Tipsania, what do you think would have happened?'

'How the hell should I know?' I snapped. 'I ran away about ten minutes after you pissed off. It was the best thing I ever did.'

A shadow crossed his face. 'I didn't know you were going to do that,' he said. 'All I knew was that if I showed you kindness, Tipsania would take it out on you later. I was trying to get her to leave you alone. It was clumsy and probably did more harm than good. Honestly though, I wasn't being mean to you.'

I scanned his expression. He seemed earnest; hell, he seemed more than earnest. 'Why her?' I asked. 'If she's such a bitch, why are you with her now?'

He cursed under his breath. 'She's not a bitch, although I can see why many people think that. I'm not *with* her either. I just hang out with her sometimes. Really, it's all politics. Her father has money.' His eyes narrowed unhappily. 'The Moncrieffes are broke.'

I tried to keep my expression blank. It wouldn't do either me or him any favours to point out that I'd worked that out already. 'How can you be broke? You're the most powerful Clan.'

'My father hasn't gone into details but he's alluded to plenty. Buying loans, paying for expensive penthouse suites and drinking pink champagne doesn't help,' he said, shooting me a wry look. 'And it's not easy keeping the other Clans in check.'

I glanced ahead. The Kincaid kid and the Darroch woman, whose Gift was dowsing, were bickering loudly. 'I've seen that,' I admitted. 'So he's spent the Moncrieffe fortune because he's the Steward. Why not give up the title? Pass on the reins to someone else?'

Byron let out a sharp laugh. 'I've asked him that. He's hell-bent on being his responsibilities, though. He doesn't think it would be fair to quit.'

My eyes fell on Aifric's back. He seemed relaxed but if I looked closely, I could just see the line of tension down his spine. 'Maybe the Clan-less don't have it so bad,' I commented.

Byron smiled sadly. 'Maybe not.'

'Is that why you sleep around?' I asked curiously. 'Because you don't like Tipsania in that way but you can't tell her directly?'

The atmosphere between us shifted abruptly and he dropped my hand. 'I didn't say I didn't like her. And I'm not the one who sleeps around. I rather think that's you.'

'You mean Jamie. That wasn't a sex thing.'

His emerald eyes flashed. 'You could have fooled me.'

'You're the one with the playboy reputation.' And the one who continued to flirt outrageously with me.

'And,' he said, his voice dangerously soft, 'I'd have thought that with your reputation, you'd know better than to place credence on such matters.'

'So you've never cheated on poor Tipsy?

Because, Byron, we came pretty close.' I knew there was unreasonable anger in my tone, but I couldn't help it.

'I told you, I'm not with her. Besides, you wanted it a hell of a lot more than I did,' he growled.

He had me there. 'Oh, I wouldn't dwell too much on that,' I spat back. 'After all, I drop my knickers when any man so much as looks at me.'

His expression darkened. I had the feeling he was tempted to drag me off poor Barbie and shake me. If it hadn't been for Lily's timely interruption, he might have.

'This is fun, fun, fun!' she exclaimed, dropping back. 'Can you feel the crickle crackle, Chieftain?'

'I'm not a chieftain, Lily,' I said tiredly. 'What crickle crackle do you mean?'

Byron nudged the black stallion and sped up, joining his father at the front. He didn't look back.

'Him,' she said, in a tone that suggested she was pointing out the obvious, 'and you. Lots of crickle crackle.'

I stared at Byron. That was certainly one way of putting it. Me and my big mouth.

Chapter Twenty

We finally made camp a few hours after dusk. Byron had resolutely refused to speak to me since our argument and Lily, while fun to have around, was often flighty, taking off in mid-conversation to gallop after a butterfly or a beam of sunshine or whatever happened to take her fancy. I tried to ask her several times what she could tell me about my parents but, whereas before when I hadn't wanted to know she'd practically begged to tell me about them, now she didn't seem interested.

I started wishing I could bring Bob out, just so I'd have someone to talk to who wasn't going to go off on a tangent or sulk. I even wondered if it would be really bad to teleport myself to the Foinse and do my bit then leave. Perhaps the others wouldn't notice my absence.

Of course, it didn't help that my arse was incredibly sore. After hours of bouncing up and down in the saddle, I could barely stand when I slid off Barbie. For her part, she seemed unconcerned, nudging me curiously when my legs gave way and I crumpled right next to her. She proceeded to grab a mouthful of my hair and chew on it. The Darroch dowser, whose name I discovered was Diana, found that very funny. I dragged myself up, using Barbie's bulky frame, rescued my hair, and started muttering.

'Diana Darroch dowses dutifully. Diana

Darroch dowses dutifully. Try saying that five times over,' I called out to her. 'It's a great tongue twister.'

She sniffed and turned her back on me. It was better than the sniggering. I didn't want anyone sniggering unless it was at one of my jokes.

Once I'd untacked Barbie - which took me far longer than anyone else because I was hurting so much - I watched with interest as Byron used pyrokinesis to light a fire. While the others started cooking, and Lily curled up next to the fire and promptly fell asleep, I wandered off and tried to do the same as Byron. No matter how hard I concentrated, I couldn't create a single spark. That answered one question at least: it wasn't enough for me to be in the vicinity of someone when they used their Gift; to learn it - if that was even what I did. I tapped my mouth thoughtfully.

'Bob,' I whispered. 'Are you there?'

There was no answer. I slid out the letter opener and glanced around again to double check that I was on my own. It was just as well that I did because Aifric suddenly appeared from out of the trees,.

'Integrity! You ran off very quickly. We've got some food. Come back and join us. We don't often cook for ourselves, you know,' he added with a wink. 'You should enjoy the moment while you can.'

I smiled at him, smoothly returning the blade to my pocket. 'You're right. Highborn Sidhe doing the job of a servant? What is the world coming to?'

Aifric appeared very easy going for someone in his position. 'The others wanted to bring more people along to serve us,' he confided.

'You didn't want them?'

'The groves are sacred. The Foinse even more so.'

I licked my lips. 'It regulates all the magic, right?' He nodded. 'And the magic affects everyone in some way or another, whether they have Gifts or not.'

'That's true,' he agreed.

'Well then, don't keep the Foinse hidden away. It shouldn't be a matter of privilege. Everyone should be able to see it. It would solve your problem of these soul keys if that were the case.'

He looked speculatively. 'You're a lot like your father.'

I blinked. I wasn't expecting that. 'What do you mean?' I asked, carefully.

'He always thought that power should be spread more evenly. He advocated opening the magical barrier and letting the Clan-less come and go as they please. The other species who work for us receive a higher wage, thanks to his efforts.'

Apart from Lily's ramblings, this was the first time I'd heard someone say something positive about my father. 'What was he like?' I asked, suddenly desperate to know more.

'He was a good man,' Aifric said heavily. 'A very good man. Better than the rest of us put together – but what he did was wrong. It changed the course of history, and not in a good way. But his wife, your mother, died during childbirth and he just couldn't take it. He went mad.' Something dark crossed his eyes. 'Not like the Macquarries, you understand. Theirs was true insanity. No, something dark took hold of your father and wouldn't let go.'

'Like a demon?'

Aifric looked at me sympathetically. 'I've heard that story too but it wasn't that. It couldn't have been.' He shook himself. 'Such a waste,' he muttered.

I wasn't sure I wanted to hear any more. 'What about my mother?' I asked.

He smiled, although his eyes were tinged with melancholy. 'Everyone wanted your mother. She was truly beautiful, inside and out. There were a lot of happy men around the day she rejected the Bull. Of course, she only had eyes for your father.' He shrugged his shoulders. '*C'est la vie.*'

I twirled a strand of hair round my finger. I needed to tread carefully. 'I was in the library the other day. The Cruaich one, I mean. I couldn't find anything about the Adairs. Anywhere.'

Aifric took my hands. 'It was a difficult time in our history,' he said. 'We tried to keep it as quiet as we could. There are a lot of people in the Clans. We didn't want the Clan-less to realise we were vulnerable and we definitely didn't want anyone else getting ideas.'

'Ideas of genocide?' I was confused.

'Some things are better forgotten.' He squeezed my fingers. 'Anyway, will you come and eat?'

I was tempted to try and hold him back, to pry out more information. From the look on his face, however, I'd pushed him as far as I could for now. Nevertheless, I decided that it might be worth cultivating my relationship with Aifric Moncrieffe, no matter how his son felt.

I was passed a plate as soon as I sat down. My fingers brushed inadvertently against the Kincaid Chieftain's as I took it from him. I'd never seen anyone flinch so obviously.

I cocked my head. 'Do you think that you'll catch a disease by touching me?' I asked. 'Or are you afraid that I'll take offence that you touched me and murder you tonight in your sleep?'

His younger Clan companion joined him, expression blazing. 'Adair,' he snarled. 'You think you're important now. Once the Foinse is dealt with, you will crawl back to the dirty hole you came from. You're no one.'

Aifric threw an arm round his shoulders. 'Relax, Malcolm. We are all friends here.'

Malcolm Kincaid didn't look happy but he didn't throw off Aifric's arm either. He subsided in a series of grumbles before eventually going to the other side of the fire –as far away from me as possible.

Aware of Byron watching me, I picked up a hunk of crusty bread then said to no-one in particular, 'A man asked his friend, "Want to hear a joke about butter?" His friend was like, "Sure." The man thought about it then changed his mind. "Nah, I butter not tell you. You might spread it."'

They all stared at me. 'Not my best, I admit,' I said, then ignored them all and ate my dinner.

*

The next day, as we started to ride again, my muscles screamed with pain. I couldn't stop thinking about Darth Vader. He was evil. In fact, he was arguably one of the best science fiction villains ever created. When Taylor introduced me to *Star Wars* not long after I joined him, I was utterly terrified. But I was convinced that, while I might tread on the wrong side of the law and I was far from perfect, I wasn't evil. And, in the end, as well as the beginning (although I refused to dwell too much on those films), Darth Vader wasn't bad. He was also Luke Skywalker's father.

Darth Vader and my dad were not all that different. It'd be nice to think that my father didn't go in for the whole heavy breathing thing, though – that was just creepy.

'I'm Luke,' I said decisively to Lily, who was dreamily gazing up at the sky. 'I don't have a light saber – and I wouldn't want to use it even if I did have one –but I think I'm Luke.'

Barbie whinnied in agreement.

'Lookee, lookee,' Lily hummed.

'Of course,' I grumbled, 'people generally liked Luke. No-one bullied him. He was a hero.'

'Gale Adair was a hero,' Lily said.

I froze. 'Was he?' I asked carefully. 'Can you explain why?'

She gazed at me, her expression reflecting a clarity I'd not seen since we set off yesterday. 'He saved people,' she said. 'They say he didn't but he did. He was a good man.'

I stared at her. Unlike everyone else I'd seen so far, her aura was continually changing colour like a kaleidoscope. Right now, there were shimmers of blue not all that different to those I'd seen for Speck. It was frustrating that I had this key to people's souls and I still couldn't unlock it. 'What happened, Lily?'

'He was betrayed, Chieftain. Make sure the same thing doesn't happen to you.' Her aura changed again, settling into a cloudy white.

'Lily,' I hissed, 'this is important. How was he betrayed?'

She placed her finger to her lips. 'Shhh,' she said. 'There are ears. Ears of corn. Bunny ears. Big ears.' She winked.

I looked up and noticed that both the Kincaids and the Darrochs had twisted round in their saddles and were frowning at us. I clenched my fists - and my entire body tightened. Barbie, sensing the movement and misinterpreting it, abruptly sped up into a canter. She narrowly avoided Diana Darroch's huge bay gelding and made a beeline for Byron's black monster. I tried in vain to pull her up but I guess his swishing tail just looked too tempting to eat.

Byron's horse was unimpressed. He swung his round to take a bite out of Barbie.

'Hey! Leave my horse alone!' Okay, she started it but still, he was at least double her size.

'Then keep your pony under control,' Byron hissed.

Aifric smiled. 'Help her out, Byron.'

Byron muttered something under his breath and pulled back. 'You're still doing it all wrong,' he observed calmly, although the dark jade in his eyes suggested he was feeling something different.

'Frankly, it's a miracle I'm doing it at all.' I rubbed my aching arse for good measure. 'I don't understand why anyone bothers with all this horse malarkey.'

Byron pulled up his reins, bringing the stallion to a halt. Barbie, of course, kept going. I twisted my head. 'What are you doing?'

Byron's eyes were fixed on my bum. 'Curvy. You have some padding there.' He scratched his chin. 'It can't be that sore.'

I glared at him. 'Wanker.' Was he deliberately trying to get a rise out of me?

There was the faintest grin. He nudged his horse forward again and gestured at the horizon. 'Look at all that. Why wouldn't anyone want to do this?'

I followed his finger. We were surrounded by undulating hills, each one cloaked in a myriad of colours, greens and browns and even purples. I focused on one distant patch of wild thistles. Even from here, the colour mimicked the aura around Byron's head.

'Okay,' I conceded. 'It's pretty.'

He was watching me. 'It's more than pretty,' he said quietly.

I sucked in my breath. One minute he was all snarly and the next minute he was flirtatious. I didn't understand him at all.

'I'm sorry I was so touchy yesterday,' he continued. 'You have an uncanny knack for winding me up.'

I shrugged. 'Hey, I guess I have a gift after all.'

He still didn't look away. 'Whatever impression Tipsania might have given you, we're not romantically involved. We're just friends.'

I raised my eyebrows and thought of the necklace. 'Perhaps you should tell her that.'

'She knows.'

I wasn't so sure about that.

'I'm single, Integrity.' His eyes glittered. 'For now.'

There was a tight knot in the pit of my stomach. I cleared my throat and pointed at Barbie. 'Aren't you going to tell me what I'm doing wrong? It would be nice to be able to stand up when I get to the Foinse.'

For a moment he didn't answer. I was about to repeat my words when he finally said, 'Sure.'

Other than the mechanics of riding, he didn't say anything else for a very long time.

Chapter Twenty One

It was around eleven when the path we were following began to narrow. Although I was more comfortable astride Barbie after Byron's help, I could still feel tension across my neck and shoulders. Every time I turned round, either the Kincaids or the Darrochs were spitting silent venomous looks in my direction. Once the Foinse was fixed, I definitely wasn't going to stick around to find out whether they would make a move on me. It might be paranoia but they certainly appeared to hate me enough to want to get rid of me for good after I'd served my purpose.

Forced into single file, we meandered down the valley. With our goal getting ever closer, everyone dropped into a meditative silence. Even Lily ceased her humming. I supposed it made sense; this was a pilgrimage that no one had completed for years because of the difficulty in getting together at least four different people from four different Clans to make it. For once, I wasn't at a disadvantage; I didn't think anyone knew what to expect.

The path gradually changed from worn dusty grass to sharp stones. The horses were forced to slow down and pick their way down carefully. It seemed to suit Barbie; for once she wasn't at a disadvantage. As the sides of the valley grew narrower, however, I wondered if her wide girth would make it. I could feel claustrophobia setting in when the slopes at either side became so steep that the blue sky was nothing more than a strip above our heads.

We eventually emerged into a small circular clearing, deep within the hills. The cliffs were just as craggy and foreboding and the atmosphere remained oppressive. All the same, a wash of relief overtook me. It wouldn't be long now.

The others jumped lithely off their horses. I stayed where I was. I wasn't convinced that, even with Byron's helpful advice, I'd be able to walk without bowed legs. I was going to take my time.

'Look,' Diana Darroch said softly, pointing ahead. 'There it is.'

I frowned. 'It' was another gap in the landscape leading to another narrow passageway, almost identical to the one we'd just left. The only difference was that this one was even darker and even more of a tight squeeze. I eyed the gap then glanced at Barbie. There was no way she'd fit. Hell, I wasn't even sure if *I* would fit.

Malcolm strode forward, halting right in front of it. He placed his palm flat against the air. That was when I saw what had really grabbed the attention of the others. There was a ripple in the air, almost like heat rising - but this was Scotland in October. It might be a sunny day but it was still damned cold.

As I watched, he pushed his hand further in. It was as if he was pressing against a vast, invisible force. He shivered and quickly withdrew.

'We're here,' he announced. 'I can feel it.'

My skin prickled and when I glanced down, I saw goosebumps on my arms.

'We shall have to leave the horses here,' Aifric said.

'How far is it to the Foinse?' I asked. If it was going to be a long hike, I wasn't sure my aching muscles would make it without a hot bath and long massage first. I looked at Byron. Perhaps he could…

'I don't know,' Aifric replied. 'A few hours, I expect.'

'We should eat first,' Diana said. 'Then we can leave the rest of our supplies here.'

He pursed his lips. 'Good idea.'

Byron walked past me. He was whistling and carrying some wood which he must have collected from the campsite. He turned up and gave me an arch look. 'You're going to have to get off sometime,' he said. His mouth curled up in a smile. 'Barbie needs the rest. Would you like some help?'

I had a sudden vision of falling on top of him because I couldn't hold my own weight any more. He'd definitely be carrying some wood then, I'd straddle his chest. It would be similar to our position in the penthouse - except the ground was hard and there was an audience.

'It's fine,' I sniffed. 'I can manage.' I looked helplessly round and caught Lily's eye.

She beamed at me and danced over. Byron's smirk grew then he continued on his way.

'How are you, Chieftain?' she asked.

'I'm okay, Lily but I might need a bit of help getting down. I'm rather stiff.'

'I wouldn't worry about it too much,' Malcolm interrupted. 'I'm sure after the Foinse is opened, you won't feel any pain at all.'

Lily and I stared at him. I licked my lips. 'And why is that?'

He gave me a long look filled with cold amusement. 'It'll be so reinvigorating that'll you'll forget all about your aches.'

Or I'll be an unfeeling corpse, I thought. I'd received his message loud and clear. I glanced at Aifric who was murmuring to William, the Kincaid Chieftain. Would he step in? Would Byron?

'Give me your hand, Chieftain,' Lily said. 'I'll help you.'

I realised that her aura had changed again. It was a crisp green that reminded me of spring. 'Are you sure? I don't want to squash you.'

She flexed her muscles. 'I feel very strong.' She tapped her head. 'And the cobwebs have gone. It's good here.'

'It's the Foinse,' Diana said. 'It's affecting her.'

I heard Byron grunt. 'It's affecting me too. I can't light the fire.'

We turned to him, watching him flick his fingers. No matter what he did, nothing worked. He grinned ruefully. 'Does anyone have a lighter or some matches?'

Aifric grimaced. 'I was afraid of this.'

I watched them warily. 'Afraid of what?'

'We're too close to the Foinse. Its hold here is too strong. Our Gifts won't work.'

Diana's brow furrowed. 'How are we going to fix it then?'

'There will be a way,' Aifric said.

'How do you know?'

'Because there has to be,' he replied simply.

Tension uncoiled deep within me. How could this have happened? How could they be so poorly prepared that they'd not thought about this eventuality? It was beyond ridiculous.

I made an effort to get off Barbie and swung one leg round. Sharp needles of pain shot through my legs and I thought better of it.

'You should never walk into something without knowing what the possible outcomes are!' I said, throwing my hands up in the air even though it made me wobble dangerously and almost fall off the saddle. 'We might make the Foinse worse instead of better! I put my trust in you lot. I thought you knew what you were doing!'

'Shut that bitch up,' the Darroch Chieftain muttered.

In a flash, Byron was in front of her. 'Don't call her that. She didn't have to come here and help us.'

Actually, I kind of did, Byron. You forced me into it.

'Yeah,' sneered Malcolm, 'you don't want to annoy her. She might go nuts just like her father and murder us all.'

'That's enough!' Aifric roared. 'I understand tensions are running high but this is neither the time nor the place! We have far greater things to worry about. This young lady has endured two attempts on her life and yet she's still here. Do you remember when you found the adder in your bed, Dorienne? You didn't leave your lands for a year after that! She's here helping and she's braver than the lot of you.'

I felt flustered at the attention and unhappy that my outburst had caused a scene. All these Sidhe wankers - myself included - had a lot of pent-up frustration. Maybe I should recommend yoga?

'We'll go to the Foinse and see what the situation is,' Aifric continued. 'If we can't fix it without our Gifts, then at least we can try to understand what the problem is. If we need to go back to the Cruaich and re-group then that's what we do.'

I was alarmed. I didn't want to spend any longer among this lot than was necessary, even if a delay meant there was less likely to be another attempt to kill me. Besides, if I stuck around to find out what had really happened to my parents and the rest of the Adair Clan, I wanted it to be on my terms, not because I was forced to wait for someone to come up with a solution for the Foinse.

I looked at their faces. There was a lot of anger towards me, bitterness towards Aifric and resignation that our quest was already doomed. Taylor was a great believer in positive thinking when it came to heists. If we walked into a job thinking we were going to fail, then we would. What was needed around here was some optimism.

I drew in a breath. 'I'm sorry. I spoke out of turn. I am sure that our combined intellect can find a way to restore the Foinse. You guys are the best and brightest of your Clans. Of course we can do this.'

'Go Chieftain!' Lily yelled.

I winced at the sour expressions on the faces of the Kincaids and Darrochs. Yoga was out and a group hug was probably not a good idea, either. We needed something - however temporary - to band us together.

'Let's take a photo!' I burst out. 'All of us together. Then we'll have it for posterity.'

There were a few grumbles. 'Good idea,' Byron said briskly. 'Do you have a camera?'

Shite. I thought quickly. 'No, but I've got my phone.' I dug it out of my pocket. 'You lot get together and I'll take it.'

Lily shook her head solemnly. 'No, Chieftain. I will not travel any further from here, so I'll take the photo. The Saviours of the Foinse together!'

The others looked at Aifric. He smiled and nodded. 'Come on then.'

I slid down from Barbie, using Lily as a crutch to stop my knees from giving way. Then I handed her the camera. Aifric took centre stage and placed his arms round the shoulders of the Darroch and the Kincaid Chieftains. Their smiles were fixed and forced – but at least there were smiles.

Diana and Malcolm joined in. I stood awkwardly to the side until Byron beckoned me. He placed his arm round my waist and grinned. Malcolm leaned as far away from my body as possible. Subtlety was clearly not his thing.

'What did Cinderella say when she left the photo store?' I asked Malcolm. Byron's arm tightened. I tried to ignore the way he drew me closer and that his hand was holding me possessively.

'Everyone say cheese!' Lily said.

'Some day my prints will come,' I said, pasting on a huge smile. 'Cheese!'

We posed. Diana extricated herself from the group and grabbed the phone to examine the result. 'It's good,' she declared. 'We're beautiful people.'

Byron and I exchanged amused looks. I shrugged, banking down the desire to stay where I was. He still smelled far too good. I pulled away, gave the photo a cursory glance and tucked the phone back into my pocket.

'I'll make sure you all get copies,' I promised. 'Or we could set up a Foinse Facebook page. Every year we could meet back here and have a reunion.'

'Don't push your luck,' Malcolm muttered. Aifric shot him a warning look.

'Is there any food we can eat before we set off that doesn't require cooking?' he enquired.

Diana rummaged around in her bag. 'I've got fruit.'

'Perfect. Ten minutes, fill your stomachs and then we shall depart. Lily, you are content to stay behind and look after the horses?'

She nodded eagerly. The animals didn't look particularly thrilled. I leaned over and massaged my aching thighs, willing some life back into them. I had the feeling I was going to need it.

Chapter Twenty Two

The first up were the Kincaids. They conferred briefly and then Malcolm walked up to the shimmering barrier. Everyone else took several respectful steps backwards, including William. Just to be certain I couldn't be accused of listening out for his true name, I shuffled as far away as possible and stuck my fingers in my ears, but I still watched carefully. I wanted to see how this worked.

With his back to us, Malcolm leaned in. I could tell from his shoulders that his breath had quickened and he was feeling more nervous than he wanted us to know.

There was a sudden, blinding flash of light and a faint chiming ring. Something wriggled in my inside pocket. I gritted my teeth.

'I hadn't realised there would be light like that as well,' Diana said to Aifric.

I cursed inwardly. Thanks a lot, Bob. The genie continued to wiggle around as Malcolm turned round and looked at me suspiciously. I folded my arms to try and prevent Bob making a bid for freedom and smiled.

Malcolm sniffed. 'The Kincaid key has done its job,' he intoned, spreading his arms wide.

I rolled my eyes at the melodrama and, taking my place at the rear, followed the others in. I looked back at Lily. She beamed and waved at me. 'See you soon,' I called. Or so I hoped.

Bob took advantage of my momentary distraction and shoved his way upwards, appearing at my collar before hopping down my arm.

'I'm bored,' he mouthed.

I glared at him and tried to grab his tiny body. He danced away. 'Get lost!' I hissed.

William Kincaid, directly in front of me, turned and frowned. I tried to smile at him but it came out as a grimace. He turned back, fortunately without noticing Bob, who was stretching languidly.

I lunged for the genie and he leapt backwards.

Trying to convey the importance of the situation to him, I glowered and put my finger to my lips. He smirked and nodded, then lifted his hands to mimic a rolling camera. Eh?

He held up two fingers. Exasperated, I realised he was playing charades. I tilted my chin, pointedly ignoring his antics. When he finally worked out I wasn't going to play, he tutted loudly, making Kincaid turn round again. I took advantage of the moment, seized Bob's squirming body, then thrust him behind my back.

'Sorry,' I apologised. 'I almost slipped.'

'Don't you dare fall into me,' he hissed.

I started to nod, just as there was a painful nip on my index finger. I let out a cry. This time everyone turned round.

'Is everything alright?' Aifric called out from the front.

'Fine! Fine! I was just making sure you were all

paying attention!'

I received a few scowls. Oops.

Once they were facing ahead again, I pulled Bob out. The little bastard had bitten me. I mimed pulling his head off and he pouted. He pointed to my ear and gave me a pleading puppy-dog expression. Sighing, I lifted him up. He perched between my ear and my skull and I pushed my hair forward to cover him. That was when his incessant chatter began.

'I've been paying close attention, Uh Integrity. These guys are very dull and most of them really don't like you.'

Tell me something I don't know, I thought, concentrating on not tripping on the sharp scree as the path grew steeper and more precarious.

'The only who thinks you're alright is that Byron fellow. The one you want to cover in whipped cream and eat for dessert. The Diana woman is starting to soften too. Everyone else hates you. Even the fat pony.'

Unable to answer him without drawing attention to myself, I grimaced.

'It's kind of cool that I can come here though. I thought I'd be blocked, but because I'm a supremely magical being I'm clearly allowed to enter.'

Either that or, by using his key, Malcolm had opened up the path for anyone who followed. It was a shame that Lily had stayed behind, if only because she would have proved to Bob that he wasn't as unique as he liked to think.

'You should make a wish now,' Bob whispered. 'To test the magic. If my magic works here, I'm obviously far more powerful than any Sidhe. And you need to know if my wishes still work for when they all try to kill you and you can't teleport yourself away.'

Crapadoodle. He had a point - although they'd find it a damn sight harder to do me in without their Gifts. As long as I kept my wits about me, I'd be fine. Anyway, I had a back-up plan; I *always* had a back up plan.

Several stones skittered down, knocked loose by our feet. I could hear William Kincaid breathing heavily as he braced himself against the sharp mountain walls. I reached out to steady him but he flinched away. His choice.

Although technically we were still outdoors and the sky remained visible, the angle of the slopes on either side of us meant that we were almost completely shrouded in darkness. Only a chink of light allowed us to see where we were treading. The passageway grew narrower until we were forced to sidestep down it.

'Your ancestors really made it hard to get to this Foinse thing, didn't they?' Bob commented. 'They didn't trust anyone.'

I considered this. Bob was right; trust appeared to be the one thing that was seriously in short supply where the Sidhe were concerned. The Clans, who'd put the Foinse here and made it so that no one person could reach it without the support of others, hadn't trusted anyone. And the Moncrieffes didn't trust anyone enough to tell them they were essentially penniless. And they all seemed to distrust me.

My foot slipped, sending a tiny avalanche rumbling down.

'Be careful!' Aifric snapped from the front. The stress was obviously getting to him.

'Can you do something more interesting, Uh Integrity? I've been cooped up for days. Go and trip that dude in front of you. He doesn't like you anyway and the Kincaids have already done their part. You don't need him any more.'

I resisted the urge to strangle Bob. Anything to shut him up, though. Spying an expensive watch round William Kincaid's wrist, a fit of mischief took me. He was so focused on not falling that he'd never notice. It was time I lived up to his lack of trust.

Counting my breaths so I timed it perfectly, I let my foot slip again. This time, however, I cried out sharply and fell against William. My right hand grabbed his wrist, ostensibly to stop me crashing into him and making us all topple like a line of dominoes.

William grunted back and tried to pull away but I looked at him desperately. With more scree sliding around our feet, he also lost his balance and was forced to grab me. By this point, I'd loosened the watch enough for my purposes. Expensive ones like these, with leather buckles, were always the easiest. Keeping my finger in the right spot to avoid the prong from slipping back in, the buckle detached completely and I palmed the watch.

'I'm so sorry,' I said again.

'Aifric said to be more careful!' Kincaid snapped.

I hung my head apologetically. As soon as he'd righted himself and was following the others down, I passed the watch back to Bob.

'Uh Integrity,' he whispered in my ear. 'You are a goddess.'

I smiled and took out the letter opener, gesturing to it and hoping he'd do as I asked.

'Very well,' he said. 'But only so I can examine this beauty in more detail.'

I shook my head and pointed ahead. I needed him to wait until the next key was used. A flash of light here would be impossible to hide.

Sensing rather than seeing him nod, I flicked my hair out to cover both the watch and him. There was a sliver of light ahead. At least we were almost at the next lock.

'We've made it to the cavern,' I heard Dorienne Darroch say.

'Thank fuck,' Kincaid muttered.

One by one we squeezed out. The relief of getting back to a more open space was overwhelming. I gulped in air and looked around. The light was deceptive. Rather than natural light filtering in from above, it was an eerie glow reflecting from thousands of green lights in the roof of the cavern to the dark pools below.

'Glow worms,' Bob hissed in my ear. 'Nasty unfriendly creatures.'

Diana gasped. 'Is it magic?'

'Glow worms,' I said knowledgeably. 'Lovely little things.'

She sent me an approving glance. Perhaps Bob was right and she was feeling less antagonistic. The genie, however, was unimpressed at my showing off and flicked my ear lobe. I jumped half a foot in the air.

'I'm still a bit stiff from all that horse riding,' I explained when the others looked at me, puzzled.

'You or me, boy?' Aifric said, addressing Byron.

Byron gestured ahead. 'Please.'

Aifric gave a tiny smile and stepped up. Just as before, we stood back to give him privacy. I put my hand on the letter opener to remind Bob to make tracks – but this time he timed it rather badly. The flash of light came about three seconds after Aifric whispered his true name.

Aifric looked round, a strange expression on his face. 'All I've done for months is research this journey. There was nothing about light flashes when the keys were used.'

I tried to look stupid. It must have worked because his gaze slid over me to his older companions. Neither Dorienne Darroch nor William Kincaid had a clue, of course.

Aifric shrugged. 'Let's hope there's nothing more up ahead that I don't know about it,' he said.

'Fixing the Foinse is going to be hard enough.' With that, he straightened his back and plunged in, the strange light from the glow worms throwing dappled shadows across his body.

Byron raised his eyebrows at me, as if to check I was okay. I flicked back my hair and threw him a kiss. His emerald eyes glinted then he turned and joined his father. The two Darrochs followed then Malcolm Kincaid plunged in. William, however, hung back.

'Don't get any ideas about the Steward's son,' he hissed. 'You won't be around long enough to see them come to fruition. In any event, he's spoken for.' The spite in his voice was unmissable. For good measure, I blew him a kiss too. He snorted loudly and strolled into the cavern.

I watched him go. If anyone was going to make a move against me when this was over, Chieftain Kincaid seemed to be the most likely. Vowing to keep a close eye on him I followed him. I hoped that whatever he was planning he'd do it quickly. I wasn't sure I could take much more waiting around for the stab in my back.

The cavern was rather pretty. The green light cast by the worms should have created a horror film effect; instead, the place was soft and welcoming. I sidled between the stalagmites (or was it stalactites? I could never remember) and enjoyed not being squashed between walls of stone. It was like walking through a grand cathedral; I wouldn't have been surprised if organ music suddenly bellowed up ahead.

With more space to manoeuvre, the others abandoned single file. Their heads bobbed as they conferred: Byron and Aifric, William and Michael, Diana and Dorienne. I tagged along at the back, taking in the scenery. Even without the hushed voices of the Sidhe, the cavern wasn't silent. There were splashes of water falling from the smooth, rounded ceiling. There was also a strange but not unpleasant whine that whistled past my ears. When the others stopped moving and I realised where the sound was coming from, my stomach dropped.

'Shite,' I whispered.

There was a rope bridge stretching from the edge of the cavern across an abyss. I couldn't see the bottom but I bet it was a long way down. Picking up a loose stone, I threw it over the edge. It was a good ten seconds before it struck something. For the first time since this journey started, I was glad that Brochan, Lexie and Speck weren't here with me. Speck would have a heart attack.

'That rope must have been here for decades,' Diana said in a low, worried voice. 'How can we be sure it's safe?'

I waved my hand. 'I'm good with heights,' I chirped. 'Once the Darrochs have opened the way, I'll go first.'

'The hell you will.'

I glanced at the source of the growl. Byron. Why was I not surprised? 'We need you for the final section,' he said, his face dark. 'The rest of us can afford to slip and fall. You can't. Someone will have to go first to make sure it's safe.'

Out of the corner of my eye I spotted Malcolm Kincaid looking disgusted.

'I'm lighter than the rest of you.'

'No.'

Looking at his son curiously, Aifric spoke up. 'I'm sure it's safe. I'll go first. But make sure no more than one person is on the bridge at any one time. Dorienne, will you do the honours?'

The older of the two Darroch women bit her lip and nodded. By now I was finding the whole true name thing rather dull. I dutifully stepped away and covered my ears. She did her thing, leaving everyone puzzled when no flash of light followed.

'Is that a good sign or a bad sign?' she asked, her eyes wide.

Nobody answered. I would have patted her on the back reassuringly but I was tired of everyone flinching away from me so I simply shrugged and smiled.

Aifric's first few steps were slow and shaky. He gripped the ropes as he shuffled along. It wasn't until he was about halfway along that the group's breathing returned to normal. So much for the Foinse being the only difficult part of this journey.

Encouraged by Byron, I went next. I wasn't a complete fool. I tested my weight first, gingerly taking the first section. When I was sure the rope was secure, however, it was very satisfying to skip across in a fraction of the time that it had taken

Aifric.

When I reached the other side, he smiled. 'You really do have a head for heights.'

I grinned back. False modesty wasn't my thing. 'Yeah,' I agreed, 'I do.'

The others followed one by one. Despite his muscle, Byron was pretty fast. From his quickened breathing when he came off, though, he'd found it harder than he was letting on.

'Are you alright?' I inquired solicitously.

'Oh, I'm perfect,' he replied, straightening up. His eyes glinted as if he dared me to disagree.

'Of course you are,' I said quietly.

The Darrochs were both slow but steady. Malcolm Kincaid crossed with so much sweat streaming off his forehead and into his eyes that I was amazed he could see anything; his father struggled even more. His skin turned white as he inched his way, the ropes swinging dramatically on several occasions as he struggled to keep his balance. When he finally arrived, he threw me a nasty look even though my expression was bland.

'You want to say something, Adair?'

'It's Taylor,' I reminded him. 'My name is Integrity Taylor.'

He flexed his fingers. Considering how tightly he'd grabbed the rope, they had to be stiff and sore. 'Yes,' he sneered. 'I'd be ashamed of my Clan if it were yours.'

I didn't deign to reply and turned my back. 'I guess I'm up next,' I said lightly. 'Let's go.'

After the rope bridge, the ground was fairly even. There was enough space to walk comfortably and even the scree underfoot was less of an issue. All the same, my stomach was twisting in nerves. Whether it was because I was worried about the Foinse or because I was about to acknowledge the importance of my true name - and therefore my Sidhe heritage - by passing the final hurdle, I wasn't entirely sure. At least the tunnel we were moving along was getting darker so the others couldn't see my tension.

The first indication I had that we were getting close was when we rounded a corner and I felt a breeze on my face. My eyes might have fully adjusted to the gloom but I still couldn't make out anything that might be Foinse-shaped. I imagined that the Foinse would be like a small fountain with streams of multi-coloured magic bubbling up instead of water. Unfortunately, everything ahead was a dark black well .

I sniffed the air. For a long time, in fact since we'd entered the cavern, it had been growing gradually staler but now there was something different about it. It was almost fresh. I picked up my pace. We were almost there; I could feel it.

When we turned another corner, the Foinse was there. It was a huge chest bathed in light, although goodness knows where the light was coming from.

Diana, who was close behind me, gasped. With the chest perched on a stone pedestal and the light cascading from above, it was like entering an ancient temple to pay homage to a god.

I felt the final barrier before I saw it. When I was less than ten feet away from the chest, I could no longer press forward; there was an invisible force field around it. It was clear, though, where the light was coming from. Hundreds of metres above us there was a round hole. If I squinted, I could make out a dash of blue.

'We're in the centre of the mountain,' Malcolm said, awestruck.

Byron drew a breath. 'It's your turn, Integrity.'

I nodded, glancing at the others to make sure they were going to give me the same privacy that they'd been given. There was a calculating expression in William Kincaid's eyes but Aifric gripped his elbow and pulled him back. Giving them a tight smile, I turned my attention to the last lock. I pressed my palms against the barrier and marvelled at the magical craftsmanship that must have gone into making it.

I squeezed my eyes shut and breathed my name. 'Layoch.'

The sensation of the barrier shattering was extraordinary. I felt a wash of power surge through me. Basking in its glow, I smiled. For the first time, I felt what it was to be Adair. I revelled in the moment - until Malcolm pushed past me, making a beeline for the chest.

He grabbed the corners and lifted. Nothing happened. I watched his shoulders strain and heard him grunt but the chest didn't budge. Byron joined him, as did Diana. The three of them heaved but it still refused to open. Aifric, Dorienne and William joined them, all six of them scrabbling and straining. I folded my arms and kept back. There was no visible lock on the front, other than a simple iron latch. Sheer muscle was going to be a waste of time. There was a lightly coloured panel of wood on the left-hand side that told me everything I needed to know.

'Aren't you going to help us?' William Kincaid spat.

I arched an eyebrow. 'If six of you can't open it, one more person isn't going to make any difference.'

Aifric stepped away, his shoulders sagging. 'She's right. There has to be another way. We must have missed something.'

Diana joined him and pursed her lips. One by one they moved back until only Malcolm remained there, huffing and puffing. 'It has to open!'

'It's not going to. We'll have to take it with us and find a way to pry it open back at the Cruaich,' Aifric said decisively.

'It's massive! How will we carry it?'

'We'll just have to manage.'

The six of them took up their positions and attempted to lift the chest off the dais. It didn't budge.

'It's stuck fast,' Byron grunted. 'This isn't the way.'

Aifric cursed. 'There must be another key. It shouldn't be this hard.'

William Kincaid kicked it. 'Blasted thing!'

I smirked, wondering how long this would go on for. Really, they were lucky they had me with them. For now, I amused myself by watching their wasted efforts.

It was Byron who noticed first. He glanced over and clocked the expression on my face. He abandoned the chest and marched over. 'There aren't any records of a container like this. It's obviously not ancient like the Foinse is.' He eyed me. 'You know what to do to open it.' It wasn't a question.

I smiled. 'I'm a thief, Byron. I do this for a living.'

Both irritation and amusement flitted across his face. 'Go on then.' He cleared his throat. 'The rest of you need to get back. Give Integrity some room.'

Malcolm snorted. 'She won't be able to open it if we can't.'

Aifric looked at me. 'Step back,' he ordered. He gestured at me. 'On you go.'

I rubbed my palms together. Malcolm and William rolled their eyes but Diana simply looked curious. 'You're going to have to give me some room,' I said. 'I need the light and you're blocking it.'

I walked round the chest, examining it from every angle. Although it looked heavy and cumbersome, the craftsmanship was superb. It was designed to appear deceptively simple. The reality was anything but. I couldn't help feeling a tinge of admiration for our long-deceased Sidhe ancestors who'd placed it here. They didn't just want the four strongest Clans to prove they could work together to reach it. They wanted them to prove themselves worthy of it too. They'd obviously decided there was no point in throwing open the source of the country's magic to a bunch of people who didn't even have the smarts to open a box.

I ignored the latch at the front and focussed on the left-hand side. I'd noticed earlier that it had a band of faintly discoloured wood.

'She's got no damn clue,' William hissed.

'Shh!' Byron admonished.

I hunkered down and carefully ran my fingers across the front. There was a knot at one end, which was out of keeping with the rest of the chest. Pressing into it with my thumb, I kept my body out of the way. A heartbeat later, a long drawer sprang open and brushed against my midriff. The others' astonishment was audible. Both Kincaids rushed forward but I frowned, forcing them to falter.

I sidestepped, tapping the back of the chest and listening. Then I nodded and went to the right-hand side. The panels of wood here were more evenly coloured. Closing my eyes and using my fingertips, I located the second hidden latch within seconds. As soon as I pushed it, another drawer opened.

'Chinese boxes,' Aifric said. 'Find the hidden latches and open them in the correct order or don't open the chest at all. Cunning bastards.'

The third panel was at the front, concealed beneath the large rusty latch that Malcolm had been tugging at. My fingers only had to brush against this one and I heard a click. I smiled and returned to the back of the chest and another drawer slid open easily. This one was both wider and deeper and when I pulled it all the way out and peered inside the gap into the centre of the chest, I knew I'd hit the jackpot.

I rested on my heels and gazed up at the others. Even in this dim light, their auras were still clear. Byron's was a rich purple, Aifric's was a sharp scarlet. I could see flickers of the same red colour in both Dorienne and William's auras, although they weren't so pronounced, and I wondered if red was a chieftain thing. When I spotted it flickering against Malcom's grey aura too, however, I wasn't so sure.

I looked at the Foinse. It had an aura as well, as if it were as alive like us. The Foinse, which wasn't like a fountain at all and was actually more of a sparkly orb, had a sickly yellow aura that wasn't far off the colour of bile. It was definitely sick; even I could work that one out.

'What is it?' William Kincaid demanded. 'What can you see?'

I reached inside. It was warm to the touch and, when I cupped my hands round it, I felt a flicker of soothing energy. I pulled back and stood up, displaying it to the others. Then I grinned.

'Take that, bitches.'

Chapter Twenty Three

There was considerable debate about what to do next. Most of the discussion took place between the three Chieftains, William, Dorienne and Aifric, with Malcolm occasionally interjecting his opinion. The rest of us stood back.

'We don't have the means to solve the problem here,' Aifric said. 'We should take the Foinse back to the Cruaich and deal with it there.'

'If it goes back to the Cruaich,' Dorienne pointed out, 'then by default the Moncrieffes end up with the ownership of it. We cannot allow that to happen.'

'My dear, the Cruaich belongs to us all. It's not as if I'm scurrying away with it to the Moncrieffe Clan lands. You'll know where it is.'

'That's all very well, Steward, but the Cruaich is hardly close to Kincaid lands. We have a lot of skilled people in our Clan who will be well placed to heal it.'

'I'm not giving that kind of power to the Kincaids!'

The argument went round and round in circles. I eyed the Foinse that was now being cradled by Aifric. If I looked closely, I could swear that its sickly aura now had a slightly different tinge.

'How long has the Foinse been held here ?' I asked Byron in an undertone.

He shrugged, his expression displeased as he watched the to-ing and fro-ing between the Clan heads. 'A thousand years, give or take.'

I considered the chest. It was an old piece but I'd estimate it was no more than two hundred years old. The aura around the Foinse suggested that it was a living being. And, speaking for myself as another living being, I didn't think I'd do particularly well trapped inside a box. I'd probably get sick after two centuries of darkness too.

I craned my neck upwards at the shaft of light. It was less strong now, indicating that the end of the day was approaching. I wondered whether the position of the box beneath the light had been deliberate. Unless you were a stoor worm used to the dark depths of the ocean, chances were you'd need sunlight.

I glanced at Byron. With his head in the beam of light, his bronzed locks were burnished and gleaming.

'Do me a favour,' I said, 'and bring the Foinse over here. Your father's more likely to hand it to you than me.' And Kincaid and Darroch would be less likely to complain about Byron taking it as well.

'What are you thinking?' he asked.

'I just want to try something out,' I prevaricated.

With a shake of his head, Byron did as I asked. Aifric appeared reluctant to let it go, as I'd surmised but he was hardly going to say no to his son and heir.

'I'd thought it was going to be bigger,' Diana said, as Byron brought it back over. 'It's still pretty, though.'

'It's warm,' he said, surprised. 'And I can feel it almost ... pulsating.'

'Can you hold it up to the light?' I asked.

His brow furrowed but he stepped over and allowed the sunlight to filter down. Not only did the Foinse seem to glow more strongly, but its aura began to change. It still didn't look healthy but I could definitely see an improvement.

'Can I hold it?' Diana asked eagerly.

Byron shrugged. 'Sure.' He passed it over.

She hefted in her hands. 'Just think,' she whispered, 'this tiny thing is responsible for all of us. For all of our gifts and all of our magic.'

'The best things come in small packages,' I agreed. I held up my palms. 'May I?'

She handed it to me, taking great care not to drop it. I smiled as I might at a gurgling baby. Aware that the three Chieftains had interrupted their conversation to watch me, I made sure I didn't appear overly possessive. 'Have you ever read Harry Potter?' I asked casually.

Malcolm's lip curled but Diana nodded. 'You know Quidditch?' I said. 'What's the name of the flying ball that they try to capture to win the game?'

She smiled suddenly. 'You're right! It's exactly like that! The snitch. That's what it reminds me of. If it had wings, it would be a perfect match.'

'Mm.' I let my fingers brush against the Foinse's

warmth for another second. Then I threw it up into the air directly into the sunbeam.

They all gasped in horror. Byron lunged for it while Aifric and William sprang forward. Dorienne appeared to be frozen in place.

'You idiot!' Malcolm screeched. 'What have you done?' He flung himself at me, slamming me down to the ground. Despite the painful crack of my spine on the stone, I kept my eyes on the Foinse.

They say that what goes up must come down – but the Foinse definitely wasn't coming back down. In fact, it was gathering speed, rising up and up and up. As Malcolm drew back his fist and punched my face, I saw the Foinse reach the hole in the top of the mountain, wink once against the failing sunlight and disappear. Then my nose exploded in pain.

I felt Malcolm's weight being dragged off me and the smack of more flesh on flesh. Blinking away tears, I struggled to my elbows, just as William Kincaid grabbed me and yanked to my feet.

'You've doomed us all!' he shouted. I got a strong whiff of garlic from last night's stew. 'You're just like your father after all!'

I pulled back. Malcolm's nose was streaming with blood, much like my own. Byron had his hand on Malcolm's shirt as if he were afraid he was going to hit me again. Saved by Golden Boy. I supposed I should be thankful. I wiped away the blood with my sleeve and gazed at the angry faces. Aifric, in particular, appeared to be incandescent with rage.

'It's the source of all the magic,' I said quietly.

'It doesn't need to be rescued by us. It can fix itself. When we get far enough away and the Kincaids can use their precognition again, they'll be able to tell us that everything's going to be fine. The Foinse's free and so is the magic. No single Clan has to be in charge of it. You don't need to worry about putting more safeguards in place to stop someone misusing it. All your problems are solved.'

My calm explanation didn't appear to dampen the group's ire. Only Byron looked at me speculatively. Everyone else wanted to murder me. That wasn't much different to an hour ago; now they were just more open about it.

'Don't you know what we could have done with the Foinse? The good we might have achieved?'

Considering that none of us could use our gifts in its vicinity, the only 'good' it could have achieved would be for one Clan to hold it to ransom over the others. I wisely kept my thoughts to myself.

'I want to go back to the Cruaich now,' I said carefully, reaching down into myself. Unfortunately, even with the Foinse no longer close by, my teleportation still wasn't working. Shite.

'If we get back,' William spat, 'and the magic is still failing, I'm going to string you up by your nipples.'

I winced. That sounded painful. 'Aw, and I thought you were my breast friend, Willie.'

Aifric exhaled. 'She might be right, you know,' he said, his anger disappearing as quickly as it had arrived. 'She might have saved the magic for everyone.' He clapped his hands once. 'We won't know until we get far enough away from wherever the Foinse is now. We need to move quickly so we can recapture it if need be.'

The fact that the benevolent Steward used the word 'recapturing' as if the Foinse was a Sidhe prisoner spoke volumes to me.

'Then let's go,' William snapped. He jabbed me with his finger. 'You stay in front of me. I want to know where you are and what you're doing at all times.'

I swept a curtsey. 'Of course, Chieftain,' I said mockingly.

'There's no need for that,' Byron interrupted. For a moment I thought he was scolding me but I realised he was addressing William. 'She can be trusted.'

'She's given us no evidence of that yet,' he ground out.

I put my hand on Byron's arm. 'It's fine.' I needed to get away from here as quickly as possible so I could teleport myself to safety. If that meant having William Kincaid at my back then that's what I would do.

Aifric strode off, his pace brisk. He held his head high but I noted that his fists were still clenched tightly. No matter what he'd said, he was struggling to give me the benefit of the doubt. Without further ado, everyone fell into line, William bringing up the rear with me directly in front of him.

Byron was touchingly worried about what was happening and kept swinging his head back to check on me. Every time he did, I gave him a wide smile. I had few doubts that I'd done the right thing with the Foinse. What happened from here on in, however, was anyone's guess.

We marched back to the bridge. Silence reigned, which suited me perfectly. I was aware of William Kincaid's every breath and footfall. I wanted to know what he was going to do before he did it. I reckoned it was pretty obvious where the attack would come. They'd have to be pretty nimble, though. Even if the Kincaids teamed up with the Darrochs, when it came to heights I was better than the lot of them.

At some point Aifric and Byron swapped places so, by the time we reached the rope bridge, there was an interesting shift in order. I hung back as Byron crossed, then Dorienne and Diana, followed by Malcolm and Aifric. I could hear my heart thumping in my chest. Before William changed his mind about staying at my back, I leapt in front of him and virtually sprinted across, keeping every sense alert.

When I landed on solid ground, I was almost disappointed. Perhaps they'd realised that trying to take me out here would be a waste of time and would reveal their intentions. I gritted my teeth as William began his wobble across the bridge. Now I'd have to be on my guard more than ever.

'The Cruaich,' I whispered, earning a strange look from Aifric. I remained where I was but didn't feel the slightest tug on my body. The teleportation still wasn't working. These Gifts were sodding useless.

In a reverie as I tried to guess where the next danger spot would be, I almost missed it when William's foot slipped. A second later he cried out, his hands frantically snatching at the ropes on either side of the bridge to stop himself from falling. Dorienne shrieked in alarm. William threw one leg up, hooking it over the bottom rope, while his hands clung onto to the two higher ones. He was sweating, though, and with moist palms, he couldn't hold on for long if he didn't haul himself upright. The precarious bridge was swinging dramatically from side to side. My eyes snapped to the muscles straining in William's arms. Crapadoodle. He wasn't going to make it.

I didn't think. Instead I shot back along the rope bridge towards him, using my own body weight to counter the swing and give him more stability.

'Hold on!' I yelled, lunging for his hand.

I was too late. His fingers had already slipped into the air and he was hanging down, head first, with only one leg stopping him from falling into the chasm below. If I'd had any doubt whether this was a staged accident, his look of white-faced terror laid that thought to rest.

'Integrity!' Byron shouted, as I jumped over William's leg to twist myself back and grab him from a better angle.

'Don't! Don't come on here! Three people will be too many. I've got this! Just trust me.'

Using my elbow as an anchor, I swung into the air. William's arms were flailing around. I tried to snatch his hand but he was panicking too much.

'Calm down,' I hissed. 'Stop jerking around and I will catch you.'

'I'm going to die,' he muttered. 'I'm going to die! I'm going to die!'

'You are *not* going to die.' I gave another swing and slapped him hard across his cheek.

He stared at me in shock. 'Stay calm,' I repeated. 'If you get hysterical, this is going to take much longer. I will pull you up.' I looked him in the eyes. 'William, I will get you. Got that?'

He nodded mutely and relief rushed through me. 'Can you lift your arms up? I need to get your wrists. If I grab your hands, they'll be too sweaty and you'll slip. Understand?'

He nodded again and stretched upwards. Shite. I still wasn't close enough.

'My leg,' he whispered. 'It's not going to make it.'

I looked up. He was right. He was hanging on now by his ankle. Cursing to myself, I pulled up and looped the less taut section of rope round my right ankle. It would give me the length I required but it wouldn't hold for long. I had to do this quickly.

Ignoring the shouts from the others, I swung

down once more. With a burst of adrenalin, I stretched out my arms and curled my hands round William's wrists. He gasped in relief.

'You know you really reek of garlic,' I told him. 'Remember that when you want to give me a grateful kiss later on.'

He managed a shaky smile but, feeling tremors ripping through his flesh, I wasted no more time. 'We're going to swing back upwards, William. On a count of three, you'll go right, I'll go left and then we'll meet in the middle. Got that?'

He gulped for air. 'Yes.'

'When we're close enough, be prepared for me to release your left wrist. Then I'll grab the rope and get both of us back up.'

'Don't drop me.'

'I won't. I told you, I've got this. Ready? One, two, three!'

I pushed upwards. William's frame wasn't exactly slight and his fear made it hard for him to find the energy to gain sufficient momentum. From somewhere deep within himself, however, he managed. With my hands half a metre away, I dropped his wrist and swung harder, only just managing to snatch hold of the rope and heave William's body up.

I freed my foot from the loop and got back to my feet, yanking him to me as I did so. The moment his feet touched the rope, he almost collapsed in relief. I was forced to steady him again before he fell once more.

The yells of relief overtook us. William began to turn, lifting one hand from the rope in acknowledgment of his close call. As he did so, and as his body blocked my view of the other side, someone else stepped out onto the bridge.

'No!' I yelled in alarm.

The weight of a third person made the bridge swing once more, this time with even more force. The rope jerked to one side and William lost his footing again. I lunged for him. I'd have caught him if the other person on the bridge hadn't pulled back in alarm, and leapt off the bridge to safety. That movement caused the rope to switch directions so I was flung off balance too. Instead of William's hand, all I grasped at was air.

In terrible slow motion, his eyes bulged and he reached towards me. His mouth opened to scream but nothing came out. A second later he was swallowed up by the darkness. Malcolm Kincaid shrieked his name but it was far, far too late.

The inevitable thump as he reached the ground made me double over, as if I'd been kicked in the stomach. Retching, and with hot tears streaming from my eyes, I stumbled blindly back across the bridge. The horror etched on the faces confronting me mirrored my own.

'I didn't realise,' Aifric mumbled. 'I thought I could help.'

I stared at him. He'd been the one to step out on the bridge then. Anguish lined his face. Ripping away my gaze, I looked at Malcolm. He was kneeling on the ground, tearless sobs racking his body.

Byron put a hand on his Malcolm's shoulder and he stumbled to his feet. He lifted up his head and addressed me. 'You killed him,' he said in a clear voice. 'You killed my uncle. You killed my Chieftain.'

'She didn't,' Byron said. 'It wasn't her fault.'

I put my hand up, forestalling him. Grief was never a rational thing and this wasn't the time for recriminations. Still feeling sick, all I said was, 'Let's get out. Now.'

Chapter Twenty Four

We stumbled back out into the stone clearing where Lily greeted us with a faltering smile. She looked from one of us to the other, her eyes eventually landing on me and staying there.

'What happened, Chieftain?' she asked. 'Your nose is purple.'

I rubbed my forehead. 'Integrity,' I said tiredly. 'Call me Integrity. And my nose will be fine.' I could hardly complain about it given what else had occurred.

Lily glanced at the rest of the group. 'Where's Chieftain Kincaid?'

'He's gone.'

She absorbed this information then bobbed her head. 'He was a bastard anyway,' she said succinctly.

I glanced at Malcolm. His features were wan and drawn. 'It doesn't mean he deserved to die.'

Lily touched me gently on the arm and turned away.

Aifric frowned. 'Malcolm's in no fit state to do anything. We need to get him away from here as quickly as possible.' He threw me a hard look. 'We still need to find out what's happened to the Foinse and the magic.'

'If their gifts were precognition, how come they couldn't foresee what was going to happen?' I said, as much to myself as anyone else.

'Some futures don't reveal themselves,' Byron told me quietly. 'And William's reluctance to cross the bridge the first time around…' His voice trailed off.

I nodded. Maybe he had foreknowledge that he'd kept to himself.

'We're going to need to get Malcolm back to the Cruaich as soon as possible. But we have to untack William's horse and clear up here.'

I saw an opening. 'I'll sort out the stuff here and follow you.'

Byron looked troubled. 'I'm not convinced that's a good idea. Someone is probably still trying to kill you.'

I laughed and waved at the steep mountainsides surrounding us. 'I'll see them coming before they see me. Anyway it's probably be better if I'm not around Malcolm.'

His eyes searched my face; there was something unfathomable lurking in their depths. 'You won't catch us up on Barbie.'

I checked on my horse. She was edging towards Byron's black stallion again with a look of determination. 'Don't underestimate her,' I said. 'But if I can't get to you along the way, I'll find you back at the Cruaich.' I half turned to go but he grabbed my arm and pulled me closer.

'Are you okay?' he asked.

I bit my lip and nodded.

'I mean it, Integrity. That would have been a traumatic experience for anyone. There wasn't anything you could do.'

I jerked my head at Malcolm. 'Tell him that.'

Byron sighed and ran a hand through his hair. 'You won't run off, will you?'

'No.' I wasn't going to run anywhere. I was going to teleport.

He released me reluctantly and went to speak to his father. Aifric glanced at me and nodded. 'Good idea,' he said briskly. He dug into his bag and pulled out a bottle of water and some jerky. 'Take this. With any luck, you'll catch us up along the way. As soon as Malcolm is up to it, we'll check on the Foinse.'

'Thank you.'

Aifric's bright blue eyes met mine. 'If I hadn't walked out onto the bridge, he'd still be here.'

I looked away. 'We could spend our lives wondering "what if?". What's done is done. Look after Malcolm. He'll be alright but he'll need some time.'

Aifric straightened his shoulders. 'Yes.'

I gazed up at the sky. Dusk was falling. Other than a few wispy clouds and the faint outline of the moon, there was nothing to be seen. 'The Foinse will be fine, too. You'll see.'

Aifric's mouth twisted. 'We will.'

I hung back, watching as Byron helped Malcolm onto his horse and the diminished group trotted back off through the narrow path. Lily stayed with me, refusing to join them.

'You should go,' I told her. 'I'm not safe to be

around.'

'I can think here. Everything's clearer.'

Perhaps the Foinse hadn't spun off as far as we'd imagined. Its magic was still affecting Lily and there was no sign that anyone's gifts had returned. 'You can't stay here forever, you know.'

She smiled enigmatically in response. 'Tell me a joke,' she said.

My chest tightened. 'I'm not sure this is the time.'

Barbie snickered and Lily reached out. 'Please?'

I stared after the departing Sidhe and thought of my role in William Kincaid's death. 'I'm sorry and I apologise mean the same thing,' I finally said. 'Except at a funeral.'

Lily swung her hair. 'That's not really funny.'

'No,' I agreed sadly. 'It's not.'

Working together silently, we untacked William's horse. Lily unclipped a rope on his bridle and connected it to Barbie on one side and her white mare on the other. She patted her horse's mane. 'I really would have liked those bells.' She shook herself.

I scooped up the last of the rubbish and glanced around. 'I think that's it.' I took out Aifric's jerky and offered her a piece. She examined it for a moment then shook her head. 'I'll take some of that water though.'

I unscrewed the bottle and passed it over. Lily stared down at its contents, a tiny smile playing around the corner of her lips. 'You need to avenge your parents,' she said suddenly. 'You can't let him win.'

Uneasiness rippled through me. 'Let who win?'

Her smile grew. 'Bottoms up.' She tilted her head back and gulped, draining the entire bottle then wiping her mouth with the back of her hand. 'Everything will be alright, Chieftain. You'll see.' All at once she started to choke.

'Lily?' I slapped her on the back, assuming she'd swallowed some water the wrong way but she only got worse. Becoming more alarmed, I grabbed her shoulders. Her cheeks were turning puce. 'Lily? Lily!' I shook her.

Saliva frothed at the corners of her mouth. Her eyes met mine in one final smile and then she slid out of my grasp and crumpled in a heap. I knelt down, moving her head to one side, hooking my finger inside her mouth. My hands were shaking and desperation clawed at me. Perhaps something was caught in her throat. I thumped her chest but nothing happened. She let out a faint gurgle.

Without thinking, I grabbed the letter opener and rubbed it furiously against my thigh. 'Bob!' I shrieked.

He appeared in an instant, his gaze sweeping from me to Lily's prone form.

'I wish for you to save her!' I shouted. He didn't move. 'Bob!' I said again. 'Do something!'

His expression was sorrowful. 'I can't. I can't change death, Uh Integrity. That's beyond even my powers.'

'She's not dead! She was just here! She was fine. She…'

'She's gone.' He flew up to my face and pressed his little hand against my cheek. 'I'm sorry.'

'But… but…' I stammered. I stared down at her. Her eyes were wide and unseeing.

Swatting Bob away, I tilted back Lily's head and began mouth to mouth resuscitation. I thumped her chest again. 'Come on, Lily!'

'She's not coming back,' Bob said.

I ignored him. 'She has to!' I breathed into her mouth again. I could taste something bitter on my lips, followed by a strange tingle. Rubbing my mouth with the cuff of my sleeve, I spat on the ground.

'Integrity,' he said, using my name correctly for the first time. 'She's dead.'

Tears blinded me. I rocked back on my heels. 'I don't understand,' I sobbed. 'I don't get it.'

My hands fell to my sides, knocking over the bottle of water that had fallen when Lily had. I looked down at it blurrily and the bottom drained out of my world.

Chapter Twenty-Five

'What did you do with the horses?' Taylor asked, handing me a cup of tea. 'I know a guy who deals in premium horsemeat, you know. I could have taken care of them for you.'

I threw him an irritated look. He grinned in return. Now that his debts were cleared, his normal insouciance was returning. I curled my fingers round the cup's warmth and sighed. 'I left them in the courtyard at the Cruaich just before I returned Lily's body to her Clan and retrieved those two.' I nodded towards Lexie and Brochan who were sitting opposite with Speck perched on the arm of the sofa next to them. All of them looked grim, their mouths tight and tell-tale shadows under their eyes.

'You'd seemed to think you could trust Aifric.'

My head drooped. 'I should have known. He's the Steward. A lot of his power might be inconsequential but he still has more of it than anyone else.'

'Maybe it wasn't him. Someone else could have spiked the water.'

I dug into my pocket and threw him my phone. 'Look at the photos,' I said dully.

The last one was the group photo that Lily had taken. Taylor examined it. 'They don't look happy, I'll admit, but…'

'Look at Aifric.'

She'd snapped it at just the right moment.

When you enlarged the photo, it was easy to see. Aifric was fingering a tiny silver ball with veins of red running through it. I'd seen one of those before – Charlie had tried to give me one. It was filled with poison.

'I was a fool,' I said. 'I thought it was the Kincaids who hated me, the Darrochs too. But it turns out that Aifric Moncrieffe is an excellent actor. William Kincaid was collateral damage. And so was Lily.'

'What about his son? Byron, is it?'

Something clutched at my heart. 'I don't know. I don't think he's involved but I can't be sure. I can't be sure of anything any more.'

'I found out a lot when you were gone,' Lexie admitted. 'The Moncrieffes are destitute because Aifric's been forced to pass a lot of money to some of the other Clans. He's been doing it for years.' She swallowed. 'Ever since Clan Adair.'

'Bribes. To cover up whatever it was he did.'

'You think he's responsible for what happened with your father?'

I shrugged helplessly. 'It seems that way.'

Speck shifted. 'The vast majority of the Clan-less don't give a flying bejesus what happens with the Sidhe but...'

Taylor broke in. 'But anyone who met Gale Adair has nothing but good things to say about him. No matter what he might have done.'

My eyes flew to his. 'Why didn't you tell me?'

'If you'd dwelled on your life with the Sidhe, I

would have. But you wanted to forget that part of you had ever existed. You were just a kid, Tegs. You needed to heal. If you didn't want to know, then I wasn't going to stir up the past for you.'

I understood the sentiment. But while I might have needed Taylor's protection when I was eleven years old, I certainly didn't need it now. My world had been turned on its head and nothing would ever be the same again. 'Did you find anything at the Adair lands, Brochan?' I swallowed. 'At my lands?'

He took a moment before answering. 'There's definitely still evidence of an immense battle. Old scorch marks, rubble that no-one's cleared up. That kind of thing. It's been too long though. I can't say what happened with any certainty.'

Speck looked at me with dark, worried eyes. 'He's going to know you're still alive. He's not going to stop trying to get rid of you. I don't know what his reasons are, but with the Foinse out in the open and no issue any more with the magic, he has no cause to keep you alive. Especially now that you know he tried to kill you.'

'He's much more dangerous than the Bull ever was,' I agreed. 'Aifric is intelligent enough to manipulate people into believing that he's a decent guy.' I took a deep breath and stood up. 'But he's not going to be sure whether I know his true nature or not. He'll expect me to suspect him but he doesn't know I have proof. I can use that. I need time to find out more about what happened all those years ago. If I'm going to expose him, I'll need evidence of what happened to my parents and the rest of Clan Adair. Not to mention why it happened.'

'What's the plan?' Lexie asked. 'Because whatever it is, I want in.'

'Me too,' Speck piped up. 'There's no way I'm letting that blue-haired pixie get all the glory.'

'I'm in too,' Brochan agreed. 'Aifric Moncrieffe isn't going to get away with this.'

Taylor stood up as well. 'So Integrity? What *is* the plan?'

I looked at him. 'You're normally the man with the plan.'

He smiled, although his smile was tinged with a sad pride. 'I think the student has become the master. You held it together through all this. I'm the one who fell apart.'

I squeezed his arm.

'All you need to do,' Bob drawled from where he lounged on a cushion, 'is wish for…'

'No,' we chorused. 'No wishing.'

I looked at them all. 'You have to do bad shit to get ahead. I'm not going to fight Aifric. But I am going to be smarter than him. We'll sort out things with the money and lull him into a false sense of security. Then we'll go back to normal and act as if nothing's happened.'

Lexie's brow furrowed. 'How's that going to help?'

My eyes gleamed. 'Because it'll force him to

come to me. He won't be able to help himself. Bit by bit, I'm going to make Aifric Moncrieffe my bitch. And then I'm going to destroy him.'

Bob lazily got to his feet. 'And his son?'

I looked away. 'Sometimes there's collateral damage.'

Chapter Twenty Six

I strolled in through the gates of the Cruaich three days later. I didn't have the welcoming committee I'd endured last time but I still received a lot of startled looks. I caught a few hushed whispers and was unsurprised at their content. The others were being hailed as heroes for first saving the Foinse and releasing it. I was being cast as the person who allowed William Kincaid to die and possibly murdered Lily Macquarrie in the process. I didn't care what they said; I held my head high.

My intention had been to make a beeline for the hall. Whether all the Clan Chieftains were there or not made little difference. My words would get back to the people who needed to hear them no matter what Aifric tried to do. I was stopped in my tracks, however, by a familiar voice.

'I thought you weren't going to run away.'

I turned, drinking in Byron. He looked rumpled, the shadow of stubble across his jawline. For once his hair wasn't so perfect but his emerald eyes remained bright. I forced down the irritating prickles of desire that danced through my veins. I wasn't going to believe the worst of him yet. Jumping to conclusions wouldn't aid my cause but whatever was behind that sexy façade, I couldn't let myself trust him. Not when I knew the truth about his father.

'Circumstances altered my path. How's Malcolm?' I asked.

'Grieving.' He took a step towards me. 'What happened? The Macquarries sent word that you appeared like a bat out of hell carrying Lily's body.'

'Lily's corpse,' I corrected quietly.

A shadow crossed his face. 'For what it's worth, I'm sorry.'

'You don't think it was me who poisoned her then?'

'No.' He met my gaze and held it. 'I don't.'

I shook out my hair. 'It was the water,' I told him. 'There was something in it. It was obviously meant for me.'

Byron sucked in a breath. 'But…'

'It must have been William Kincaid,' I continued blithely. 'He hated me with every fibre of his being. He'll be spinning in his grave that he missed his shot.'

Byron's jaw tightened. 'The magic is fine,' he said. 'As you assumed. Wherever the Foinse is, it's no longer broken.'

I liked to the think of the source of all Scottish magic as a 'she', rather than an 'it'. Kind of like Mother Nature. 'I told you so,' I said, raising an eyebrow.

He didn't rise to the bait. 'Why are you here now, Integrity?' His voice was low and husky. There was an odd light in his eyes and I realised he was searching for a particular answer. I shrugged. Whatever.

'Here,' I said, thrusting out a brown envelope. 'That's what Taylor owes you. Including your unreasonable interest.'

He gazed at my outstretched hand. 'You don't have to do that. It was a mean trick in the first place.'

I cocked my head. 'Beggars can't be choosers, Byron. Your Clan needs the money and you have his loan paid in full. We're all leaving town and I want to make sure there are no loose ends before I go.'

'Leaving? Where are you going?'

'I was always going to be leaving. I have a new job.' I smiled. 'This one is on the right side of the law.' I wasn't quite so sure that Lexie, Speck, Brochan and Taylor would adhere to that but they weren't his concern. I checked my watch. 'In fact, my train leaves in a couple of hours so I don't have long.'

A muscle throbbed in his cheek. 'You're Sidhe. You don't have to work among the Clan-less.'

'No,' I said cheerfully, 'I don't.'

A door opened at the far end of the corridor. It was difficult to be sure with the light behind them but it looked like Aifric. I forced myself to stay relaxed and raised a hand in greeting. I didn't check to see whether he waved back.

'Anyway,' I continued. 'This is for you.' I took out a small velvet bag from my inside pocket. 'I thought you might want it back.'

Byron was genuinely surprised. 'Is that the Lia

Saifire?'

I inclined my head. 'It is. And it's all yours. Clan Moncrieffe can do whatever they wish with it.'

'I thought you'd sold it on.'

I smiled. It had been a piece of cake to steal it back from the human who'd bought it. He'd shoved in a display cabinet in a showy castle up in the north. There was a vast collection of artwork and other jewels alongside it. I bet it would be months before he even noticed it was gone. Teleportation made everything easier. It was just as well I was changing professions; I'd be bored out of my wits if heists were always so simple to pull off.

'I'd like to say it's been a pleasure knowing you all,' I said lightly, 'but I can't deny that I'm glad all this is over.'

He took another step towards me. 'Is it? Is it all over, Integrity?'

'Of course it is.' I paused. 'What did the beaver say to the tree?'

Byron frowned. 'Integrity…'

'It's been nice gnawing you.'

He didn't acknowledge my joke. There was no appreciation for the finer art of humour these days.

'Goodbye Byron.' I tossed him the bag with the Lia Saifire in it, turned on my heel and walked out, whistling. I'd be back.

Author's Note

Although Scottish Gaelic and Irish Gaelic are very similar, many of the spellings are different. Technically, the Scottish version of Sidhe (prounounced 'she') is spelled Sith but to avoid inevitable comparisons with Star Wars characters, I've taken some poetic liberty in using the Irish version.

About the Author

After teaching English literature in the UK, Japan and Malaysia, Helen Harper left behind the world of education following the worldwide success of her Blood Destiny series of books. She is a professional member of the Alliance of Independent Authors and writes full time although she still fits in creative writing workshops with schools along with volunteering to teach reading to a group of young Myanmar refugees. That's not to mention the procession of stray cats which seem to find their way to her door!

Helen has always been a book lover, devouring science fiction and fantasy tales when she was a child growing up in Scotland.

Helen currently lives in Kuala Lumpur, Malaysia with far too many cats – not to mention the dragons, fairies, demons, wizards and vampires that seem to keep appearing from nowhere.

Other titles by Helen Harper

The *Blood Destiny* series

Bloodfire
Bloodmagic
Bloodrage
Blood Politics
Bloodlust

Also

Corrigan Fire
Corrigan Magic
Corrigan Rage
Corrigan Politics
Corrigan Lust

The *Olympiana* series

Eros
Lyre

The *Bo Blackman* series

Dire Straits
New Order
High Stakes
Red Angel
Vigilante Vampire

The *Dreamweaver* series

Night Shade
Night Terrors

Printed in Great Britain
by Amazon

56882265R00208